PICTURING

WILL

PICTURING

WILL

Ann Beattie

RANDOM HOUSE
NEW YORK

Library of Congress Cataloging-in-Publication Data
Beattie, Ann.
Picturing Will / Ann Beattie.
p.   cm.
ISBN 0-394-56987-3
I. Title.
PS3552.E177P53   1989
813'.54—dc20   89-42781

Manufactured in the United States of America
Book design by JoAnne Metsch
24689753
First Edition

For Lincoln

PART I

MOTHER

O N E

At night, when Jody had trouble sleeping, Wayne seemed, in his sneaky way, always to be there in the shadows, his smooth voice still a whispered undertone of the breeze. They had divorced years ago, and except for talking to him on the phone periodically to arrange for Will's visits to Florida, she had no contact with him at all. His image had become blurry. She was confused about whether his gaze seemed more intense when he wore his glasses or contact lenses. She could remember that he was tall, but not what it felt like to stand beside him, let alone to be held in his arms. She could remember the pattern of the plaid shirts he wore in the winter, but not if he had tucked them in or left the shirttails hanging out. The only absolutely distinct memory she had—whether she was awake or during the many times she dreamed it—was of the day they married. They had gone to a justice of the peace. His brother, and a girlfriend with whom she had since lost touch, had been the only witnesses. After the ceremony, she and Wayne had walked out the door with an arm around each other's waist and made a happy race for the car (his brother had overtaken them and managed to throw open the car door, bowing as if opening the door of a gilded carriage). There had been a split second when she looked down to where Wayne's fingers curved around her waist and suddenly saw their future as clearly as anyone looking into a crystal ball. His fingers were perfectly placed, but you could see how lightly their touch registered. Either the thing he touched was ephemeral, or his touch made it so; this many years later, she still wondered which. But in that instant, she had realized that she would slip through Wayne's fingers.

She had known him for only a few months before they married—months during which there was such frantic activity that by the time he proposed, Jody had begun to think that marriage must have been what they were headed for from the start. Their eyes had met when they passed each other, walking down a crowded street. Only a few steps beyond him, her heel had snapped. He had been looking over his shoulder—giving her the evil eye, she now believed—and when she stopped to take off her shoe, she was stopping for years. Years in which she'd move to the country, marry, and have Wayne's child. The thin little leather heel she held was the shed tail of a captured lizard.

She should have seen through it—the bullying and bravado—but the bullying was always accompanied by charming coercions (so many flowers he couldn't afford), and the bravado seemed at the time like real intensity. Wayne had always been *about* to create a life for himself, and for her. He borrowed money from his brother to go to school, then quit. He railed against city life—everything from the cracks in the sidewalk that caught the tip of your heel to the political wheeling and dealing that determined the city's character. For Wayne, the plaster gargoyles on the buildings were always blowing an ill wind, but the night sounds of the country were the music of the spheres. They lived in a tiny house on a farm, where she looked after the horses, and Wayne read books—not to expand his horizons, as he said, but to reinforce the limits of what he believed. His brilliance, he claimed, would someday light up the world, but in the meantime he rewired lamps for a living and worked as the odd-jobs man on the property. And for quite a while she had been entranced with him, and with that life. Without knowing much about him—without even knowing, until they applied for a marriage license, that he had been married before, without ever pausing to consider how strange it was that he had no friends and that his own brother was mystified that he had been asked to attend the wedding, without any knowledge beyond what she saw in his eyes and what she felt when she touched his body—she was willing to leave behind worried friends, argue with and finally stop speaking to her parents, and view her own ambition with skepticism. Though it now seemed impossible that she had ever been under his spell, she continued to feel chastened by the experience. Still disturbed enough to roam the house at night, checking like some crazy worried lady to make sure torn-up love letters hadn't reappeared as untouched sheets of stationery, that the roses hadn't taken root to bloom again at the bottom of the trash.

Wayne left without leaving a note, when roses he had given her were only slightly wilted in the vase. She had awakened to Will's cries one morning in a house that felt intensely empty. She couldn't convince herself that he had gone out to fork hay for the horses. Or that he had decided to call it quits with his attempts to repair the car and had taken it to Smoky's garage. The horses were quiet, and the car was gone, and on the table by the door was his house key. Outside, dawn was breaking.

And she had Will in her arms—Will, who smelled of the night's sleep: that mixture of damp diaper and Johnson's baby shampoo and sweat and powder that for years she thought she would never get out of her lungs. She had stood there by the closed door as if it were transparent and she could look out and see Wayne's car in the distance. Because even before she saw the key on the table, she knew that he was gone. He was gone and at the end of the month she and Will would be gone too, with the money she had borrowed from her father, whose note was so kind that she had crumpled it and thrown it away before finishing it. The gardener's wife had put a picnic basket—as if they were going for a day's pleasant outing!—in the backseat of the old Buick she had bought with her father's money. She drove an hour farther south and spent the next two weeks at a girlfriend's house in Charlottesville—a house that was miraculously empty, because the girlfriend had put it on the market and was on her way to join her boyfriend in New Orleans. It was a lie to think that photography and good luck had saved her, but it was still too painful to think that her father's small savings account had been the factor—or even that her girlfriend's generosity in leaving her not only the house but a series of friends she asked to call Jody (one of whom had invited her to the party where she met Mel) had foiled Wayne's plans to ruin her life.

Now she lived with her son—their son—in the same small Southern town she had driven to almost randomly, and she had gone from being a clerk in a camera store to working as a much-in-demand wedding photographer. Prowling through the house at night, a drink in hand for consolation, walking quietly in her stocking feet so as not to awaken Will, she was often mesmerized by what she had created. Not that it was particularly lovely or even expressive of who she was, just that it existed at all: the tripods and strobes and drop cloths, the entire dining room transformed into a photographer's studio.

She would feel her way around that room in the darkness: the pegs next to the fireplace, from which she had hung antique wedding dresses and straw hats; the mantel, where her lenses were lined up like soldiers; the built-in corner cabinet with her cameras inside and her light meter dangling from the front latch; the window seat Duncan had extended so she could lower the ivory-colored velvet curtain and photograph brides-to-be sitting prettily in the little niche; the chair bought at the Salvation Army and reupholstered (no modern chairs had such wide seat cushions) so the bride and groom could be shot sitting together without looking like Edgar Bergen and Charlie McCarthy. Was it possible that at the end of the day doctors turned out the fluorescent lights in their offices and ran their hands over their stethoscopes and tongue depressors and syringes and felt perplexed at the unfamiliarity of those cold items and plastic packages? Did bakers take a secret finger-swipe at perfectly scalloped icing, taste it, and then repair the damage with their pastry tubes? Didn't people sometimes hover a bit above their lives, see that they were stranger than they seemed, and then—with their hearts fluttering—answer the ringing phone, say the perfunctory good night, continue on the same path?

Rhetorical questions were some help, but when Jody was awake—when it seemed that she was totally alone in the house, in spite of her child sleeping upstairs and her lover sleeping in New York City and dreaming dreams of her—only the slight absurdity, and the awkwardness of having created this life, seemed pertinent. She could have turned on the lights, but then everything would have looked too stark—the room would be obliterated by such brightness. She could have stayed in bed and thought about all this, but one of the advantages of being an adult was that she could rise and claim her territory without being challenged.

She sat alone in the big chair and listened to the sound of

the trees blowing in the night wind. An irregular patch of
light from the street lamp jutted across the wood floor. She
studied it as if it were a slip of test paper: What would be the
proper exposure to register every gradation of white to black?
It was a luxury, she knew, to be able to speculate, to seriously
put observation before action. To be neither the harried
mother nor the beleaguered artist.

She put her empty glass on the kitchen counter and looked
through a pile of papers ready to slip into chaos. She got a
large manila envelope and put into it the bag from the pharmacy, with the receipt stapled to the outside, that had held
a bottle of eardrops for Will, and a crumpled receipt for the
Chinese takeout they had eaten the night before. Will loved
wonton soup. He loved the special spoon that came with it
and had as much interest in the wontons sunk to the bottom
as a fisherman looking at trout in clear water. Jody also
dropped in a note she had no intention of responding to,
from a woman whose wedding she had photographed, which
asked for a written reminiscence of the day. There was also
Will's printed request for another G.I. Joe, the letters enlarging and sloping as the pencil came near the edge of the
paper; a computer letter offering Jody two free days in a
Key West condo if she agreed to consider buying; the cartoon that came with a cube of bubble gum; a grocery receipt
with a smudge of strawberry juice that looked like blood;
another postcard from the Electrolux dealer, urging her to
reserve a date for a demonstration; Hershey's Kisses wrap-
pers; a Polaroid of Will holding one pajama leg high, trying to
look elegant in a pair of pink satin high heels; a note from
Will's teacher expressing her concern that Will's attention
drifted too often; a place mat imprinted with a picture of a
cardinal, the state bird, crayoned on by Will, who drew a stick
figure pointing a gun at the bird's beak; the label from a jar of
black currant jelly that Will had asked her to soak off and then

had lost interest in. In the morning she would stop at the post office and mail the envelope to Wayne. She took some pride in her audacity, even though there would be no acknowledgment, even though she might as well be sending it to Mars. She just wanted him to know things: the price of a quart of soup, the fact that medicine had been prescribed. She thought of some of the things she enclosed as wide-angle views of their lives and other things as close-ups. Nothing much could be made of a parking ticket—a common enough occurrence—but there was something almost intimate about sending the pharmacy bag.

She ran her finger along the flap of the manila envelope. The first time she mailed one to Wayne, she had realized what a devilish thing it was to do. But after the second and third, when he never responded, she realized she had found a way to confound and intimidate him.

She sealed the envelope tightly, licking until the glue of the top flap became wet enough to adhere perfectly to the dry strip of glue underneath. At the same time, she took care not to cut her lip on the paper. This was what the careful kisses of years ago—the lightly placed night kisses, meant to register without awakening Wayne—had become: a lick along a line of glue, and a flap folded and pressed in place with the strength of one person strangling another.

When she finished putting things in the envelope she began to straighten up a bit, even though she knew Mel would say that of *course* she couldn't be expected to be the perfect housekeeper when she was raising a child and supporting herself. Mel understood final notices and took fines for not paying on time in stride. He urged her to be even-tempered when cops stopped her for speeding, and he didn't hesitate to run out into the rain to tip the paperboy at Christmas. Mel was nobody's fool and came close to being ideal. He was a more patient lover than Wayne and found Will's laughter contagious. He loved

her and had let it be known that he was very sad that she had
not yet chosen to marry him and move to New York.

That was a good part of the reason why she stayed awake at
night, pacing like a lost person. Because she suspected that she
would have to relocate, be lost, capitulate, in order to keep
what she had. She was feeling another version of the anxiety
that had made her pace through the house years ago, mesmerized by late-night fears about what would become of her and
Will. Though she had found a way to make a stable life for
them, she still felt everything could become precarious. That
once again she would walk out her door and be a night trav-
eler, but that this time she would have to go it alone because
she wouldn't dare awaken Will. When Will was a baby she
had held him in her arms and taken him for walks. If he
couldn't sleep, she couldn't sleep. It always surprised her that
there were not other mothers who were nightwalkers. At three
or four in the morning she and Will would start down the hill,
and along the way she'd ask, "What's this?," and really the
question would be as much for herself as for him. The Indian
cigar tree did look surreal at night: something of a mix between an upside-down birthday cake whose candles improb-
ably stayed stuck in the icing and the mobile that had once
dangled over Will's crib. "What's this?" she'd say, pointing at
the sky, and they'd both say, in unison, "The moon." Even on
the coldest winter nights they'd wander through a strange
dream that distorted the daytime world, noticing what was
highlighted by streetlight or by starlight. There was hardly
ever a noise. Sounds, certainly—the cat darting out of the
bushes, leaves rustling in the breeze—but the overall impression was of quiet. The neighbor's old blue car glowed lavender
when the moon was full. Falling snow looked as solid as pearls.
Tar could look like satin. Sometimes her own voice would
imitate the breeze; lips on top of Will's ear, she'd whisper,
"What's that?," drawing out the last word so that the *a*'s,

exhaled, caused their own air current. "Whose baby are you?" she'd say, and Will would say, "Yours." She'd point: "Whose house is that?," and he'd say, "Mine." A kingdom to be claimed. Who could have blamed him for feeling powerful? Moving through the night, she became for him a galloping horse with an unerring sense of direction. Smell the air: danger there. Feel the breeze, coming from the north.

Without him, she would have perished. Only a baby—someone who truly needed her care—could have made her rise to the occasion. Held tightly against her chest, Will became her buffer against the world. When he had bad dreams and she consoled him, the warmth of his body had made her relaxed enough to sleep. Now there was enough money to get by, enough time to work and to play, and there was Mel—even the person closest to her had no idea that she and Will had ever been night travelers. If she did not confide in him about that time, she would forget it sooner, she was convinced. Why remember your vulnerabilities? It was a great advantage that her accomplice in those days had been a baby, who would forget the wind blowing through his hair and the rush of hot and cold as she put her lips to the brim of his stocking cap and tried to breathe evenly, getting over her anxiety about how they would live and what would become of them. That would all be as lost to him as the moment of birth. It would matter no more than a lost marble mattered a month after its disappearance. Your secrets were always safe with babies. With adults—and sometimes even with yourself—they were not at all safe.

T W O

The day after Jody photographed a wedding on an estate east of town she called the housekeeper to see if she could return to rephotograph the grounds. Something about the house—nothing architectural; some nebulous *something* that seemed to be in the air—had gotten her attention. She was not sure herself what she wanted. She only knew she wanted another opportunity to poke around.

Though she photographed weddings for a living, her real interest was in the photographs she took for herself. She had gotten good enough, she knew, to start thinking seriously about showing her secret work. Photography had been a fascination at first—nothing she thought she would ever be involved in. Will had been an infant then, and her marriage had just about collapsed. She would buckle Will into a car seat and drive into Washington every week to see photography shows, or to browse through museum bookstores and look at books she couldn't afford. How vulnerable she must have seemed to anyone who noticed her: a pretty young woman with an infant in a Snugli slumbering on her chest, attention riveted to the book she was examining, as if it could provide her with clues about the rest of her life. Where had the photographers positioned themselves, and why? The photographers' preoccupations became clear, their level of aggression measurable. In the best photographs, the photographer's presence was palpable. Though she had revised her thoughts now and was inclined to think just the opposite, she was interested, then, in trying to understand what the photographers revealed about themselves. The risks they took were the ultimate fascination. She had tried to figure out when the photographers thought they were hiding, and to what extent this was true. Sometimes the photographer disappeared as unconvincingly as a child playing hide-and-seek who couldn't help peeking around the corner to see how the game was going. Other times you couldn't help thinking that the photographer had orchestrated the moment in order to make a personal statement, which did not express the subject's feeling at all. Looking at photographs was a little like sleuthing, but in so many cases the mystery transcended anything that could be explained.

She bought photographs from the Library of Congress.

Wayne asked her why she wanted pictures on the walls of people she didn't know.

She cashed the Christmas check she got from her father and bought a Canon TX.

Wayne reacted like someone whose cat has proudly brought home a dead mouse.

She bought a developing tank and practiced prying open a roll of film with her eyes closed, trying to wind it on the reel by her sense of touch.

As she tipped the tank back and forth, Wayne looked at her

as if she were a deaf person shaking maracas that had no seeds inside.

Memories of those years could overwhelm her when she least expected it. Perhaps the road she was driving on reminded her of the road she and Wayne had lived on. Certainly it was not the sight of the wedding house itself, one of many big houses that had been kept up but not extensively renovated, painted over too many times without having been scraped, the shutters hanging a bit awkwardly. Still, there were nice things about the big white house: leaded-glass windows that ivy would have to be pulled away from when spring came; huge maple trees with gnarled roots that twisted along the ground, and ash trees, recently planted, with slender trunks no thicker than a broom handle.

Getting out of the car, she stepped on shards of gold crushed in the gravel: the plastic champagne glasses from the day before. Her friend Duncan, who often catered such events, said that pilfering had become such a problem that many of the rich people now relied on plastic for large gatherings.

Because she thought someone might be watching her approach, she did not stop to photograph the crushed plastic. It was also too obvious a thing to photograph, though she often allowed herself to work her way into feeling something about a place by photographing in a perfunctory way: documenting what was there, then moving on. Seeing the obvious through the viewfinder always sharpened her eye for odd, telling details. Photographing a tree, she would see ants swarm a bit of food on the ground; shooting the side of the house, she would catch the reflection in the window of two trees whose overlapping branches seemed to form the shape of a cross.

"Do you believe this is the same place where we had all that excitement one day ago?" the housekeeper said, throwing open the door. Jody could tell from her tone of voice that she was truly welcome. Except for the housekeeper's wiry hair, it might not have been obvious that the woman was black. She wore a black uniform—or an unstylish dress—with a tan down vest. Blue plastic earrings dangled from her ears.

"You didn't go on their honeymoon?" Jody said, smiling.

The woman shook her head. Clearly, she was more than a housekeeper. The day before, she had been sipping champagne and teasing the bride, threatening to slip into the steamer trunk so she could pop out when their ship arrived in Europe.

Jody walked in, and the housekeeper turned to pour coffee without asking if she wanted any. "He was my second choice," the housekeeper said, "but I think she did wonderful well for herself." She handed Jody a mug of coffee. The aroma filled the room. "I want to tell you," the housekeeper said, "he has got to be some nice boy for me to like him without him having no religious beliefs of any shape or kind. He told me his own parents, out in California, raised him to be an atheist."

"Who was your favorite?" Jody said.

"An Episcopal boy who's in training to be a doctor. And that has nothing to do with my personal religion, either, which happens to be Baptist. The boy she married just doesn't have the charm Taylor Tazewell has, but the both of them are kind boys, and I guess that's what's important." The housekeeper smiled. "It's not one bit of my business," she said, "but I can't tell if that ring on your finger is a wedding ring or not."

It wasn't. It was a blue enamel ring with a little strand of gold spiraling delicately through the enamel. Mel had bought it for Will to give her last Mother's Day. "I'm divorced," Jody said. "I have a son. Will." She reached into her bag and brought out her wallet.

The picture she carried of Will was several years old, a black-and-white Polaroid that had faded, so that now Will's face was indistinct; it was not obvious that he was smiling. Like all photographers, she cared most about pictures of people she loved that were in no way exceptional as photographs. Maybe there was something special about the day a picture was taken (the first time Mel got Will to climb to the top of the slide and come down without his having to stand next to it, ready to reach for Will if he toppled), or even the day it went into the wallet (Will had cut it small, with Mel's help, for the card-case of an old wallet she no longer had). The housekeeper's face lit up, though, as if she had seen an angel.

"I have two boys and would of had three, but one was taken from me in infancy with pneumonia," the housekeeper said.

"I'm very sorry," Jody said. She looked at the picture of Will. Impossible that he would be taken from her. As impossible as having aborted him to please Wayne. She looked at the ring—her hand, holding the picture. The enamel ring had cost more, she was sure, than the thin silver wedding band Wayne had given her. With the tip of her thumb, she pushed the ring closer to her palm.

"It's always easy to think there's a reason for everything, unless something bad happens to you," the housekeeper sighed. She offered Jody milk for her coffee. Jody poured some in before she realized what she was doing; she drank her coffee black. She would let the mug warm her hands a few seconds longer, then go outside and pour the coffee on the ground.

Wayne had done that, years ago: poured all the coffee out of his cup over her tomato seedlings. He had also thrown things: bed pillows, dishes, unlit cigarettes.

"I'm taking up too much of your time," Jody said. "I'll go outside for a few minutes and take a few quick pictures, if that's all right."

The housekeeper shrugged. "The outdoors sure don't belong to me," she said, smiling as Jody walked out the door.

There were times when the smell of the breeze let you know you were going to get a good photograph. A tingle in your fingertips preceded whatever was about to intervene: a breeze, a stream of migrating birds. The best of them were synergistic, or they didn't work at all except as well-composed arty photographs.

Earlier that day she had been looking through a book of At-get's photographs of Paris—in particular, the photographs he took in the 1920s of hotel interiors. The picture of the Hotel de Roquelaure would have seemed a vision of heaven to any parent with a young child whose home was a battlefield of fallen animals, marching monsters, and discarded clothes. Only the black chair sitting to the side of the tall doors reminded you there was life in the hotel. You knew instantly that the chair was covered in velvet. It was not a leather chair, or a chair covered with any other material, but a chair with a fringed velvet seat. That hint of softness humanized the entire picture. The viewer believed there was a possibility of entering that room through the open door, of sitting in a magical chair.

She set up the tripod and screwed on the camera. Why was she about to take a photograph of the side of a house? Because—unless you were Atget—you had to wait for a mystery if you did not discover one. It was all intuition and patience: A rabbit might appear from under the bush; a meteor might fall.

She moved the tripod to another location so that when she photographed the house the little ash trees would be in the picture. She leaned over to look through the lens. Until you looked through the lens, you could never be sure. That was when things took on a prominence they didn't have in life, or when details disappeared. You could find that the picture you thought to take with a wide-angle lens was really better seen in close-up. You could know the routine, use the right exposure, compose perfectly, but still—the photographs that really worked transcended what you expected, however certain the results may have seemed at the time.

It was a nice shot, but Jody didn't trust the dimming light, so she bracketed when she took the shot again. Then she let the tripod stand where it was and loaded the Leica. Its lightness was reassuring. With the little Leica in the palm of your hand you suddenly felt more delicate, but at the same time more connected to things, the way you felt when you slipped a ballet slipper on your foot.

Through the lens of the Leica, the scene was nondescript. Turning a bit to examine the world, though, she found that it was just right for photographing the remains of a bird's nest wedged between limbs above her head. No broken eggs lay below it. The ground was almost winter-hard. There would be no photograph of eggshells, and there would be no photograph of the crushed plastic in the driveway. At that moment, though, the photograph that would be taken began to exist. A rusty blue pickup started to bump its way into the driveway. She photographed the approach, as documentation. She photographed the man opening the door on the driver's side and his companion, hopping out the other side. If they saw her, they gave no sign. They walked toward the house, one tall man and one small man with a funny way of walking, never turning to look over their shoulders.

She waited until they got to the door, then began photographing in earnest. And luck was with her: the wind got in the photograph. A wind blew up, and in an almost palpable way it reinforced the empty space that surrounded the men. Then she moved quickly to stand behind the tripod and photograph the men as the door opened, the lens compressing distance until their truck was no longer a respectable distance from the house but a huge presence, large and threatening. It existed in stark contrast to the branches blowing in the breeze, overwhelming the three small people who stood in the doorway. The housekeeper was squinting against the rush of air. Jody clicked and knew she had the right picture. The photo caption would read: After the Wedding. It would be one of twenty or so pictures she took in the county that winter that, to her surprise, would make people stop dead in their tracks to stare—photographs that revealed what she knew about the world in 1989.

T H R E E

In the late afternoon, the sun moving toward the west struck the globe of the ceiling light, sending prisms of color against the walls, mottling the furniture, and electrifying the edges of the big silver mirror. Jody's camera equipment was pushed against the back wall. A tangle of cords was piled up in the corner, making her think of blacksnakes stunned in their crawl. Will liked to put his rubber snakes in among the cords. Sometimes he would wind them more neatly and place his collection of windup toys in the corral. Often, when Jody began to pull out the cords, she would topple Godzilla, or a family of apes in graduated sizes. Ah, she thought, staring at her improvised home studio, what a noble profession. She had put on hip-waders to walk into the lake amid lily pads in order to photograph one wedding couple setting sail in a canoe. She had loaned her size-eight shoes to a bride whose heel began to wobble just as she was about to walk down the aisle and had

photographed the ceremony in her stocking feet. In the beginning, when she had almost no money and hadn't believed
in her heart of hearts that she could support herself and Will
by taking photographs, she had bargained with one groom's
father for a weekly supply of baked goods in lieu of a fee. At
least half a dozen times before she met Mel she had wished
that she was marrying the man the bride was marrying. She
routinely lied in admiring wedding rings that were no more
attractive than pebbles. Camera raised, she would close her
eyes for a few seconds and pray that the marriage taking place
would last, however unlikely it might seem at the moment—
that it wouldn't become some dreary statistic of failure down
the road. She often went home with blossoms stuck in her hair
and rice in her shoes. She had also gone home and wept,
unaccountably.

Right now, Will was at his Friday-afternoon hobby class.
So far, he had made fourteen ashtrays (she did not smoke) as
well as a dozen tiny human forms with arms outstretched so
that they resembled Mel's favorite corkscrew. Mel thought
that whatever Will produced was a work of genius. Mel had
also been presented with several ashtrays and had been told at
great length about the ones that broke during firing. The ashtrays were lined up on Mel's desk at work (when they were in
New York last, he had taken Will to see them), and he assured
Will that everyone at the gallery admired them greatly. It
made Jody feel a little bad that she stored so many things Will
gave her in the corner cabinet, but really, what was she supposed to do with so many presents?

Duncan knocked on the door. He had come to borrow her
vacuum. Duncan was twenty-eight and young for his years.
Mel was sure that he had a crush on her. He asked her opinion
of cameras he would never buy, stood very tall when she
complimented his cooking, and was always available to baby-
sit if a sitter canceled at the last minute. Will assumed that Mel

could follow up in teaching him ballet steps that Duncan had been showing him. He was entranced when Duncan snipped flowers from their stems and tucked the blossoms on trays of food he prepared, and he didn't see why his mother wouldn't adorn their dinner with sprigs of lilac. Duncan was always cheerful—and so hopeful—that even Mel occasionally made fun of him behind his back, rolling his eyes and posturing the way Duncan did when he was being praised.

"Are you *sure*?" Duncan said, standing in the hallway. "If you need it to clean up—"

"It gives me the perfect excuse not to vacuum," Jody said. "Take it. Keep it as long as you want."

"Well," Duncan said, reaching into the deep pocket of his sheepskin coat and bringing out a little rectangle wrapped in foil. He thrust it toward her, the same way Will gave her something he was shy about handing over.

"Brandy walnut cake," Duncan said. "It's an improvement on the cake I made with hazelnut flour that you liked so much."

"Oh, thank you," she said. "It isn't necessary to give me something just because you're borrowing the vacuum, though."

"Not because it's necessary. Because you're one of my best testers."

"Thank you," she said again. She opened the door of the hall closet. He rushed forward and took out the vacuum. Previously, he had borrowed books, blankets, vases, and her slide projector. Since he was a caterer, he could hardly borrow a cup of sugar. When he returned the things, he always brought her something in return for the favor: beeswax candles, tulip bulbs, a brass stirring spoon.

"*Babette's Feast* is playing at the movies this week," he said. "Have you seen it? I was wondering if—"

"Thanks," she said. "Actually, I have seen it."

"Who's baby-sitting on Halloween?" he said.

"Will's going to a party."

He nodded. "I was supposed to cater that Halloween party you're photographing, but the guy canceled."

"He canceled the party?"

"No. The food. He must be using somebody cheaper. I got the feeling he didn't like my prices."

She shrugged. "Then he's a creep," she said. "Your prices are fair. Don't worry about it."

"I'm catering quite a few things on Halloween," he said. "He invited me to come to the party anyway, but I don't think I'm going to go." He looked at the vacuum. "Well," he said, "I ought to be going."

"Thanks for the cake," she said. Didn't he realize that she was anxious for him to leave? "Maybe I'll see you if you decide to go to the party."

He nodded. "You might want to put the cake in the refrigerator if you're not going to eat it right away," he said.

"I will," she said. "Thanks again."

"Let me know if it's not sweet enough. I like to get by with as little sugar as possible."

"I'm sure it's perfect."

"But let me know if it isn't," he said.

She looked at him. He looked at the vacuum. "Find out who's catering it if you can," he said.

"I could call the next day and ask if anybody else got sick," she said.

"No, don't do that," he said, alarmed.

"Kidding," she said, smiling.

He clicked his fingers. "I forgot to bring Mel's book back."

"I'm sure he's in no hurry for it," she said.

"Well," he said, "maybe I'll see you at the party."

She opened the door and smiled. Duncan lifted the vacuum and waved goodbye as he went down the walk. Like a child, he looked over his shoulder at the end of the walkway to see if she was still standing there. She was, but not because she was seeing him safely on his way. Mary Vickers's car had just pulled up to the curb. They were going to the playground to sit and talk while Will and Wagoner played, as they did two or three times a week.

Will was involved in G.I. Joe's taking over a new kingdom (a cordoned-off area of the bedroom rug, laid out by Mel during his visit the week before: a swarm of plastic cowboys and Indians, with the addition of free-standing castles that Mel had laboriously cut out of a book and glued together), but when the old Ford coasted to the curb, he began to run down the stairs. He and Wag were still too young to have inhibitions about throwing themselves in each other's arms and instantly resuming their important talk that had been heartlessly interrupted by Mary or Jody when they last insisted upon parting them. They *did* make a slight parody of their quick embraces, though perhaps it only seemed that way to Jody and they were not even aware of it. The slightly bumped foreheads and the fingers that tickled as they grabbed each other's waist might have been true awkwardness, the quickly locked eyes a conditioned response from infancy. In any case, they formed a unit of their own that always made Mary and Jody instant outsiders, so that they moved awkwardly toward each other, conscious of the lack of passion they themselves displayed.

Mary Vickers was Jody's best friend, but when intimacies were exchanged, they tended to be said with dropped eyes, and certain topics, such as Mary's marriage to Wagoner (her son was—and Jody never stopped marveling at this—Wagoner Fisk Vickers III), were never alluded to unless Mary initiated the conversation. Jody was better at not asking Mary why she didn't divorce her husband than Mary was about not prying into the reasons why Jody didn't marry Mel and move to New York. Then again, although she would hesitate to say it aloud,

Jody considered herself more in control than Mary Vickers. More of a survivor, if truth be told.

Duncan had been caught in the maelstrom of the arrival. Holding the vacuum aloft, waving to Jody, and exchanging a quick greeting with Mary Vickers, he bowed out, heading toward his car. Of course Mary Vickers and Jody agreed that Duncan was a sweet, harmless soul—someone whose positive attitude they could only be in awe of.

"Don't go upstairs," Jody called, seeing the boys' feet disappear up the stairs. "If we're going to the playground, we're going to the playground. G.I. Joe can win the war when you come home."

Will looked over the banister. "I just wanted to show him," he said.

Will had a way of always seeming moderate. He also had a way of making her remarks seem too cute. Of appearing adult, while she called out shrilly like a child.

"Show him for two minutes. Then we're leaving," she said.

Will hesitated. "We can look later," he said.

Clever. This meant that after the playground they would return to the house. Jody looked at Mary Vickers.

"Let's go," Mary Vickers said. "We want to get there while it's still light."

Will began to walk down the stairs.

"Wag!" Mary Vickers called.

He stomped down, overtaking Will.

"So is Duncan coming to the park with us?" Will said.

Wagoner stood at his mother's side, sulking.

"Duncan just came to borrow the vacuum. You didn't express any interest in Duncan when he was here."

"I didn't know he was leaving," Will said.

Was Will really hurt that Duncan wasn't going to the playground with them? Will's acting the part of the perfect host, a little late, was making her feel less than the perfect hostess. She searched his child's face: guileless. He thought whatever he thought.

"Duncan's gone," she said. "And we're gone, too, the minute you put on your coat."

The bench Mary Vickers and Jody sat on was across from the Episcopal church, whose bells rang early every Sunday morning and on numerous other occasions—so often, in fact, that the bells might have heralded the first fallen leaf of autumn and the first star of twilight. The bells were one of the things Jody always listened for, along with the daily screech of sirens, which began early in the morning, reached a hiatus around four o'clock, then sounded sporadically throughout the night. There was nothing in the newspaper to explain why the rescue squad, fire department, and ambulance constantly raced through the streets. It was Mel's belief that the sirens were turned on every time the men went to grab a burger at McDonald's. When you were driving, ambulances and rescue-squad wagons inevitably shot past, barely braking to go through the lights, weaving into oncoming traffic, stabilizing just as they seemed about to turn over in their wild trajectory toward one of the hospitals.

Will liked the sirens; for him, the potential for disaster was exciting. In his experience toppled soldiers shed no blood, and he had not been present when G.I. Joe got his cheek wound.

His own experience of pain had been the result of falling on the blacktop in back of the school, or being stricken with a sore throat or an earache, and without Jody's telling him to be brave, he had learned that he should not cry unnecessarily. The other boys had taught him that, the way they had taught him to use a slingshot and to call breasts hooters. Recently, Mel had been trying to teach him to whistle through a piece of grass held between his thumbs. Will's progress so far was what it would have been if he had been instructed to whistle through pudding. The nicely shaped little-boy hands, when the grass blade was clamped between the sides of the thumbs, suddenly looked boneless, molded from clay, and as he frowned at the blades of grass Jody had an inkling of what it would be like if she lived to see Will an old man, myopically staring at objects held close to his eyes. Mel felt that if Will could master whistling through grass, that would be a good preface to his calling "Hooters!" That was what he had said lying in bed the week before, trying to get a rise out of her. It amused Mel to pretend that he intended to corrupt Will—that he was her enemy, as was the passage of time, which would change her baby soon enough anyway.

Will and Wagoner were climbing the ladder to go down the slide, "the up-down" in Will's baby parlance, shooting to the bottom, racing around the side to climb the ladder again. Mary Vickers pretended to be an announcer telling the audience, *sotto voce*, about an upcoming show, in which Will 'n' Wag, as she called the performers, would be seen doing various amusing stunts sure to strike fear into their mothers' hearts. Sounding like an excited sports announcer narrating a batter's triumphant trot around the bases, she crossed her arms and whispered to Jody: "Now Wag's in the lead, coming down the slide, and we can see on the sidelines that the squirrel who's been watching is scared. Not so his sidekick, Will, who's four for four in successful rides to the bottom. Wag's dusting the slide—time out—and we can expect that the next ride down is going to be a particularly fast one. You know, our audience out there might be interested to know that part of the success of sliding depends on a slick slide that does *not* have a residue of sand. But back to the main action, and then at our station break, folks, an ad for Valium."

The summer before, Mary Vickers had had her first affair, with a playwright who had moved to town to team-teach a drama course at the university. Mary did not meet him there but ran into him by chance, at the all-night drugstore, where he was buying 3-D postcards of hawks floating over Skyline Drive at sunset. She had stopped at the bulletin board by the Kong game inside the sliding glass doors to see if anyone was advertising to do lawn work. The playwright came out then, slightly high on a few shots of Cuervo Gold, holding one of the postcards and snorting with appreciation. He showed her the card, as if she had been there waiting for him to exit. "Is this really out there?" he had asked. He had come to Virginia from New York for the summer. Walking to the parking lot, she suggested he take 29 south to North Garden, then cut through to route 250, as a good way to get to the mountains. Jody supposed, when Mary first told her these things, that it must have been obvious to Mary that she and the man would become lovers. It had happened between one visit Mary and Jody made to the playground and the next visit, so that when Mary sat on the bench and toed the dust like a sad horse, Jody had not been surprised—only perplexed that neither Mary nor the man thought it would last. It didn't last past the end of the semester, but during the period when they were meeting for clandestine pepper vodkas and holding hands early in the morning at Spudnuts, eating doughnuts and licking the sugar from each other's lips in the parking lot before going their separate ways, Jody had taken a photograph of Mary Vickers, naked to the waist, with a feather boa wrapped around her neck. Mary later mailed it to New York so it would be waiting for him when he went home. It was a soft-focus glamour-girl shot that Jody had sepia-toned, in which Mary—except for her sad, expressive eyes—looked like a little girl masquerading in her mother's clothes.

Not long after she photographed Mary Vickers, she had taken the boa from the shelf and shot a roll of color to explore its other possibilities. In a decorative way, it could make anything it was draped over look humorous, so she had let herself take a few of those shots, trying to work her way toward something more interesting. She coiled it so that it made a fuzzy turban on top of a melon. She photographed it weaving through her fingers. She photographed it stretched out, bouncing light off a reflector. Then she tried a twenty-second exposure, using only candles for illumination. When she studied the contact sheets later, she saw her inclination had been right. With a starburst filter, the tips of fur narrowed into threads that flashed to the top of the photograph like a spiderweb gleaming in sunlight.

On the bench near the fence, two mothers were ignoring their children and talking animatedly. The subject was former surgeon general C. Everett Koop, who, one of the women said, had apparently crept around his neighborhood with his mother when he was a child, carrying a garbage can that contained an ether-soaked rag; they would capture a cat, and the surgeon general would take it home to operate on. Whether Mary Vickers was paying any attention to the conversation was unclear, but the woman hearing it looked frightened to death. Mary Vickers was looking at the spot where Will and Wagoner crouched, studying something in the grass. Then she looked at her watch. She shrugged, because she knew Jody had seen her checking the time, and wound the scarf around her throat and pulled the end, pretending to hang herself. Jody knew that Mary Vickers envied her because she didn't have to go home and cook a meal. Will was always happy to eat cereal with fruit, or the two of them would have what Jody called a many-colored meal: She would arrange side by side on a plate a hot dog, a narrow squirt of mustard, a slice of avocado, a wedge of tomato, a carrot, a piece of green pepper. She and Will said nothing about their secret meals when Mel was there. Either they ate proper dinners she or Mel cooked, or they went out.

"It's time to go," Jody said as Wagoner ran by, arms stretched out like airplane wings. Will ran behind him, tilting his own arms and humming. Jody and Mary Vickers might as well have been monsters who had risen from the ground to claw in the boys' direction. *Please. Go back to the underworld.*

Don't be our mothers. No surrender to hooter monsters with grabby hands and obsessive ideas about the necessity of sleep. Just die! Be gone! Let us live free!

Across the playground the pilots were giggling, ready for lift-off, eager to leave the grassy runway behind.

"Maybe I should get on a plane and go to New York to visit him," Mary Vickers said, shrugging again and getting up to stare at the two boys in the distance. She plunged her hands into the pockets of her coat. "I have to admit that I envy you," she said. "Being able to plan your life so you can be gone when you want to. Being in love with somebody you can actually go and stay with."

"Mel's just a romantic," Jody said. "He's romanticized me so that he thinks I'm a great artist, and that I'd make a great wife." Her words surprised her. She was not used to expressing her doubts, even by making questions into statements.

"Aren't you thankful that somebody believes in you?" Mary Vickers said.

The pilots had expected artillery fire, but Jody was speaking softly as she came up behind them. They veered off course and were allowed to try for greater altitude one last time.

"Did Mel ever tell you he ran out of gas when he was driving Wag and Will to the lake?" Mary Vickers said. "He wanted me to keep it a secret. He thought you'd think he was irresponsible. Another time he called from New York and wanted to know what your favorite color was. He didn't know your favorite color."

Jody smiled. "You think everything he does is endearing."

"I told you," Mary Vickers said. "I think you're lucky. I envy you."

"You could leave Wagoner and do something else," Jody said. If Mary was going to keep after her, she thought it only fair that she be allowed to mention the unmentionable.

"You go first," Mary Vickers said. "Without you I'd go crazy. That would make it a lot easier to leave him."

F O U R

Jody sat next to Mel in the porch swing, pushing them gently back and forth with the tips of her toes. Mel was a tall man with disproportionately large hands and feet he was used to being kidded about. The dark brown eyes he had inherited from his Greek father were his best feature; from his English mother he had gotten his narrow lips, slight chin, and wavy hair. She had met his parents once, years before, when they visited Mel in Virginia. He had dropped out of business school and stayed around trying to figure out what to do, meanwhile writing a novel he never finished. He was rescued—if that was what it was—by his former room-mate from Exeter, who opened a gallery in New York City. Mel was in charge of the bookkeeping and administration of the gallery, but more and more often he dropped the names of the celebrities who'd come in to browse, mentioned the parties he tagged along to, discussions held below Sandro Chia's mural at Palio. Jody listened to his accounts of city life with the same mixture of affection and skepticism she reserved for Will's theory that G.I. Joes had proliferated all over the planet, so that everyone in the world but him had dozens. Will would come right out and say *I want*; Mel implied it, and could contain his breathless excitement better than Will.

Mel's plane from New York had been late, as usual. The long-promised airport improvements had nothing to do with flights; instead, bulldozers plowed up fields to expand the parking lots. It was no longer possible to abandon your car some distance from the airport to escape paying for parking. As Mel liked to point out, many of the so-called improvements in town were detractions. The city council couldn't decide whether to build a bypass or widen the highway again to accommodate the traffic. Signs saying Security Watch were posted on downtown streets as often as houses were broken into. Mel had been using these things as leverage, trying to convince her to move to New York.

When she called the airport and heard that his plane would be delayed an hour, she had rounded up Will and Wag, dumped Captain Magic Rainbow Beads into the tub, and helped the boys undress as the big bubbles rose. Blown from the palm of the hand, they stayed airborne as long as Pustefix bubbles sent sailing from the bubble wand. She launched Will's rubber turtle, which could float with a bar of soap in its back but now held a devotional candle, which she lit when she turned off the water. The two boys climbed into the tub with their Night-Viper G.I. Joes. After a few seconds, Will blew out the candle so Jody could remove the little glass cup and Joe could have a ride in the turtle's belly. It occurred to Jody that an idyll such as that might have been what some real soldier envisioned, dying in combat: to be set afloat, if not among the bulrushes, then amid the Captain Magic bubbles, safe in the hollow belly of a grinning turtle. She got wet helping them soap up and rinse off. Out of the tub, Wag exaggerated his shivering and suffering, allowing her to fold him in a big bath towel and hold him against her legs. Will took hold of his towel and shimmied, like a person about to lose a Hula-Hoop that had already slipped to his knees. Neither boy would let her come near him with a brush. Wag had pleaded to bring the big damp bath towel to play with in the backseat as she drove to the airport to get Mel. All the way there they held it high, a sail that wouldn't fill with wind but that they made to flap erratically, giggling behind it as she took the winding curves. Later Mel had gotten them to bed with almost no trouble, though he was probably wondering, as was she, whether the house didn't seem almost *too* quiet.

"No wonder kids have nightmares," Mel said. "Everything in those books has to be made literal. It says, 'The wind that night had a bite to it,' and there's a drawing of a gaping mouth with shark's teeth." He bared his teeth and gently sank them into Jody's shoulder. Then he leaned back, sighing dramatically. "It'll be his lucky day when he can read pornography under the sheets with a flashlight," he said.

Wag was spending the night because Mary Vickers's husband had come home drunk. Mel had used this information, too, as leverage, saying that people were no different wherever you went. He implied that he was a saint, compared to men like Wagoner Vickers.

"How can you compare yourself to a fifty-year-old insurance agent?" Jody said.

"How can you pretend to be excited by taking pictures of glassy-eyed girls holding nosegays when you should be taking serious photographs?"

"Don't put me down for supporting myself," she said. "I spend a lot of time photographing for myself."

He had her, though. He was only repeating what she had said to him on the phone earlier in the week, when she had been feeling blue. Mel had made the mistake of trying to bolster her with praise, which only resulted in her becoming reflexively cynical. It was easy to be admired in a small town, she had said. Reassuring to know that you could make a life for yourself. But it was also a dead end. Even the wedding photographs themselves had started to make her sad: documents that would allow people to look back and wonder about their naïveté or their self-righteousness that would one day turn to skepticism. That had been Jody's reaction when she looked back at photographs of herself and Wayne. She could see that she had romanticized their little house into something it had never been. That she had remembered the landscapes as more inspirational than they were, filled with scrub and pines and mountains too far in the distance. Even the photographs she had been so proud of in those days now seemed terribly forced: an obvious detail seen with a too-practiced eye; the beginner's conventionally unconventional cropping; filters that artificially changed what would have radiated as intrinsically complicated if photographed correctly. These days she was transfixed by one of Man Ray's rayographs of what looked like a white ship in a bottle, fuzzy enough to be a dream ship, the bottle floating against a cloudy sky, and by Coplans's incisive examination of his own aging body. She wanted to be capable of working with such exactitude. And only privacy would make that possible: no more polite comments about the weather as she worked; no bottles of champagne unless she was so proud of what she turned out that *she* went out and bought the champagne.

"Are we ever going to take that walk, or are we going to sit here with horns locked all night?" Mel said.

She went into the house without comment to get a warmer sweater. A cold wind had begun to blow. Rummaging through

the hall closet, she thought of the illustration in Will's book
and smiled at Mel's comment about everything in storybooks
having to be personified. Sometimes Mel doctored Will's
books for her amusement. In one that gave samples of things
mentioned, such as a scratch-and-sniff patch that smelled of
roses, he had crossed out the word "Straw" on one of the
pages and written "Kiefer" above it. At the end of another
book he had taped an index card with an alternate ending, in
which all the characters flushed each other down the toilet and
went to Happy Sewer Land. Will knew Mel's changes were
jokes and would never let her pass them off without explaining
them in detail. She blamed Will's crayoning in the stairwell on
Mel's scribbling in his books. Mel maintained that Will was a
budding artist. "Would you rather have him take it out on the
stairwell now or grow up and waste his time being Cy Twom-
bley?" he had said. Still, she had made the two of them re-
paint the stairwell. They had come upstairs with white paint
on the tips of their noses and brushes held behind them like
horses' tails and pranced around the kitchen. She worried that
they thought of her as uptight every time she tried to preserve
order. She had a sense, too, of how ridiculous she sounded
every time she tried to cajole Will. For some reason Mel never
sounded ridiculous, but she did, saying, "Oh, *don't* you want
to hear a bedtime story? I'll turn all the adults into funny
animals and pretend that one of your favorite TV characters is
there with them. It's a party that you can go to without having
a bath! Just close your eyes. I'll get you a puppy and double
your allowance and never again cut your fingernails if only
you'll listen to this very, very important bedtime story."
  Bedtime was always a difficult time. Sometimes she was
convinced that Will did not love her at all and that if he were
reincarnated as a cowboy he would drop a lasso around her
neck. If he became a doctor, his bedside manner would consist
of walking away from her bed. As a dragon, he would breathe

fire into her face. His desire to escape was transparent, yet she was also sure that he would marry her if she were not his mother. As it was, he pushed her away when he could stand to, hurt her when he couldn't stop himself, and nestled against her at night when he was too tired to be anything but her baby. Sometimes he crept into the bedroom early in the morning, on the run from having been imprisoned in some dream. Other times he put his toy stethoscope around his neck and listened to the heartbeat of the table leg, the porcelain vase, the amaryllis stalk—those mysterious, silent rumblings that went on in the adult world all the time. He watched TV and imitated the stance of cowboys about to rope a steer, although what Jody noticed were the scars on his knees. He had fallen on the blacktop at school so many times. You would think that a gathering tornado drove him to race for the distance, at a speed no one could sustain.

She felt a strong bond with Will, but it was Mel who adored him *sensibly*, Mel who was flexible enough to use common sense instead of preconceived ideas, Mel who could silence Will by looking pained by what he was doing quicker than she could stop him by grabbing his hand and pulling him. Mel was gracious—it was one of his best qualities; he was genuinely gracious. He said that because Will was not his child, he found it easier to go to the heart of the issue.

"I'm going to check on them," Mel said as he passed by Jody, who was rearranging jackets in the hall closet. A mummylike stillness in the room upstairs had made him suspicious. (He had come in to see if Jody had been swallowed by the silence; he should have known that she was brooding— brooding and preparing herself for an argument if he didn't back down and stop pressuring her to move.)

Mel walked close to Will's perfectly straight body, put his nose lightly on the tip of Will's nose and Will rose up, squealing. Wag also gave up his pretense of being asleep.

"We were playing mole," Will said. One of their favorite
games was mole. They burrowed deep into the covers Jody
piled on the bed—she had a horror of awakening cold with not
enough blankets—and twitched their noses, following the
scent of buried treasure, or quickly flapping back a corner of
the covers and letting the wind tell them the best route to
escape from their enemies.

"Finish playing mole and go to sleep before we get back, or
we'll both be in trouble," Mel whispered.

Coming downstairs, he took his scarf off the banister, where
he had draped it when he arrived. It was going to be too cold
for late-night walks soon. The rustling of leaves would end.
The mountains would be easier to see, fading from gold to
bluish gray.

Jody got off the porch swing when he came out of the
house. She had been worrying that if they married she would
take him for granted. Not that he would take her for granted,
but that she would take him for granted. He wanted to have
a child with her, and she did not want more children. This
meant that she would let him down and be disappointed in
herself, while he would no doubt survive with his feelings
intact. He always encouraged her. If she succeeded as a photographer, she feared, she might not need his encouragement
in the same way. She needed to need him. Need enforced
manners on people. It was only children, who made no dis-
tinction between what they needed and what they wanted,
who were confused enough, or honest enough, to give in to
thrashing in the presence of whoever foiled them.

He put his arm around Jody's shoulder. She had a sudden
thought, turned, and locked the door. He saw her questioning
look and folded his hands as if in prayer. She hadn't been in
the house when Will spoke, so she didn't know the boys were
awake. He put his cheek on his hands and closed his eyes,
letting her assume, from the gesture, that Will and Wag were

sleeping the sleep of angels. He felt a twinge about deliberately misleading her, but finally it seemed a minor matter: sniffing moles or slumbering angels. They were safe in bed.

He thought about telling her that he had made inquiries about the possibility of Will's attending Collegiate. That he thought they should move to a larger apartment in New York—farther downtown, where you could see the sky. That she could have a darkroom in the same building where he worked, in SoHo.

Her head was resting on his shoulder. They had taken this walk so many times. He had resolved, so many times, that he would succeed in persuading her to marry him. Silently, he began to rehearse his opening line, so that he was surprised himself when only a tired "I love you" came out, and then nothing more.

F I V E

King Kong was a mystery, but Jody suspected the frog was Bob Walsh, because it was quite tall and had Walsh's way of walking. Many people had taken off their masks or headpieces, but King Kong had revealed nothing of himself. She had taken a photograph of him holding his hairy costume away from his chest and shaking it to allow some air to circulate inside.

Jody was photographing a Halloween party at an abandoned church twenty miles outside of town. She had been hired by one of the men who owned the hundred acres and planned on tearing down the old clapboard church. Earlier in the year she had photographed the same man's daughter's wedding, which took place in an orchard adjacent to his Earlysville property. He had made it clear that if she hadn't been involved with someone, he would have liked to have an affair. Will had been along that day, dressed in a gray suit that resembled Mel's favorite suit, because at the last minute the baby-sitter had canceled, and she couldn't get Duncan or Mary Vickers on the phone. She had promised Will a Lego train if his behavior was impeccable, and as the father of the bride tried to ingratiate himself with Jody, Will kept coming to her side—and her rescue—with visions of train tracks and imaginary puffs of smoke rising in his eyes. Lowering his voice, as if his whispered tones would escape Will's notice, the father of the bride suggested having a drink, in order to offer her some advice about real estate investments in the county. She was curt with him because she wasn't interested, but also amazed that he thought she had that kind of money. The following day, three dozen irises had arrived, and that afternoon Will's new train whizzed through Iris-land: water glasses filled with flowers meant to approximate trees the train would pass by.

At the wedding, she had moved away quickly once the man's intentions were clear, walking across the grass, holding Will's hand. She wondered how many times women tempted Mel in New York. Mary Vickers's expression about Jody's refusal to make a permanent commitment to Mel was that she was "playing with fire." Hardly a unique way to express the idea of danger, but over time Jody had come to interpret what Mary Vickers meant by "fire" as having to do with all the matches carefully cupped in waiters' hands as they ignited the white candles on your dinner table; all the flame-haired beauties who had back-combed and sprayed their hair to make it wild and electric; all the hot tips you got every day, about as-yet-unannounced corporate mergers, about which doorman would tell you honestly how many tenants might be about to die. Mary insisted upon seeing New York as either burning or smoldering, whether it involved physical passion, or the burnt-rubber smell that rose off the streets from so many slammed brakes, or lunatics who wired themselves and blew apart on the subway. Of course Mary Vickers feared and hated New York so much because she had convinced herself that it was the city—anthropomorphized as a burning witch—that had taken her lover away from her. She was sure that if Jody didn't watch out, time and the city could well do the same with Mel.

Jody looked at Mel across the room. He was dressed as a stalk of celery. He had borrowed the costume from a ballerina whose husband was one of the new artists represented by his gallery. BAM popped into Jody's mind, and she smiled. She didn't think Mel would turn to ashes. She still was not sure that marrying him and moving to New York was the right thing. Though she would never say it to Mary Vickers, her hesitancy had less to do with the vague feeling that the moment wasn't right than with the belief that the more she withheld, the more Mel would desire her. She did not think it was necessary to be withholding in a physical way, but she hesitated to talk too much, to have too many discussions. She and Wayne had talked their relationship to death, but when he left, he had taught her an important lesson by leaving unexpectedly and silently. It had been a rude awakening, but later a relief, to find that saying nothing could be the strongest way of communicating—and also the strongest way to flirt: A hesitant shrug or narrowing of your eyes in concentration as you listened could make a man's heart beat harder. You could honestly say "I don't know" and have any number of men assume that you only wanted to keep your sphinxlike secrets. From the moment she started studying photographs she had given herself permission to move farther and farther away from Wayne. It had driven him crazy when she taped on the walls photographs of people she did not know. He hated it that she began to submerge herself in a world of nameless faces. He saw himself losing her to a drug called silver halide.

But they stayed lovers. That was the other part of the trick:

to get as close physically as the other person wanted. To jump into the tub when they were showering, pull cold champagne from under the bed, announce on the way to dinner with another couple that you were not wearing underwear. If you came through physically, men would give you a lot of time to decide whether you would marry them, because some part of them would foolishly think that you had already chosen.

She stood by one of the narrow, drafty church windows and realized that it would probably be easy to reenter the church some other day, even if it was locked. There might be enough Halloween souvenirs and enough character to the run-down church itself to make photographing the empty interior worthwhile. The church faced west; late afternoon would be the time to come. She unscrewed her camera from the tripod and began to take a few last pictures with the lens wide open, holding the camera above her head, aiming down and guessing about what would make it into the frame.

Mel came up beside her, the leafy celery top hanging down his chest like a pale green jabot.

"I just called the Careys'," he said. "Will's on his second pair of fangs. Nothing seems to be winding down over there."

"Where did you find a phone?" she said, surprised.

"I struck up a conversation with a guy who had a phone in his car." He nodded toward the door.

"You found somebody with a cellular phone in *Charlottesville*?"

He shrugged. "You're the one who's always telling me it's not Siberia. If I had my way, we'd be in New York right this minute." He put his arm around her shoulder. Jody was dressed in 1950s regalia: a crinoline, over which she wore a skirt embossed with a poodle that flashed blue rhinestone eyes; a pink blouse with a silver circle pin; white bobby sox; loafers with bright copper pennies. She had pulled her hair back in a ponytail.

"You know," Mel said, "you look like the type who wants to party all night but won't put out."

"Not true," she said. "As silly as this seems, it's work. And if you remember—"

He put his fingers over her lips as Bozo strutted by, honking his bulbous nose. Bozo had acquired a fur cape and a wife who had pushed her eye mask to the top of her head. She was trying to steer Bozo toward the front door, but he was drunk and got away from her, swirling his fur like a bullfighter's cape as she went toward him.

"I remember," Mel said.

Before leaving the house, they had had sex in the shower while Will marched his new G.I. Joe (his fourth) around the living-room floor, making it do maneuvers over such obstacles as Mel's running shoes and his own plastic-wrapped bubble-gum Dracula fangs, which he was to put in his mouth later that night. Will loved Halloween. The costumes and shrill cries at the door for candy that had frightened her as a child had never intimidated him. It was interesting to see what a child feared on his own, what fears were communicated to him, and what he was absolutely fearless about. The first time he tasted a soda he had been as shocked as if he'd drunk acid. He shrank from cats but would pat any dog. Halloween was a breeze, but as a small child he had not wanted the overhead light to be put off when the Christmas tree lights were turned on. Vampires were shocking but fascinating. Joan Rivers would make him run from the room. He loved cap pistols but was afraid of the vacuum. The flamingo night-light was scarier than being left in darkness. Will was afraid to put his face in water but fearless in the seat of a bumper car. He once cried because he looked into a man's mouth and saw gold fillings and thought he could catch them, like a cold.

The band had switched from rock and roll to the big band sound, and Richard Nixon led King Kong onto the dance floor, both stepping aside to avoid colliding with Bozo the matador, still swishing the fur cape. Here was a roomful of people, Jody thought, most of them parents, behaving as if they were children so out of control they had to be threatened. Monsters that all parents swore existed only in their children's nightmares cavorted with one another, plotting mischief, entering the den of smoke, uncorking bottles with no regret, even if genies were trapped inside.

Mel smiled at Jody. "Too caught up in this craziness to take pictures?"

"No," she said. "I was just wondering who'd have a cellular phone in this town."

"Would you like me to get you one?" he said. "Maybe in lieu of an engagement ring? Keep up with the times?"

She shook her head no.

"A cop," he said.

"A cop?"

"A private investigator."

"What are you talking about?" she said.

"That's who had the phone. A guy who's a private investigator. He's doing what you're doing: taking pictures. But he's got a tiny hand-held job. Some woman who's off in Aruba hired him to get a picture of her husband with his lover. At first he thought it was going to be impossible, because everybody was in costume, but he came anyway and got the big payoff because the guy's in regular shoes. They're the only shoes the guy ever wears. He said he already had a dozen pictures of the guy and the secretary, and that the guy was always wearing those same black wing-tips."

"You're putting me on."

"Why would I be putting you on? It's not to my advantage to make this place sound exciting."

"But how did he happen to tell you that?"

"I went outside on the off chance there was a phone anywhere in sight. He was talking on the phone in his car. I hung around, and he let me use the phone. He was happy that he had what he needed and could split."

"You just walked up and asked if you could use his phone?"

Mel nodded. "What's so strange about that? I said I wanted to make sure my kid was okay."

She felt a pang when he said "my kid." Will really did seem to be as much Mel's child as her own. He had Mel's way of sitting with his legs uncrossed, both feet dangling because he could not yet plant them on the floor. He bit his bottom lip when he was concentrating, like Mel. He had Mel's way of saying no without shaking his head as an accompanying gesture. Both of them often threw their pillows on the floor when they slept. And of course they never drank the right beverage from the right glass. For a drink of water Will would take a tiny glass; for an inch of apple juice he'd reach for a beer glass. It was just the cast of his eyes that sometimes reminded her of Wayne—that way of looking slightly down and to the side, even when nothing important seemed to be happening there.

"Guess who!" a flamingo said, stepping in front of her. She could smell alcohol on the flamingo's breath. Like the private detective, she looked down and saw Duncan's worn Adidas, though she could have told from the voice alone.

"Duncan," she said, and he nodded without taking off his headpiece. A palm tree stood next to him: someone in a badly made outfit fashioned out of a sheet painted to look like wood. Big green-painted cardboard palm fronds protruded from the shoulders. The person wore a black eye mask, with a small painted moon curving over one of the eyes.

"Take our picture," Duncan said, stepping in front of the camera. He put a pink wing around the palm tree. "Mel," Duncan said, "I really enjoyed that Harry Mulisch book you let me borrow. I keep forgetting to bring it back."

Jody inclined her head and looked into the camera. There

they were: two happy, silly people who had no doubt given great thought as to how they would appear. They didn't seem that different from the engaged couples who put on their best clothes and sat side by side to smile for posterity.

As Duncan and the palm tree walked away, a dog came up and sniffed Jody's leg. A fireman tugged at the dog's leash, smiling at Jody and Mel and saying that the dog was really a rabbit in disguise, but that he was a real fireman.

"I'm the woman in the Toulouse-Lautrec painting," a blue-faced woman announced, butting her way in front of the camera.

Jody looked through the lens. The woman stood very still, chin resting on her shoulder.

"Got it," Jody said, looking up. But she had not taken the picture. There was something about the woman she didn't like—something deeper than the paint and the rakish hat. As the woman moved away Jody moved the tripod a little to the side, centering Mel in the picture. She did not take that picture either, because when she cared about someone, she didn't like to waste time taking pictures that didn't reveal him. Mel was sure that he was being photographed, though. He put the celery top back over his head and stood very formally, hands at his sides. Was it mock seriousness, or was he really so used to being accommodating? For a moment she felt vulnerable and sentimental, as if she wanted to rush into Mel's arms.

That was the good thing about having a camera between you and the rest of the world: It afforded some protection, a way to stall for time. She walked forward and gave him only a quick hug. She could almost hear Mary Vickers's voice: *Playing with fire.* She kissed Mel quickly on the lips. His lips were cool, as was his hand, which he put briefly on the back of her neck as they kissed.

She looked around for Mary Vickers, who had come as Cinderella, to say goodbye, but the room was very crowded.

It was possible that Mary Vickers had left early with Wagoner, who, as usual, had gotten drunk. Those thoughts flashed through her mind in the few seconds it took Mel to bend and zip her camera bag. Camera bag over his shoulder and tripod in her hand, the celery stalk and the American Bandstand cutie started out into the night.

As they left the church, Mary Vickers was about a mile ahead of them down the road. She had quarreled with Wagoner (if you could call it that—she insisted he turn over the car keys; he tossed them at her and walked off). She had sat in the cold car for a few minutes, expecting that he would come to his senses and reappear, but as she waited she got angrier and thought that he could find his own way home. One of his drinking buddies could escort him. One of those men whose faces got mottled by drink until they turned as rosy as the madras pants they wore.

Mary passed over a small bridge and looked at the moon glowing over a field. She drove by a trickle of a brook that passed under some willow trees. The spring before, during Will 'n' Wag's short-lived fascination with butterfly hunting, she and Jody and the boys had picnicked under those trees. Jody had described to her a photograph of Nabokov, running forward with a butterfly net—Jody could make other people's photographs seem more real than what was actually in front of her as she spoke—and they had agreed that, at the boys' early age, it was impossible to say what interests would keep up, what hobbies were worth investing money in. Mel had fashioned the butterfly nets from netting that held the padding around busts that had been shipped to the gallery in New York, and sturdy sticks he had collected on a walk. In spite of everyone's complaints that there were no available men in New York, when you did find a New York man, he seemed too good to be true. It was her ex-lover she was thinking of.

Licking her chapped lips, she remembered his taste for alcohol that burned going down—drinks meant to get you wired, none of those diluted bourbon-and-waters that Wagoner sipped until bedtime. She tried to think that she had been attracted, yet again, to another alcoholic, but that was an oversimplification. She had been attracted to someone who was energetic and a little crazy, and who had ventured to involve her in his flirtation with danger.

A sepia shadow spread in front of the car. She found it difficult to believe that what she saw was real, that it wasn't just some externalization of what had been going through her mind. It was as if Impossibility had materialized—taken real form—so that she could hit up against it. What had been going through her mind? The willow trees sprang up. She had bit her lip as the car slammed to a stop. There was the cold taste of blood in her mouth.

She had hit a deer. All in a second, her thoughts and her car collided with a deer that ran in front of the headlights. She touched her seat belt to make sure it was fastened. She looked out the front window. For a vertiginous second, the shadow rose and twisted before it crumpled, like something in a horror movie. She fiddled with the shoulder strap of the seat belt like a lady lightly fingering her corsage. Below her fingers, her heart was racing. She said—probably out loud—"My God. I hit a deer."

There were no other cars. She kept searching the rearview mirror. She looked out the window on the passenger's side and saw the moon again, but no cars coming in either direction. In a few seconds headlights flashed into the rearview, but by then it seemed she had been sitting there for an hour. She was too shaken to get out of the seat. Rather than having an urge to bolt, she felt glued in place: a heavy person, a ludicrous statue, a woman in a formal dress sitting behind the wheel of a car, a deer crumpled in front of her headlights.

Lights began to blink behind her. A man in a tuxedo who had been at the party was tapping on the window, asking if she was all right. His round-faced wife, who had dressed as Mao, was standing behind her husband, her hands clasped over her mouth. Eventually she lowered one hand and made a circular motion.

The window rolled down, but Mary Vickers didn't remember having done it. New York, she thought suddenly, but what she was saying was "No. I'm fine." She was fine, but she had hit a deer. Mao's hand was now clasping her hand, which gripped the seat belt.

As more cars stopped, Mao helped her out of the car. A real estate agent dressed as Peter Pan ran past everyone and bent over the deer. "Stay back," he shouted. "You don't know what's going to happen." He said that he had a rifle. That he had a rifle, but he didn't think he was going to have to use it. Suddenly Wagoner had come from nowhere and was looking at Mary, perplexed. Or maybe he was worried. Or angry, because people in front of the car were assessing the damage. One headlight shot off to the side, cockeyed. There was the moon, over to the right, and the beam of light to the left from the headlight.

The deer was dead. Wagoner, as if he had been just a moment's apparition, had suddenly disappeared (later, he would tell her that once he saw she was all right he ran down the hillside to take a piss before his bladder exploded). "Let's move the cars," Batman was saying. "We'll have a real pileup if we don't."

The wind blew a swirl of leaves against Mary Vickers's leg as she stood shakily outside the car, and she jumped, thinking that something had stabbed her. She could smell the dead deer's blood, and taste blood inside her mouth. Mel stood beside her, frowning and examining her cut lip. If Mel was there, then Jody must be there. She looked down and saw that the side mirror had broken. Glass beads spread out in the road as though fish had spawned there. Was this the same world in which little boys chased butterflies? She turned and looked at Jody.

Jody had been moving fast. She had a roll of 1000 ASA in her camera and was in the process of taking photographs of Casper the Ghost as he crouched with Peter Pan by the car headlights. As she moved the camera and Mary Vickers's startled look suddenly became the central image of the frame, she clicked quickly. Thank you, God, she was thinking, for the invention of the autowinder. The next shot she took was the photograph that would later be blown up and hung on the large wall to the right-hand side of Haveabud's gallery in New York—the primary display wall, the place people always looked as they began to find their way into the depths of the gallery: Mary Vickers's eyes, bright enough to bore a hole through the camera lens, full moon shining to one side, people clotted together on the road, and in the background the large form of a ghost, white body billowing in the wind, looking down at who knew what.

≈≈≈

Of course you do not want the child to be a ventriloquist's dummy, but if there could be a bit more sitting on the knee, a little less of the back of the head and more of the profile as you spoke, that might be all the better. The child that reminds you of your own mortality needs so much tending to—so many wisps of hair brushed off the forehead, so many dollar bills handed out, so many anklet cuffs turned down, so much humming to accompany the soprano-sung solo—that it is almost impossible to decide whether to be as quick-talking as an escaped convict, or as patient as a penitent.

It is understandable that parents play a little game of self-deception and think they know everything about their child—that with their peripheral vision and with their ear inched backward an extra bit to listen they need not turn to see the child's predictable expression: the gleeful smile, the lowered eyes. In this way, they miss the unexpected. They make the mistake of thinking children are simpler than they, and *that therefore they have children figured out. (The children know better. They know that at least some of the time they can rush toward danger faster than their parents can stop them. That the parent who confiscates the water gun has failed to notice the slingshot in the back pocket. That tying shoelaces is a reassuring activity for parents. That off-key bedtime singing should be tolerated because it helps parents unwind.)*

You have created the child, but you could not have anticipated the child's power. Because the child's presence and desires are so constant, it becomes the course of least possible pain to persuade yourself that being subsumed is synonymous with parenthood. You can only pray that by early evening the child's eyelids will grow heavy with sleep. Then you hope that the sleeping child will not loom large in your own dreams, that once the night-light has been switched on, that beam of light alone may guide the child to dreamland.

In the silence of the house, you can sort out the day's failures and successes. You can admit that you have approached the child with a mixture of awe, regret, and envy. Wouldn't it be nice to scream louder than the child? To plead for peace as diligently as the child pleads for adventure? Couldn't the tables be turned, and couldn't you be found hiding underneath?

Parents can endure only so many tears before they become impervious, can listen to only so much pleading before whatever is being requested—the smooth peanut butter, the puppy in the pound—begins, cosmically, not to matter. It is predictable that the child denied a mongrel will contort its face into a version of the thing it most desires.

Fact: The child is your child whether or not the crib seems some days like a sinking ship. In order to proceed, focus your attention even though the haunting lullaby you sing distracts you. Grab on to the diaper as if you were clinging to the mast of a ship. Ignore the Sirens' song tinkling on the child's music box that would lure you into drowning in memories of your own childhood. Consult the experts and let them steer the way; call a sympathetic friend whose child is six months older.

There are so many books published to advise you about the child's upbringing, so many predictions about patterns you will notice and pleas to which you will be subjected. Psychologists will speak to you on early-morning television shows, mothers in the park will disagree, relatives will try to pull the rug out from under whatever you believe, the pediatrician's calm may turn to poorly disguised mystification, and the comic on late-night TV will effectively satirize the creature whose existence you care so much about.

The message is always to change doubt to certainty and proceed. *Sit by the sandbox with newfound strength. Embrace the squirming child and urge him to behave differently. Insist on eye contact when you speak. Do not let others turn the child upside down. Check the baby-sitter's references. Lock the cabinet that contains the cleaning products below the sink. Regular visits to the doctor. Two security blankets, so one can be washed. Check toe room in shoes regularly, by depressing the leather underneath your thumb. Comb tangled hair from the ends up. Speak out against environmental hazards. Look out for danger, but do not communicate your fear to the child. Buckle your seat belt. Cut down on consumption of red meat. Learn a jingle called "The Toothbrush Is Your Friend." Advise him not to bother kitty when she's eating. Try to make a game of gathering up toys with the child. Don't overdramatize the scary parts of books. Do everything right, all the time, and the child will prosper. It's as simple as that, except for fate, luck, heredity, chance, the astrological sign under which the child was born, his order of birth, his first encounter with evil, the girl who jilts him in spite of his excellent qualities, the war that is being fought when he is a young man, the drugs he may try once or too many times, the friends he makes, how he scores on tests, how well he endures kidding about his shortcomings, how ambitious he becomes, how far he falls behind, circumstantial evidence, ironic perspective, danger when it is least expected, difficulty in triumphing over circumstance, people with hidden agendas, and animals with rabies. With these things in mind, you will watch the child hopscotch from certainty to uncertainty, throwing the stone of trust before him, going all the way to the end by hopping one-footed, then turning and hopping back, full grown, much taller, with a puzzled expression that may not leave his face whether he is succeeding or failing.*

Does it seem impossible that the child will grow up? That the bashful smile will become a bold expression? The sparkling eyes in need of corrective lenses? That fevers will subside, that there will be no more bloody knees, that a briefcase will replace the blue security blanket? You must resist the tendency to think ahead; wishing for peace is not the same as wanting things to change forever, and when all is said and done (a state only songwriters believe in), the child will never really be gone, even though he grows up. You will find that although the child may be remembered in association with one or two prized toys, more likely the child will be remembered alone, standing with his legs parted, his arms dangling at his sides, pants fallen down a bit so that only the toes of the sneakers are visible. He will be standing the way he stood in the snapshot, with an expanse of field—or maybe the beach—around him. A little thing, but you will remember that distinctly without having a photograph in front of you. That will be the way, in fact, the child will stay: a visual image—one that, even at the time, you squinted to look harder at, whether or not a camera was raised to your eye.

When you are thirty, the child is two. At forty, you realize that the child in the house, the child you live with, is still, when you close your eyes, or the moment he has walked from the room, two years old. When you are sixty, and the child is gone, the child will also be two, but then you will be more certain. Seeing pictures of your child at different ages, you will not hesitate for a moment. You will point to the two-year-old, not the ten-year-old or the twenty-year-old. He will always be that high. With a nick above the eyebrow. Those eyes, at that point a bit too large for his face, so that, in remembering the eyes, you are sure that your child possessed startling intensity. He might be wearing some article of clothing purchased for a special occasion, but unless the picture of the shirt with the anchor and the sheepshank knot is right in front of you, you will not think much about that. He will be in typical little-boy clothes, smiling or looking straight at the camera with a tolerant expression that may show a hint of fatigue: Another picture? Why do you want it? What can it mean to you? He will be there with you without special costumes or toys as the years go by: the child alone, more and more a fact. Your life before the child seems too long ago to think of. What happened with the child, something of a blur. There were late-night walks in the summer heat, weren't there? Didn't the child once assume that you could give him pointers about how to fly? Didn't he think he was recreating the rumbling of Vesuvius with the plastic straw in the glass of chocolate milk? You go on—and the child goes on—but you change, as the child sees you. You do, but he does not. He stays the same, no matter how many marriages, mortgages, dogs, and children he may surround himself with—he does not change, so he is not vulnerable. It becomes difficult to remember that he ever was. That the dog snapped at him, and he was afraid. That the cut got infected. That night after night, the same blue-bodied demon flicked its tail in his dreams. Sticky fingers. Wet sheets. Wet kisses. A flood of tears. As you remember him, the child is always two.

S I X

In New York, every crack in the sidewalk seemed to Mel to portend disaster. Wouldn't panes of glass be blown out of skyscrapers? That had happened so often with the John Hancock building in Boston that for a long time people were not allowed to walk beneath it. The situation with the homeless was already so grim you didn't want to have to think about buildings tipping over, construction accidents, small things gathering speed and force as they dropped to earth. If you thought of New York as precarious, it would do you in; the way to keep going was to take big strides even if you felt like shuffling, to come on stage like the MC even if you were only the warm-up act.

Step on a crack, break your mother's back, Mel kept thinking. His mother had been dead for years. Then maybe bad luck would befall his father? Nothing had befallen his father so far but a woman twenty years his junior, who lived with him in his Scottsdale, Arizona, condominium. His father had stopped smoking, joined a country club, and was taking flying lessons. Step on a crack or not, the world was an unpredictable place. He was back in the awful pattern of finding fear in a handful of dust, when he should have been savoring life in every egg of caviar he spooned onto his tongue.

Mel was on his way to the second meeting with D. B. Haverford, who had bought him lunch at Petrossian the week before. Haverford was moving his gallery uptown and wanted Mel to work for him. He must never know that childish rhymes went through Mel's mind, that over the weekend, after a cold walk during which Mel had again not gotten up the courage to ask Jody to marry him, he had cried. That Mel had seriously been thinking about going to a psychic at the Ansonia Hotel. That because the woman Mel loved wouldn't marry him, he was even thinking about leaving the city and going to her, to see if that would impress her. For D. B. Haverford, Mel had put on his Charivari suit, with a moss-green shirt and no tie. The more audacious he was in his dress, the more compliments he got. Being a graduate of Dartmouth was a great embarrassment to him, but he covered for it by being the first to bring it up, shaking his head and saying that he had turned down Yale (not the truth; he hadn't even applied) because in his youth he had only wanted to ski. When Mel shrugged, he looked as helpless as someone forced to stand and recite something he hadn't memorized. At Dartmouth he had been the lead in two plays and the applause had made him seriously consider becoming an actor, though he had eventually capitulated to his father's demands that he go to business school at his alma mater, U.Va. His father had also been an excellent skier, and Mel had never learned how to outski him, though for years he had dreams in which he did, leaving his father behind, buried in avalanches. Years before, he had tried to write about the competitiveness that existed between them, but probably he had tried to write for the wrong reason: to exorcise demons instead of trying to court them and see if, in a fair fight, they won out or the writer did. The analyst he saw during those years pointed out to him that he was very goal-oriented. In the novel, the analyst became a humorous figure who listened to his patient's stories about skiing and replied with anecdotes about tennis. As he was writing the book, and during the time he saw the doctor, he found the courage to quit school and to try to envision something to do with his life other than what his father would have liked. Mel's grandfather left him a house in Williamstown and some money when he died. He sold the house the same spring he met Jody. She had just moved south and was figuring out how to make a living. Jody had seemed to him genuinely sad—so much so that he was surprised she didn't turn out to be a transient, that she stayed in town, placed ads in the paper and started a business, functioned like a person who was not oppressed. All the particulars of her sadness intrigued him, so that he would have fantasies about Wayne and the bad way he had treated her, imagine her other suitors who fell short of the mark as keener competition than they were. He had thought she was younger than she was, so he had lied about his age by a couple of years—an entirely pointless thing to do, because women never minded that men were older. He had no reason to trust her, so he told her about the sale of the house but not about the money he had also been left after his grandfather's death—also pointless, but he didn't know then that she had very little interest in other people's money. He pretended that his novel did not mean much to him, though she probably would not have asked to read it anyway, being hesitant to ask anything that might seem to be a favor. He never mentioned his analyst, but since Freud and Jung were among her books, it was doubtful that she would have thought less of him for seeing a psychiatrist. She had always turned out to be other than he expected.

A few weeks after Mel first met Jody, he loaned her money. To get the roof repaired, to buy the new camera lenses she needed, whatever was necessary to make her house habitable and to get her career started. He slept with her the second time he saw her—the first time he saw her alone, really, because he had first met her at a party. He had dismissed his life story by saying that his father was overbearing and that he had too often given in, so that it was only recently that he was getting his life together. She whispered when she talked about her life. There was something very seductive about that, and at the same time consoling, as if he were being told a fairy tale. The next night, when she was also whispering to him in bed, he teased her about it, and she said that she was whispering because she didn't want to wake Will. He pointed out that the thunderstorm earlier that evening hadn't awakened Will. "You're right," she said. "I guess I'm whispering about things Will and I have lived through because I like to think he doesn't know about them."

She still whispered at night, but now she whispered because of shared intimacies, or because the two of them were planning strategies or conferring about Will's upbringing. Upbringing—what an antiquated way to think about someone's childhood: as if the two of them were slowly and competently stretching Will like taffy, when in reality it was all either of them could do to keep up with his energy, his questions, and his desires.

He was thinking about Will in Will's calmer moments— usually when he was tired, at bedtime. He gave his mother a hard time about going to sleep, but when Mel was there he never minded going to bed. Halloween night, Will had wanted both of them to tell him stories, though. He had wanted to cling, even though they had said nothing about the accident, made no mention of danger. Like all smart children, he had sensed their disquiet. He had let it be known that he thought *Where the Wild Things Are* was a story for babies. Mel sat at the foot of the bed, chin resting in his cupped hand, while Jody read Will a poem by Auden.

Who was Icarus? Will had wanted to know.

A mythological creature (her soft voice). A boy who tried to fly, but his wings came too close to the sun (matter-of-fact; no preaching to the child), so the wax that had been used to attach the wings to his body melted, and he fell to earth (Mel, hoping to make this less ominous, had whistled on the intake and made a little downward spiral with his index finger).

When they left his bedroom that night, Jody had whispered to him, "It's so easy to answer questions when all you have to do is recite information."

Will had looked at his mother so calmly. If the explanation of Icarus's plight and Mel's finger whirling through the air hadn't pleased him, her voice certainly had. Mel knew what it was like to have that voice settle calmly in his own heart: It was the antidote to the sharp sounds of the city, the smooth assurance that she had infiltrated his body to echo even when she was not present.

What he wished, walking along the street in New York, was that it would become clear to her that she should marry him. But since that did not seem likely, he had decided on a strategy—something that would be done at his expense, but perhaps not at so great an expense. Something that might even be like a game that could be well played. As he watched the sidewalk to make sure he did not step on any cracks, he continued to consider carefully Haverford's offer. It was well known in the business that the mercurial Haverford usually got his way. He had already offered Mel a significantly larger amount of money than he was making at his friend's gallery, but Mel thought that money alone should not be the deciding factor. Haverford also knew Mel was thinking that. If another price could be struck, however—if, to be specific, Haverford might take an interest in giving Jody a show—that might be the incentive Mel needed to join up with him.

In addition to the enlargements Jody asked Mel to get from the photo lab, he had had four shots blown up to sixteen by twenty and had paid for a rush job. He now carried those photographs in a portfolio he had bought earlier that day at Charrette. People passing him would have thought him an artist, if they paused to look. A thought suddenly went through his head: that the Queen of England always carried a change purse, even though there was nothing in it.

If he could get Jody a show, her self-confidence would soar. And if the Halloween photographs wouldn't do it, nothing would.

Stepping carefully, he turned the portfolio vertically to hold it like a shield against his chest as he went through the revolving door.

Haverford was there, on a barstool. Tiny bubbles floated up in Haverford's champagne flute. Haverford smiled, and Mel smiled back. That was it: two people who believed they knew each other so perfectly—who thought they could predict things about the other so well—that they didn't even need to shake hands.

S E V E N

On an unusually warm April day, Jody took the bus from the airport to Grand Central, got on the subway, exited at Twenty-third Street, walked crosstown to Ninth Avenue, and continued to Mel's street. Will was spending the weekend with the Vickerses. Jody was supposed to meet the man Mel was considering going to work for—a man whose last name made him sound like a character in a Henry Fielding novel, a name she could not remember, no matter how hard she tried. One of those men named Lord So-and-So, who would wear what they called drawers, and whose days would always be characterized by high propriety.

She smiled to herself. Whenever she imagined people in excessive detail it made Mel nervous, as if she were really hallucinating and bound to bring trouble on herself. But the joking protected her; otherwise, a gallery owner whose name, she'd been told, was often mentioned in the society pages might be a formidable and intimidating figure.

Mel lived across the street from General Theological Seminary, behind which stretched a long courtyard with grass so green it shocked you into remembering the country. Mel had befriended one of the seminarians and had in his possession a key that would open the big iron gate if you reached through the bars, inserted the key into the lock on the other side, and turned it counterclockwise. Some dexterity was needed for this, and some nerve—though the few times someone had spotted her and Mel sneaking in, the person had not batted an eye. Perhaps the seminarians thought there was nothing wrong with finding a way into the courtyard, which might be analogous, to them, to finding a way into heaven. The key could not be duplicated, though, and Mel had the key, so she would have to wait for Mel in his apartment. Also, SoHo Wine was delivering a case of chardonnay for dinner that night, and a woman named Angela, who had run away from Oklahoma to become a Rolfer and had a catering business on the side, was coming over around five to drop off the dinner Mel would serve that night. Jody had met Angela before, at a party she and Mel attended, when she went to get a drink of water in the kitchen. Angela had told her that she had lost her mother when she was a child and had grown up on a ranch in a family of four brothers who treated her like one of the horses. Jody did not ask exactly what this meant. By the time she left the kitchen, she had Angela's card, and Angela's boyfriend's card. Jody could either get Rolfed or get legal advice. Angela had her own staff, which included the dishwasher, who was a teacher of the Alexander Technique and with whom she was two-timing her lawyer boyfriend, and a fleet of people who served the food, among them a dwarf who worked nights when he was between movie-stuntman jobs. He went around tapping people's knees to see if they needed their wineglasses filled. Jody had wished that Will was with her. Why read fairy tales to your child when you can take him to a party in New York? If he understood that Rolfing and the Alexander Technique were similar to spanking in slow motion and to being made to stand in the corner, he might not have liked that, but he would have liked the dwarf in his blue cap, carrying a bottle of red wine in one hand and a bottle of white in the other. The dwarf was doing just what Will was not supposed to do: carry two drinks at once.

What did Mel think about Jody's being in his apartment while he was at work? Apparently, it was fine with him. She'd already seen the secrets (such as they were) in the medicine cabinet. Everything else had been put on display to show her how tempting life in New York could be, so she would move in with him. Did she like his crystal champagne flutes, hung upside down under the kitchen cabinet as if they were ordinary wineglasses, which could be hers if she married him? What about the stereo (they could compromise on the volume), the mattress (they could get one larger), the bath towels (if she didn't like brown, they could buy them in every color of the rainbow).

As she came to the end of the row of brownstones, she saw the man who lived in the garden apartment sitting on the front steps, watching his dog play with a bone on the little patch of cement inside the front gate. Daryl was a good-looking man in his late fifties who had retired from NBC, where he had worked as a cameraman, to devote his time to his great love: the acquisition and repair of jukeboxes. The garden behind the brownstone prospered because it was cared for by his sister, who came from her apartment in Hoboken two or three times a week to plant and prune. His sister was responsible for ending—or almost ending—the springtime ant problem in Mel's apartment. The ants had climbed the twisting wisteria boughs and come through the screens until Estelle ingeniously designed an upside-down funnel that fit around the base of the vine and sprayed it with chemicals to repel ants. "All he has to do is remember to douse it every couple of days, but I know he slips up," Estelle had said to Jody when she last visited. "All his life he's put his cereal bowl in the sink 'to soak,' which means that he was too lazy to wash it. All men are the same about their cereal bowls—as if they'd be washing a part of themselves down the drain if they cleaned them. Cereal bowls are sitting in sinks all over America, filled to the brim with water." Naturally, Jody was crazy about Estelle. She loved to be invited to walk in the garden behind the apartment to see the little plants and flowers. From the fourth floor, most of the flowers were only a pastel haze.

"She's not here today," Daryl said. "I thought I'd take the opportunity to sit out front. She gets insulted if I want to see some city life instead of flowers." He picked up the blue leash the dog trailed behind it. She smiled down at the little dog, whining happily to see her at the front gate. Will had been asking for a dog. She suspected that Will and Mel were in collusion.

"The tulips are up," Daryl said. "The ones with the green centers."

"Parrot tulips," she said.

Daryl gave her the look a parent gives a child who has said a dirty word the parent would like to disappear from the child's vocabulary: a glazed-over look, with the trace of a prim smile.

The dog ran up the steps behind her and stood panting at the front door. Daryl got up and brought the dog down the stairs again. She put her key in the door and pushed it open— it always stuck on the ugly carpeting—then closed it behind her. The half-table in the hallway had a vase of dried flowers on it, and the gray rug had been recently vacuumed. This was because the second-floor apartment was empty. The landlord always put out flowers and hung a painting in the stairwell when an apartment was empty. When it was filled again, the painting would disappear and the flowers would be left to crumble into confetti on the tabletop.

Climbing the stairs, Jody thought about the peculiarity of walking into someone else's life. Now the dog downstairs knew her. Just like that, she was greeted by the small things that surrounded Mel's life. You never merely took on another person, you drew all the things surrounding that person to you like a magnet—the postman's nod, the gas station attendant smiling through the windshield at both of you, the waiter who asks, "How are you?" and looks to both faces, the colleague's wife who asks you to lunch. Before you knew it, there would be a drinking glass that was your favorite; the lipstick you left behind would be put in a dish on the back of the toilet. He'd hide your toothbrush so you'd go home and have to buy another, and then there the toothbrush would be, in the holder, the next time you went back. You'd know that you were in deep when your things began to proliferate in the apartment: things he bought for you, to be *yours*, if you did not leave enough behind. When he stopped taking his blue shirt to the dry cleaner and started tossing it in the wash because it had become your favorite nightgown. When he bought you a plant instead of cut flowers so you would call to make sure it had been watered. When cotton pullovers became unisex and got jumbled together. When pictures of the two of you were put on the refrigerator. When other women called and he didn't close the door or lower his voice and, when he hung up, acted as if your conversation hadn't been interrupted.

That was the thing about taking photographs. About taking wedding photographs, at least: that the people you were seeing wanted so sincerely to belong. It was desperation rather than vanity that made them look soulfully into the camera, because the camera had the power to stop time and to verify that they were part of a tradition. That was why brides wore their grandmothers' wedding dress (a little too tight in the waist, and the shoes were *always* too small; few brides could walk down the aisle in their grandmother's size-five shoes). It was a celebration that all generations were invited to witness, and sometimes the dog as well. The bride was always asking an implicit question: Don't you remember this? Even if you don't understand my life now or know me very well, doesn't this ceremony constitute a link between us? Isn't this your engagement ring I'm wearing? Haven't I styled my hair with the waves that swept my mother's cheeks at her wedding? Isn't this the wedding cake we've always eaten, even though we've never had dessert together? The figurines at the top are generic. The bubbles in expensive champagne don't vary in size. I'm in love. Don't you remember being in love?

At a wedding she photographed recently, some relative of the groom had said to her, "Love is like a feather in the breeze." People often said startling things at weddings, so perhaps it was just the dreamy—no, deranged—look on the woman's face that had made Jody force a smile. As the old lady walked away from her, Jody had thought several things in quick succession: Love, that exhilarating and exhausting state, is whatever anybody says it is, so stop the poetry and end the song; love is, indeed, like a feather; love is nothing like a feather; the word "breeze" might have been indicative of the lady's attitude, because a feather in the wind would be another matter entirely.

Jody put her key into the lock and opened the door. A flight of steep black-painted steps rose into Mel's apartment. Except for two rooms in the front, under the steep pitch of the roof, the area was open space, with an off-center stairwell surrounded by a high railing. It was like being in a treehouse; tall windows at the back overlooked the tops of ailanthus trees growing below. In the kitchen there was a skylight through which wisteria had pushed its way. When it rained, the top of the stove would be moist, and occasionally tiny flowers would be scattered over the stovetop. When Mel turned on the stove he ignored them, but she always brushed them away, as if they were alive. She sat for a minute, a little out of breath, on the sofa that curved around the room. No sofa in New York rose higher than midback.

Mel had left a note for her on one of the sofa cushions. Apparently Duncan had called to say that his former room-mate, who lived on Christopher Street, had just gotten very bad news from a blood test. What was she supposed to do? Call some man she'd never met? She pushed the note aside and wandered away. Tucked in the bathroom mirror was a picture of Will, straddling Mel's neck, proud of his new red sneakers and looking as secure, perched there, as the driver of an armored car. Recently, Mel had instigated the silliness of nicknames. Some days Will wanted to be Ace, some Butch. She thought that on the day the picture had been taken he was Ace. Ace in need of a haircut. Ace, who swung as hard as he could and still didn't raise a bruise on Mel's bicep. ("Of course you can't hit me in the stomach," Mel had said to him. "You'd hurt me.") She looked at the lipstick on the saucer on top of the toilet tank. Mel would like it—he liked any profession of affection, however corny—if she scrawled I LOVE YOU on the bathroom mirror. The lipstick had cost ten dollars. Ten dollars for lipstick! She took off the cap and put lipstick on her lips but didn't write on the mirror. She filled a glass with water and rose on tiptoes to water the spider plant. Putting the glass back in the holder, she remembered one of Mel's peculiarities: wiping the glass, after use, with his bath towel. How could men be so neat about some things and so haphazard about others?

She tried to remember the name of the man she would meet that night. Could it really be Haveabud? His first name was probably Steve or Ed. No, there were no more Steves or Eds

in New York. They were now Steven or Edward, whether
they were gay or straight. If they had money, they didn't have
a nickname. Everybody was into high seriousness, so that now
even dogs were named Humphrey and Raphael.

When Angela buzzed and Jody let her in, she was dressed
in stone-washed jeans, probably about a size three, and an
enormous sweatshirt with a green-faced, red-lipped Oriental
on it and raised red letters spelling SUMO. Her hair was
yellow—not any shade of blond but yellow, Crayola-crayon
yellow. Pink ballet slippers. No socks. On her wrist a coiled
bracelet that ended in the triangular head of a spitting snake.
An earcuff and a diamond stud in one ear, a replica of the
Empire State Building dangling from the other.

"I've left my old man, but it's a good thing. I just don't want
him *inquired* about ever again. But wait, you weren't here
when he came to help out last time, were you? Tell Mel that
it's over, and to *please* not ask how he is, because that's as
boring as somebody calling you to tell you how their day
went. The thing I'm handing you now"—Jody had stopped on
the second-floor landing as Angela rushed up the stairs two at
a time, heading for the top—"is a date-and-prune tart. The
prunes cut the sweetness of the dates, but don't tell anybody
about the prunes because they won't eat it. They think prunes
are those things they bring you in wet bowls in Miami Beach,
and prunes actually don't cause you as much trouble as corn,
but try telling that to anybody. So. I'm double-parked, and if
you can help me carry stuff upstairs I can leave the car at the
curb. It's salmon mousse for the main course. And I *love* that
lipstick. That's going to look fantastic by candlelight." Angela
smiled a beatific smile. The waves that surrounded her face
looked more like a corona than overdyed yellow hair. "Room
temperature," Angela said, handing the platter to Jody. She
put her hand over her heart. "As if we know no seasons in
New York. As if each moment is purely invented."

———

After the party that night, Mel listened to the message tape. Duncan was flying to New York in the morning. Jody shrugged. "Why does Duncan think I'm going to get involved in the problems of a man I've never met?" she said to Mel. Then they fell into bed and drunkenly made love.

In his dream Mel sank, to the bottom of the ocean in a submarine. At first it was one of those submarines the tourists get into to see the coral reef and the fish swimming around, but a few seconds into the dream everything changed, and suddenly there was a commanding officer who was quite annoyed with him for thinking of the submarine's downward path as "sinking." "We are *descending*!" the man shrieked shrilly at Mel, who suddenly had to endure the stares of the other Navy men. One woman from the first part of the dream was still there: a tourist in a pink pants suit, taking a picture of a flat yellow-and-blue fish that floated by. Then there was the carnage: the deer on the road, again; the Halloween revelers squatting and standing in the glow of the headlights. The bright eye of the deer. A body too large to have been supported by such delicate legs.

He kicked his feet backwards, out of the covers.

In the next part of Mel's dream the small dog who lived downstairs was sniffing the corpse in the road.

Mel opened his lips, exhaling to blow the scene away, but the deer stayed still. The October cold made him shiver. His lips closed.

The small dog sniffed and sniffed, and then it became apparent that there was a second dog, identical with the first, and that they were not partygoers on Halloween night but damned souls in Hell.

He had some consciousness of his mouth. Was he drooling on the pillow? But then there was confusion: It was the dog who was drooling—the dog in the dream—and that dog was Cerberus, who was guarding the gates to Hell.

The small dog had an owner, but Mel could not imagine

who among the costumed partygoers that could be. It was not Richard Nixon, because Richard Nixon's dog was named Checkers. It must be Will's dog, then. He and Will must have persuaded Jody to get a dog.

Mel turned onto his side.

Just before the dream ended, dogs were floating past the window of the submarine. In the little corner of his mind that fought to become conscious, Mel knew that if there were a cartoon caption—if Gary Larson were in charge—everything that was dreadful could be amusing. But the unconscious mind won out, so he knew that if he laughed it could be a death sentence: It would attract the rabid dog, and once bitten—once his leg had sprung a leak—it would be impossible for the submarine to rise again. Even the woman in the pants suit was alarmed. She had been photographing fish, and then drowned dogs began to drift by. Then Will was in the dream, looking at him as if he had known all along how grotesque this would become.

Mel drew his feet inside the covers and moved his knees up, toward his chest. His eyes darted left and right, behind closed eyelids. Like little fish, Jody thought. She was propped up on one elbow, looking at Mel. The aspirin she had taken was slowly dulling the thud in her head that was the result of too many drinks too late at night. Now Mel's REMs had subsided, though she still looked sleepily at him in the gradually brightening bedroom. A line from "The Waste Land" came to her: *Those are pearls that were his eyes.* She had read Keats and Auden to Will, but did not think "The Waste Land" would hold his attention, even though a few of the lines had end rhyme. What was the line before that line? The world could indeed be a perilous place, she thought as she was falling asleep, if you could not remember those things that came first. She remembered that someone had drowned but not the line itself.

E I G H T

Lord Haveabud raised his glass—topheavy, so that it was easier to curve his fingers under the bowl and forget about the stem—and swooshed the blue margarita through the air like a courtesan about to make an elaborate curtsy. The toast was all eye contact and no words. The deal had been decided on (though Jody, who kept forgetting his last name, didn't know it was a deal), the deed as good as done (though Haveabud wanted to see the entire shoot, not just the enlargements Mel had shown him at Palio), and now all that remained was for Haveabud to buy a tie—lately, he didn't like what Alexander Julian was up to—to wear to the opening. Photographic galleries, like Witkin, were showing paintings, so why shouldn't he show photographs? Haveabud believed that new ties brought him luck. Also, whenever he flew, he carried with him in some pocket a small geode he had bought in a previous life, when he and his second wife visited a gift shop near the Grand Canyon. Being an agnostic, he recited silently to himself, in times of stress, a litany of introductory adverbs, in alphabetical order: after, again, also, as, before, besides . . . He fancied himself something of a character, wearing a Swatch instead of a Rolex, but spending more on Missoni socks than most people spent on an entire outfit. Haveabud bought his ties well in advance of openings and put them, still in their boxes, in his filing cabinet under the artists' names.

When he first came to New York he had been married to his high school sweetheart and had worked as a clerk in a store specializing in art books. He became so trusted that he was left behind in the store to take inventory and to create his impressive displays after the others had left. When he was done, he threw two switches to activate the alarm, then got out the front door and locked it, all within fifteen seconds. Those few seconds were never a problem until he started drinking champagne after hours. The champagne came to him as gifts from women—daytime browsers who were searching for more than oversized books on Monet's water lilies. It was classier to meet someone in a store such as the one Haveabud worked in than to go to a high-class bar. And if the women didn't meet anyone else, or if they just took a fancy to the earnest young man with a body he imagined to be better than it was (now he worked out four days a week, swam on Thursdays, and jogged on weekend evenings around the reservoir in Central Park), they were likely to ask him over for a drink after work—the husbands were always away on business—or to try to please him with enough gifts of bubbly so that he'd ask them out for a drink. Much to Haveabud's surprise, you could often have a beautiful woman lusting after you just because you had special-ordered a book on Christ's sexuality or a biography of Courbet. In fact, Courbet was Haveabud's favorite painter, but he would not reveal this to anyone. He had his secrets: his geode, his visions of Courbet's landscapes, his package of French ticklers in the file under *S*. He might never have been in the position he was in today if he hadn't been fired from the bookstore. In the good old days, he and a few of the other employees (now they hired clerks who looked like people in a Grant Wood painting. Where did they find them?) had opened bottles of champagne and played baseball in the buff on the second floor of the store, using the handle from the toilet plunger to bat rolled-up wads of duplicate inventory slips. This had never been discovered, but a jealous husband had had a tête-à-tête with the owner, and Haveabud was fired. "You don't want to hear whether I deny having an affair with her?" he had asked the owner. "No," the owner said. "I knew that anybody as knowledgeable and personable as you was too good to be true."

There had been months of anguish after he was fired, but finally he had gotten a part-time job proofreading, and the excellent job he did with one manuscript resulted in an admiring call from an editor at the publishing house who, when she heard Haveabud's plight, called a friend who owed her a favor, and zip, Haveabud began working part-time in a gallery on then-still-unfashionable West Broadway. The rest was history. History was personified in the form of Luther, a.k.a. Jake Markson from Brooklyn, an overweight overachiever from the Queens College art program whose talent Haveabud knew he could market. He put Luther on a protein diet and called twice a day to make sure he was drinking the daily gallon of Poland Spring. By the time showtime rolled around Jake Markson didn't exist anymore and Luther, twenty pounds lighter, pores cleansed at Dr. Mario Badescu's for extra radiance, stood in the gallery in his jeans and white shirt—a shirt that had cost Haveabud two hundred dollars— to start a new tremor in the downtown art scene. Around him were hung photorealistic paintings of enlarged cash-register receipts, including the smudged thumbprint of the clerk who ripped one out of the register, or the spot where it had been slightly torn, the numbers in black ink or purple, some so pale they could hardly be read. The Tx./Tl. show was the rage of the moment, pronounced upon even by Andy Warhol, who said, "Money is very important, but usually artists don't keep good receipts." After the opening the two-hundred-dollar shirt was handed from Luther to Haveabud the way a bullfighter folds his cape and gives it to a worthy lady. Haveabud's cut of the sold-out show was fifty percent, and he and Luther did a pas de deux to Dean Witter Reynolds to find out about shelters. As anyone might imagine, fame went to Luther's head. In trendy restaurants he offered to autograph the bill for the dinner he and his hangers-on had eaten, in lieu of payment. Though many places would not go for this, Luther found that star-crazed waitresses themselves would often foot the bill for the dinner in exchange for a fuck. One of those waitresses nabbed him, of course: a nobody from Lyme, Connecticut, who had come to New York to study acting—a young woman who dyed a green streak in her hair long before it was fashionable and went by the name Thalo. She became Luther's Yoko, and eventually he was lured from Haveabud into instant obscurity, after doing a recording with Thalo that consisted of the sound of whips cracking, punctuating a two-way whispered argument, as a boys' choir soared to high soprano in the background. The bitch got pregnant instantly and had twins. When she and Luther divorced, Luther attempted to work his way back into Haveabud's affections, and when he could not—Haveabud believing that those who turned their back on people who had helped them did not deserve a second chance—ended up working in his brother's restaurant, though later Haveabud heard that he had gone to Paris, to the Left Bank, where he made take-out *ceviche* that was praised in *Le Figaro* and French *Vogue*. *Quel dommage*, Haveabud said, with malice instead of sincerity.

But life is strange, and years later he became reacquainted with one of Luther's sons. The bitch remarried—step, step, stepping up the rungs of the social ladder in her Manolo Blahniks—so that when Haveabud saw her again she was the young wife of a sixty-year-old multi, standing outside Collegiate, waiting for her son (the other twin being, for some reason Haveabud never got clear, with her parents in upstate New York), with a Cuban au pair who stood at her side, looking into the swarm of children leaving school with the wide eyes of one of her relatives fleeing Castro's Cuba. The bitch looked Haveabud up and down and then spread an inappropriately radiant smile on her face. What was *he* doing there? He was about to attend a meeting, with his third wife, about her nephew's progress in overcoming dyslexia. (His third wife's sister was at the Betty Ford Clinic, and Haveabud had been persuaded that he should attend the meeting as a show of support to the boy.) Luther's son turned out to be his third wife's nephew's classmate. His third wife emerged from a cab then and was introduced. The bitch said that she and Haveabud were old friends and invited them to dinner that Saturday, and his wife accepted. On a run, the seven-year-old boy rushed not into the bitch's arms but into the arms of the au pair, and a most extraordinary thing happened to Haveabud: He felt a surge of tender affection for the boy. The boy was a dead ringer for his father, so much so that Haveabud had the eerie feeling that Luther in miniature stood near him on the sidewalk. It brought back memories of the good times he and Luther had had—the shopping expeditions for clothes sure to impress, when the two of them laughed so merrily that one clerk had said, as she wrote up the sale, "You know, evening wear is not returnable." The two of them used to toke up and go for tango lessons. They had owned, together, a ski chalet in Stowe and a house on the beach in Barbados, half a mile from the Sandy Lane. They had had drunken sing-alongs with Dolly Parton records, late at night, savoring the quality of Luther's Blaupunkt, even learning an a cappella version of "Old Flames Can't Hold a Candle to You" that would have friends rolling on the floor. When Haveabud had to explain to his third wife who Luther was, Luther became an eccentric artist who had encountered fleeting fortune. He did not fill her in on their personal relationship. He did warn her that the bitch was poison, but she discounted his words because she thought he was always too harsh. The bitch's lawyer and her hairstylist had been at the dinner that night, her multi out of town on business (it gave Haveabud pause: The bitch was one of those women he would have encountered years before in the bookstore, who would have given him a bottle of champagne), and she and Haveabud's third wife chatted merrily about house renovation, agreeing that exposed beams were as necessary for aesthetic reasons as a frame on a painting. His wife was astonished to learn, during the warmed-goat-cheese-and-grapes course, that Luther and Haveabud had enrolled in an Arthur Murray dance class. The hairdresser wanted to have a dance with Haveabud, but he declined, saying that he'd forgotten everything he'd learned. (Later that night, alone in his living room after his wife had gone to bed, he went through the dance movements.) Roederer Cristal was poured throughout the evening, and at party's end the two women kissed the air, his third wife inhaling the bitch's Graffiti, the bitch sniffing his wife's lavishly applied Joy. The two would meet again, to discuss ceilings.

Haveabud disdained the lawyer's Republican politics, but since the hairdresser—whom Haveabud had rather come to like—had given him such a rough time, Haveabud had not had to expend any energy in that direction. But the child, Spencer, he was quite fascinated by. In the boy's bedroom were hundreds of dinosaur models, some cast in bronze and arranged on a long shelf, others standing among the palm and ficus trees. An inflated Rhamphorhynchus dangled from the ceiling fixture. ("It means 'prow beak,' " Spencer said.) That one Haveabud had to be informed about, but he was able to recognize the large green Stegosaurus, and he nodded with faint recognition when Spencer told him that that particular dinosaur usually weighed almost two tons. "How long have you been collecting them?" Haveabud had asked, and the boy's answer made it clear that he would have preferred teething on dinosaurs if they had been offered in place of teething rings. Here was a child who would not plead for a pet, unlike his third wife's nephew, who would agitate himself into weeping fits, chanting corgi, corgi, corgi. In a frame was a drawing of a Brachiosaurus, which Spencer proudly pointed out, saying it was probably the largest animal that ever lived. "It was strictly herbivorous, too," the boy said. "Do you know what that means?" Assuming that the boy was asking if he knew, in point of fact, what "herbivorous" meant, Haveabud nodded yes. The implications, on the other hand . . . But the boy had rushed to pull a massive book from the shelf. "This one is about carnosaurs," the boy said, raising his lip and exposing his little top teeth. "They were *really* wicked." Haveabud was startled that the word "wicked" was in a seven-year-old's vocabulary. He wondered if at night the dinosaurs came alive for him, ranging around the room or wading into the river of his dreams.

But the au pair had come to the door for the second time, accompanied by his impatient wife, and because he had felt protective of Spencer and his reassembled prehistoric world, he quickly said goodbye and left the room to rejoin the party. He also had the distinct thought that the au pair knew he did not love his wife, an impression she later confirmed over cappuccino at The Cupping Room in SoHo. But that night he had really not planned to meet Gloria again. It was only later, thinking it over, that he realized the obvious: The au pair was his way to Spencer, and Spencer was a person he wanted to know better. How much of Luther, besides his looks, had gotten planted in the child? To his complete surprise, he began to swell with emotion, like the buddy of a soldier killed in action who must go to that person's hometown and kiss the wife's cheek, lift the child into his arms. It was surprising because, while Luther was indeed M.I.A., his disappearance was only into *le monde chi-chi* of Paris. But really, why bother to understand your reasons when you are so strongly drawn to something or someone? Sipping through the foamy milk, Haveabud knew there was something that he wanted, but he did not know exactly what that something was. Only that it involved Spencer, and staying on good enough terms with the bitch to have access to Spencer.

But that was the past, and right now Haveabud was sipping not cappuccino but a sour-sweet, fashionably silly blue margarita with Mel Anthis, from whom he also wanted something, and Mel Anthis's ladyfriend, who turned out to be a more impressive photographer than he could have imagined. To get Mel, he might have mounted a show of thumbtacks and string, but this woman, whose name he had forgotten in the haze of remembering that night, several years ago, with the lawyer, and the hairdresser, and Gloria, and the person who had served the dinner, and Stegosaurus, and . . .

The waitress asked if he would like his salt rim freshened.

"What?" he said. The Rolling Stones were singing "Wild Horses" and a group of hyperactive partygoers had just come in and were playing musical chairs around a table too small for them.

"If you would like your salt rim freshened," the waitress said, raising her voice slightly.

"I've never heard of that," Haveabud said.

She took this for a no and went away. Mel Anthis and Jody—that was her name—were frowning at him, as if he had anything to do with the waitress coming to the table.

He shrugged, indicating his own puzzlement and surprise. He was also surprised to have heard, just as the waitress interrupted, that Jody was the mother of a small child: a boy, Will, going on six. He was entering her life when she had a son just a little younger than Spencer had been when he had reentered the bitch's life. How would Will deal with his mother's becoming a star? She was a very smart, very attractive woman, and her work was stunning; this one was going to be almost too easy. He would call in a favor and get some notice on Page Six. He would ask his former assistant, to whom he had advanced money so that two thugs would not break his legs for nonpayment of a gambling debt, to find some way to borrow a gold evening dress he had just seen in the window of Charivari.

He tried to get the waitress's eye, to take her up on her offer. A little salt to cut the sweetness. Another night on the town, during which possibilities arose when you least expected them.

N I N E

Sitting under an umbrella at a table outside the Empire Diner, Haveabud took in the passing parade as he waited for Jody. A limousine driver in Ray Bans sat doing a Jack Nicholson imitation, trying hard to look oblivious of passing people and traffic. He could have been shot, stuffed, and put back in the front seat, for all the life his expression betrayed. He was not going to leer at anything, *à la* Jack. He had joined the ranks of what Haveabud thought of as New York statues. Yes, they moved, but for all intents and purposes they were statues: guards at Bendel's, doormen, hatcheck girls, out-of-towners waiting fearfully on the curb to cross the street when the lights changed. They were the startled fawns and self-contained spiritual masters, the repositories of peace in our time. Haveabud's mother, who visited once a year just before or after his birthday, searched for these buoys the way a drowning insect rides the current until it encounters a solid object to fasten its grip upon. His second wife had had quite a talent for both amusing his mother and keeping her calm, but his present wife had no regard for a woman who chose to live without being smothered by fur or anesthetized by French aromatics, and so it had fallen to Haveabud to squire his mother around, carefully leading her on a zigzag through collapsed women with ulcerated legs and Senegalese hawking imitation Rolexes. Still, she would say to him, "Whoever would have imagined that you would want to live this way?" Amid the chaos of Jackson Pollock at the Modern she would find the simple shape of the treehouse he had once climbed into. Lifting her head to see the blinking warnings to planes on the tops of buildings she would remember carrying him outside to see the stars. His mother had an unerring ability, with her sincere questions and her well-intended assertions about the value of a peaceful life, to make him question every aspect of his existence, and re- member to say his prayers at night, too. What *was* Pollock up to? Might it not have been the externalization of the body's death wish, bleeding out, so that all the world could see, onto the canvas? How *did* Diane Arbus have the nerve to poke her camera into the face of a mental patient? If Albers's colors vibrated, was there really so much value to that? It was all he could do to refrain from mentioning that he had considered suicide himself, that he had been emotionally, and sometimes physically, involved with other men. It made him nearly wild to see his mother, though he thought that perhaps he would have been driven to distraction no matter whom he had to tour around the city unwillingly. You simply had to march for- ward like the conqueror or you would be done for. The mere presence of a doubter could undercut your own confidence.

In his breast pocket was a letter from his mother, who would be coming to town in about a week. It was a half- formed thought that perhaps Gloria could be useful in entertaining her—that is, if he could think of a way to make Gloria seem just a casual acquaintance while at the same time communicating to his mother that she must not mention her name to his wife. Or even Jody—surely she would be beholden to him, but the problem was that she might be back in Charleston, or . . . shit, the name of the town, the name of the town, he simply could not remember. Charlotte. That was it. Or maybe it wasn't. Charlotte was in North Carolina, and he remembered her saying that she lived near the foothills of the Blue Ridge. Charlottes*ville*, he was thinking triumphantly when she turned the corner, leading a little dog on a blue leash. Mel's dog? Most dog owners mentioned their pets, and Mel never had. Well, no matter, he would have been happy to see her if she had been leading Quasimodo by the hand. A pigeon flapped a few feet away, clearing the path for her black Indian moccasins (oh, how he admired the *outré* trendy) and the little dog's clicking paws. She had style—there was no problem there. Anyone who had melded into Chelsea well enough to wear her lover's shirt over white painter's pants with neon-green socks and moccasins would need no coaching on how to make an appearance. Then, in a sudden jumble of thoughts as she saw him and smiled, he imagined fucking her, or, alternatively, asking her to take his mother for tea at the Palm Court. As a groundswell of desperation rose in his brain, he wondered if she was drawn to Mel for the same reasons he was: a steadfastness and dedication that had a loony spin to it, a faint suggestion that a masquerade was going on the more one revealed oneself. He was not, Haveabud firmly believed, either a drug user or—other side of the coin, and harder yet to deal with—a person who had religious beliefs. He did not seem to be reformed anything, but neither did he seem weighed down with the cynicism so chic in his profession as advisor to *artistes*. Or rather, those concerned with the fates of *artistes*. Or, to be honest, those concerned with their own fates, who trucked with *artistes*. The little dog was all bright eyes and tongue and looked as if it had lived all the sexual moments Haveabud imagined. Haveabud raised his hand to gallantly kiss hers, but she surprised him by taking his hand and leaning forward to plant a little kiss on his knuckle. Women were never what you expected, even when you thought you had no expectations. When she sat down her chair scraped the concrete. She stood again, after drawing it in toward the table, to drop the top of the leash under the chair leg.

"What is it like?" Haveabud said, searching her face. He waited for confusion to register. When it did, he moved an inch closer to her. "Being an artist but . . . taking photographs of weddings. We all have to keep ourselves amused, don't we?"

Amused? she thought. Ah, he must mean the amusement of eating. The amusement of buying your child's corduroys. The amusement of paying the electric bill.

"Because Mel has explained to me," he said, moving his hands as if cutting a deck of cards, "that the intensity of what you do is something no one would want to sustain. I myself go and scream my head off when the Mets play. I certainly do not merely immerse myself in the world of art. The intensity—I keep coming back to that word—the intensity would be too much to cope with."

Intensity? Did he know what it was like to be home with a child who had a fever and who would not keep the blanket over him and whose only happy moments came when people were crashing their cars into walls on television at ear-splitting volume, because his ears were blocked up and he could hardly hear? Could this man have any idea what her previous week had been like in terms of intensity?

But she did not answer him. She shrugged, considering a minute. She could have said that photographing weddings was not the easy diversionary activity that he supposed. You were part shrink, part philosopher, part stand-up comic. At weddings you moved snooty great-aunts shoulder to shoulder with skeptical children from the first marriage and linked them for all time in one shot. You tried to subtly communicate in any way you could that there was a sure future, that this was the beginning of a trip that would be sunny, a send-off for people who for one day, at least, had the countenance of angels. You assured the mother of the bride that her daughter's beauty was due to her; you pulled the tick off the top of the dog's head without comment; you piled napkins in puddles of champagne on the furniture. You tossed rice if you had a free hand and a free minute, danced one dance if asked, and won their hearts by taking picture after picture and by being the last to leave. Then you went away with memories of the day that *would* be larger than life because you had a machine that could do the enlarging, smiling with the assurance that you had zoomed in on details people were too preoccupied, or too nervous, to notice.

Would he understand if she made an analogy?

She told him that after the pictures were taken they were pieces of a puzzle. That in the darkroom they would float for a while, like a rose petal that had fallen into a glass of champagne.

She looked at a spot on the table where no glass was placed. He looked at the same spot.

They were images ruffled by currents, she said. Those slips of paper in the developing fluid.

"Images ruffled by currents," he said slowly.

Whatever mood he had meant to establish, she had broken it. She looked at the tabletop, secretly proud of herself. Then she looked up and gave him a smile as lovely as she could manage, being sure that it was still tinged with regret.

Haveabud knew that his momentum had been interfered

with, but he was really quite captivated with what she was saying. If she could say that when she was at his side—when there were people there who mattered—he felt sure that they would be on Easy Street.

Though any day without his mother, and before he went home to his third wife, was relatively easy.

Such a pretty girl, he thought.

She thought: This man is going to be no problem. I am not ever going to have to seriously discuss photography with him.

A waitress in a black fright wig walked out and gave them the menus Haveabud had declined until his companion arrived. He reflected on the fact that he had called her "my companion," as opposed to many other things he might have called her. He could have lied and said she was his wife. He could have called her, archly, "the lady" or even, pedantically, "the woman who will be meeting me." He could have said "my daughter" for laughs, since she was about his age.

As he smiled to himself, he was suddenly struck by the realization that he would not have to worry about his mother's coming into town for another week. The euphoria of that— the 168 hours contained in a week—lifted his spirits.

Jody ordered chili. He ordered another Heineken, and scrambled eggs, loose, with sausage, a dismissive motion through the air with fingers splayed accompanying his order. (Though Haveabud did not, and would not ever, know the waitress, this particular motion would be recreated for the waitress's best buddy in acting class later that night, and reported to her psychoanalyst. His fingers would continue to rise in her dreams, and she would confide to her girlfriends that she hoped against hope that he would stop by again and this time take notice of her. He was uptown, upscale, uptight in a way she found irresistible. But none of those thoughts and desires had anything to do with the way she pivoted and affected lack of interest, walking back inside the diner. To Haveabud, she was just a girl whose thin lips led him to suspect that she would give cold kisses.)

"You said last night that you wanted to show my work," Jody said. She touched the top of the saltshaker, letting her fingers linger.

He nodded, as if this were a foregone conclusion and not their only agreement.

Haveabud said that she must move to New York so he could launch her career. He would put in a call to Scavullo that afternoon. She could attend an important opening with him the next night. But she *must* be in New York. This went without saying, he said, then said it again, even more emphatically.

She looked a little startled, as if she had been strolling along and a stick on the ground had suddenly begun to sing to her.

Haveabud stared as if transfixed. Hypnotize with your insistence. And then—when the person was captured—throw a curve, express a little doubt. What about showing a little wit in her work? Things not quite so . . . dark.

The feather boa unfurled in her imagination. The early shots of the boa were so much what he wanted, so witty, that it might as well have been there, tickling his chin and provoking a smile. She described the series of photographs: the boa coiled; the tip of the boa dangling from the light table; the boa laid out on the dining-room table so that, against the mahogany, it seemed delicate and lost on so large a surface. The boa wrapped around Mary Vickers's neck ("a model," she called her), like a sensual noose.

Haveabud was looking at the multicolored beads on Jody's shoes, which reminded him of sprinkles on an ice-cream cone: absolutely mesmerizing, when you stopped to examine them. *If* you stopped to examine them. That was the artist's imperative, of course. Haveabud closed his thumb and first finger tightly against the bridge of his nose, squinting. The French word for beads . . . what was that word? *Ou sont les beads d'hier?* Fallen, every one, like plates from a Schnabel canvas. The waitress asked if they wanted anything else. Haveabud played rogue, raising his eyebrows and turning to look at Jody as if the question were intentionally loaded with sexual innuendo.

Jody was thinking of the flash storm that had hit the week before, soaking a wedding tent as it was being erected. Early in the morning, she had walked east to the photo district to drop off the negatives at the lab, so she could pick up contact sheets at the end of her meeting with Haveabud. She suspected that if she presented the contact sheets to him as amusing, he would see them as amusing; if she said they were sad photographs, he would see them as that.

Haveabud asked the waitress for the bill. As Jody looked away, Haveabud suddenly wondered whether his wife might be having an affair. She rarely cooked anymore—more interesting things to do in the afternoon? Instead, they ate roasted chickens she had delivered to the apartment, along with asparagus-tip salad that cost the same per pound as gold.

Two men pulled out chairs at the adjacent table and sat down. One carried a beat-up violin case with a peeling peace sign stuck to it. The other had eyeglass frames with a false nose and bushy eyebrows pushed to the top of his head. Bushy Brows swatted at his companion and told him to lighten up. "Telling me to lighten up when you're in one of your manic periods is like telling me to raise my hands above my head as the roller coaster dips down," the man with the violin case said.

"Do you think they have Bosco?" Bushy Brows said.

"What in the name of *God* would make you think they might have Bosco?"

"So," Haveabud said. "Scavullo. Any time better for you than another?"

"I have to go home tomorrow," Jody said. "A friend is taking care of my son."

"Aaaaaaah, the son," Haveabud said, letting her know by his use of the article that the child was interchangeable with an object: the chair, the phone, the stove.

She shrugged, palms up.

What a pretty woman, Haveabud thought. Nice hands. Pretty shoes. Someone's mother. Why couldn't he have been dealt such a mother?

The waitress gave him his change. He said, "That's a private detective double-parked over there. My companion is Sherry Lansing, wearing a wig."

In his daybook, Haveabud wrote: "Lunch re Scav shot $28.40," adding twenty cents for good luck. Particularities— that is, lies that were very particular—were in Haveabud's experience quite likely to convince people.

Haveabud decided he would take Jody up on her offer to accompany her to the photo lab, where contact sheets of the rained-out wedding awaited them. Even Jody could not have imagined the perfect effect of the rain-splashed filter, like a glossy membrane over everything: women clustered under an overhang, hands lifted to their faces in dismay; the chaos made by men first erecting, then abandoning, the tent. It was unclear whether rain or tears glistened on some faces, but the surprise—the shock of the sudden downpour—was there. Ultimately, one rained-out wedding hardly mattered, and because she was so sure of that, Jody decided she would play devil's advocate and pitch the photographs to Haveabud as serious business.

As his mother and Haveabud sat on the front step of a brownstone, looking at small rectangular images, Will was in Virginia, staring at a peanut butter sandwich Mary Vickers had served him. He had peeled the top piece off, to compare

with Wag the number of banana slices each had been allo-
cated.

Haveabud's lips, smacking with pleasure as he surveyed the
photographs, were echoed across the miles by the sticky lips
of two small boys who had been told to place the bread back
on the sandwich instantly and to begin eating before Mary
Vickers went stark raving mad.

Before the child can tell time, the wristwatch with painted hands is not a joke but quite acceptable. Later, he may wish to have a real watch so he can turn back the hands and make the hour earlier and not have to go to bed, or turn the hands ahead so the visit to the circus will come sooner. At first, there is no hostility to clocks. Like a puppy soothed by the regularity of a sound, the child may be consoled or oblivious—but in any case, the sound of seconds ticking away will not correspond to anything real. He may see it as something that fascinates adults: that disc on the wall that is watched so closely when a visitor hasn't arrived, when the bread has taken too long to rise, when many other people are ahead of you in the pediatrician's waiting room.

What is time? As the child experiences it, it makes no sense at all. Children have little or no sense of what goes on behind the scenes, so when things happen, they seem to just happen suddenly. Imagine how strange the world would seem if you were too young to know gray clouds meant rain, too inexperienced to realize that the dog coming toward you could run faster than you could get away. Adults become angry when they have to slam on the brakes, unhappy even if the weather report has been unreliable.

Considered from the child's perspective, life is always speeding up or going too slowly. The best ideas come at bedtime. The circus ends too soon. String beans take forever to eat. Cartoons aren't satirical exaggerations but normative presentations of everyday situations. The child also will suddenly crash into a wall, unable to correctly judge speed versus distance.

In cartoons, people drop off cliffs.

The child wakes up on the floor, tangled in covers, having toppled—who knows how?—from the bed.

In cartoons, beasts roar and devour people.

Turn a corner in a city, and a gang of pink-haired punks hurtles in front of the child.

In cartoons, buildings suddenly explode.

Remember that the child also sees TV news.

What if your world was a comedy routine gone out of control? What if you experienced the world as a dwarf? What if people saw in you a potential troublemaker simply because you were present? What if half the questions you were asked were rhetorical and the other half inordinately complicated? What if you lacked the ability to judge whether people were drunk or sober, and if your plans for the following day were changed when another person announced a change of plans? What if you lived in one house and suddenly moved to another? What if you had mysterious fevers?

Consider a typical day in the life of a child:

A Day Visit to Mrs. X

Getting up early, on an overcast day. Raincoats put in the car trunk. Finding Ozzie, the rubber turtle, when the trunk lid pops up. Ozzie, saved from oblivion! (Though the child has never been *informed of it, Ozzie has been named by the parent after Ozzie Nelson, whose short neck made him look like a turtle.) Then the road: pine trees, with all the green growth high up, which must mean they're dying. An unfamiliar smell blowing through the windows. The ride is much too long—how can adults just look straight ahead and drive? The parent's jack-o'-lantern eyes shine brightly in the rearview mirror. The child counts all the cars that are red. Probably the color of the car Santa would drive, if he drove a car instead of a sled. Checking the sky, just to see . . . but it's the wrong month. Santa never makes mistakes. He only comes out one night a year.*

Arrival at Our Destination

The child is suddenly shy when he meets X, a tall, matronly woman in a gauzy dress. When it blows in the wind, it looks like the ruffling feathers of the lavender-blue bird he saw at the zoo. They let you walk right into the cage with the birds. There are strips of plastic instead of doors. Does X know about the birdcage at the zoo?

The child tells X about the zoo.

X sits on her heels to make eye contact. She says she knew him when he was a little baby.

People say this all the time.

X says she has spent all day cleaning her house; it won't be much like a zoo. (She says this to the child, but is actually speaking to the parent.)

X rises. The parent and X embrace.

Time stretches endlessly. X brings out cookies. Raisin, not chocolate chip. The child has been told that raisins are monsters' nose goop.

Slightly embarrassed, the parent says that children are unpredictable. Who knows why they sometimes refuse to eat?

Returning Home from X's

It might not be a road but the sea. They might be in a boat, not a car. That might not be the setting sun but the North Star by which the parent navigates. Soon all the other cars will have to give sea room. Sea room means that other boats are supposed to come only so close. What if there was sidewalk room, and people were supposed to stay a certain distance away? Or bedroom room, and your stuffed animals needed to be one foot away from you? The child decides that before he goes to bed, he will see that Dobbin, Chubby, and Sheila Skunk are all one foot from his side, instead of nestled close. That is, if the hill they are about to ascend doesn't turn into a wave that crashes, sending their car far off its path. With relief, he sees that they have caught the wave perfectly. Then there is more black sea in front of them. Distances across water are farther than they seem.

Think about the odd situations and difficulties the child faces every day. With not enough information, he has to go on intuition; because of an as-yet-uninhibited imagination, the ordinary devolves into the extraordinary with phantasmagoric swiftness. And, as if the world weren't mysterious enough with its cacophony of voices and unanticipated interruptions, at day's end the child is read a fanciful tale.

There can hardly be a more serious test of a person's sanity than surviving childhood. Romanticized by adults as a time of freedom, childhood is actually the time when the child is increasingly told to repress his desires. Singled out by poets as persons who possess great wisdom, children are in actuality often silenced.

Adults keep their sanity by ruling out excessive speculation. They strive to see continuity when little is discernible. But these things do not come naturally to a child. The child is either totally involved or looking ahead to the next thing. The child always wonders, What if? The child can see continuity in a doll, a train, and a yo-yo. Though the child's room can seem a chaotic battlefield, it may have a very distinct order. How distressing that at the parent's whim villages are torn down, and all the animals in the zoo are piled in the toy box, with no regard to natural enemies.

While children spontaneously imagine, parents compulsively seek order. The lines are drawn, though fatigue can erode the strongest parent's resolve. Down on all fours, the parent may agree to help reconstruct the village. To stop the child's tears, the parent will willingly take the yellow hatbox down from the top shelf of the closet, in spite of previous explicit instructions to the child to stay away from it, and place the box at the far end of the rug, so it can shine again as a three-dimensional sun, illuminating a happy kingdom.

PART II

FATHER

T E N

Haveabud invited himself along on the trip to Florida. Mel was going to deliver Will to his father's house, then drop off the rental car and fly back to New York. At the last minute, Haveabud decided to take Spencer on the trip. As far as his mother was concerned, if Spencer wanted to miss a few days of school, so be it. She would write a note explaining his absence, using heavyweight cream-colored paper embossed with her initials and a fountain pen she would guide faultlessly through the slanting loops of the Palmer method. According to the test they had given him at school, the boy was a genius. Why did a genius need to be in school?

Going to Florida had become a common enough routine for Will. He did not dislike his father—he hardly knew him—but the reason he was excited to make the trip was to see Wag, his blood brother, who now lived there. They had pricked their thumbs and held their fingers together for the blood exchange and had peed into the toilet so that their urine made one stream.

Wag knows that Will thinks New York City is a noisy marching-ground of people who pay no attention to children. Will knows Wag's mother is seeing a psychiatrist because of something to do with having killed a deer in Virginia. Wag wants to go back to Virginia. Will would like to be wherever Wag lived.

In the motel parking lot, Haveabud rose up on tiptoes, curling his fingers in horror-movie fashion, baring his teeth. This was part of his stretching routine, *après* drive, as he said, when he climbed out from behind the wheel. As a passenger, he drummed the dashboard, leaned far to the left and tilted the rearview mirror toward him so he could examine his eye and remove a speck, changed the station on the radio constantly, rocked back and forth in the seat, poking the insides of his cheeks with his tongue. Nevertheless, in spite of having communicated to Mel that he was doing him a favor, Haveabud was having a good time. It was a pleasure to be riding in a comfortable rental car instead of being bounced through potholes in a New York cab whose suspension system must previously have hit landmines. Boys in the backseat talking about dinosaurs were preferable to cabbies raving about the mayor or about their daughters being taught communist propaganda in kindergarten. No bottle of Poppy was attached to the dashboard. No crucifix dangled from the rearview mirror. And best of all, their destination was a place filled with palms, not the World Trade Center. Florida, where the bourgeoisie sat in bamboo bars and sipped drinks swirled into a mush of coconut and rum (in a true heaven, such bars might exist to dispense mother's milk). Florida, where the planes spewing their skywriting above the beach moved faster than Walt Disney's pen. And all around you, turquoise—the color that was once the hope of the future.

"Did you know," Haveabud said to Mel, "that the signature you see when you go to a Walt Disney movie is a fabrication? Disney never wrote that way. He'd try to sign an autograph, and faces would fall. But it had been perfectly conceived: a signature to establish a persona. A wonderful idea that came to haunt the real Walt Disney."

"I only knew he was frozen," Mel said.

Spencer came up beside Haveabud and asked who was frozen.

Mel said they should register; he had a headache and wanted to stretch out for a few minutes.

"Uncle Haverford," Spencer said, "the Tyrannosaurus had a head that was over four feet long."

Haveabud rubbed his fingers across his eyelids.

"And it had serrated teeth, and some of them were half a foot," Spencer said, spreading his arms wide.

Haveabud looked at Mel, who was lifting suitcases out of the trunk. "I don't know," Haveabud said. "He wants a computer to keep track of all this information. Maybe I should buy him one."

"Please buy me a Mac II," Spencer said. "It could be my birthday present and my Christmas present."

"But I'd still have to get you a confirmation present," Haveabud said. His eyes felt gritty—strange, because the car was air-conditioned. But who knew what cars were composed of? There would probably be an announcement, years down the line, that the air grates had been made out of a substance more dangerous than asbestos.

In the hot parking lot, Will was fanning himself with one of Spencer's books about the terrain of the prehistoric world. Mel turned to hand him his duffel bag but saw that Will looked tired and hefted it himself. He started toward the entrance to register, and Will ran to his side and walked with him.

"What's a confirmation?" Spencer said.

Haveabud snorted. "I was kidding," he said. "Your mother has no religious beliefs that I have been able to ascertain. The day religion goes public and is listed on the American Stock Exchange, you may have to dress up and go to church."

"We don't go to church," Spencer said.

"My point entirely," Haveabud said. "Don't listen to me. I've told you before, I just need to talk."

As Mel was registering, Will asked whether they could call Wag's mother.

"She knows we're on the way," Mel said. "We're not going to get to your father's until late tomorrow. You've got to at least say hello before they make arrangements for you to see Wag."

Will looked skeptical.

"Look," Mel said, kneeling. "It's going to work out. If Mary can't drive Wag to see you, Corky said she was willing to drive you there on the weekend. One way or another, you're going to see him."

Will looked only slightly less skeptical.

"Look," Mel said again, continuing to talk even though his head was pounding and the clerk had finally materialized, snapping chewing gum and brushing her bangs out of her eyes. "The thing you have to do is hang out with your father and Corky for just a little while. They're anxious to see you. They know you miss your friend, but you don't want to run in and start talking about that immediately, because they're both looking forward to seeing you."

Mel finished and smiled hopefully. As he registered, Mel gave silent thanks that his own parents had not divorced. There were certain things that seemed to be generational: In his grandparents' generation, tyrants kept their wives. Anyone who lived through the Depression, as his parents had, was always wary about calling long distance. The telephone could have been a one-armed bandit; even gambling frightened them less than long distance.

"Would you like to call Wag when we get to the room to tell him about your trip?" Mel said.

Will lit up.

Mel got two sets of keys and put his hand on Will's shoulder as they walked through the lobby.

Outside, Spencer was showing Haveabud a picture in one of his books, telling him that it was drawn to scale and illustrating his point by holding up his thumb, like a painter testing perspective. In front of Spencer's thumb was a carwash with a shopping center behind it. Mel gave Haveabud's key to Will, who ran to give it to him. Haveabud called to Mel, asking if he wanted to go across the highway for ice cream.

"Aspirin," Mel said, shaking his head no. He was relieved that the room was so close. He opened his suitcase before he even looked around, shook three aspirin out of the bottle, pulled the glass out of its plastic wrapper in the bathroom, filled it with tepid water, and drank.

"Aspirin," Mel said again, aloud, hoping his body would realize that help was on the way and that the pounding would subside. He lay on the bed, flat out, and waited for Will. When Will did not appear after a few minutes, he struggled up, thinking he might not know which room was theirs, even though he had left the door ajar. He saw Haveabud, arms spread hawklike over Spencer's and Will's shoulders, steering them toward the highway.

When Will opened the door to the room he would share with Mel, he saw both of Mel's shoes kicked off and felt the air conditioner's strong, cold blast. Realizing he should not awaken Mel, he went next door to Haveabud's, knocked, and was let in. He told Haveabud Mel was sleeping. He said nothing to Haveabud about the phone call, because when he mentioned Wag earlier, Haveabud had asked if Wag was his girlfriend. Will had frowned, thinking he was being teased. Wag was his best friend, and he was not a girl. His mother had said that Wag's mother might get tired of Florida and come back to Virginia, but he wasn't sure if his mother was just guessing about that, or if Mrs. Vickers had said something to her. Wag would know—if he ever got to see Wag.

Sulking, and feeling sorry for himself that the phone call would have to wait until Mel woke up, he curled into one of the chairs by the air conditioner and flipped through the coloring book he and Spencer would work on the next day. This one was about animals in the zoo, which meant that Spencer wouldn't be very interested and that he would do most of the coloring. Spencer really only liked dinosaur coloring books.

While Haveabud showered, Will and Spencer watched TV. Commercial TV was but a paltry thing to Haveabud. He thought with appreciation of all the bars of soap wrapped in paper in motel bathrooms as he lathered up—those thin rectangles whose outer wrapping is always damp by the time you remember to take the cover off before you turn on the water. Everywhere, right now, people who had never met were spiritually united in scraping wet paper from bars of soap, reaching out to put the wad on the sink, or flicking the pieces onto the bathroom floor. All those things were downright ritualistic in America, yet one rarely paused to realize one's own place in such domestic traditions.

Haveabud's wife bought French milled soap at $7.50 a bar, $72.00 a box. Several dollars' worth of free suds were the result of buying soap in groups of ten. The good thing about the soap his wife bought was that each bar was individually wrapped in pleated paper with a small silver seal at the top—a handy thing to throw into one's pocket for a little gift during an afternoon rendezvous with one's lover, and so much more appreciated than flowers. What woman would not blush car-

rying a bunch of flowers into a hotel? And if you brought
flowers to a woman at home she inevitably had them, because
she had thought of flowers along with anointing the bedside
lamp with patchouli oil and spreading brand-new designer
sheets on the bed. A bar of soap was perfect because it showed
a woman that you were thinking of her body. There was no
telling whether a woman wanted to smell of sea breezes or of
muguet des bois, so perfume was a bad choice, but the bars of
soap had a delicate scent that anyone would like. But ah!
Those little bars of Camay in motel bathrooms! The gluey
bars of Neutrogena, like dried honey. And the infrared bathroom lights as magnificently warm as the sun on a perfect day.
The too-small towels the motel provided made you pat, not
rub, so that it seemed you were commending every part of
your body. Life was always an adventure if you adapted to
circumstances. How sad it must be for all those travelers who
wanted familiar smells, the mattress of optimal hardness, windows that opened onto their backyards, instead of parking lots
where cars of all colors and shapes were lined up for your
inspection and delight. You could find out under what circumstances your fellow human beings would brake; what puns
and slogans moved them; whether they thought women should
have control of their own bodies; what national parks they had
visited. With careful inspection, you might be able to see which
bumper sticker was applied *first*, so that their feelings about
abortion could be understood as pre-Yellowstone or post-
Yellowstone. Who would not be tempted to imagine a com-
posite portrait of the driver who kept an eye out for falling rocks,
while also asserting that gun laws were already too restrictive?
Some car owners wore their hearts on their sleeves by sticking
decals of peace signs and endangered species on their bumpers.
Their vanity license plates were effusions of the soul, succinctly
expressed; the cars' colors the ones they loved but were too embarrassed to wear. Four-cylinder, six-cylinder, fuel-injected

dreams, all lined up to educate and provoke and titillate, and what did people do but close the curtains and turn on the tube in order to hear Ed McMahon enthuse about Alpo and Johnny Carson reel off the list of the night's guests.

A set designer could not have done a better job in assembling this particular motel room, Haveabud thought. Ochre shag carpeting stopped a foot short of the heating unit below the casement window, where a yellow-slatted venetian blind dangled. The drawstring curtains were imprinted with fish and squid and what Haveabud took to be sand sharks, all in perfectly spaced configurations that would never be found in the ocean: tentacles like witches' gnarled fingers dangling at regular intervals and, interspersed in the empty spaces, mysterious sperm-shaped bits of yellow that might have been millions of worms lost simultaneously from fishing poles, or simply abstract shapes whose own erratic pattern was meant to aesthetically unite enemies of the sea.

Haveabud had once read an article that said many motels deliberately offered something for everyone, and nothing to offend. That was the explanation for pole lamps, shag carpeting, sunburst clocks, laminated-wood wood, and desks (who had a desk at home?) with neatly placed blotters and a top drawer filled with postcards of the kidney-shaped pool. The bed linen was stretched as tightly as a tambourine; lotions and potions in the bathroom smelled vaguely of gardenias; the Sani-Wrapped drinking glasses and the toilet seat with the paper band would bring back memories of the Fourth of July as the sash was snapped away or the glass was pulled from its plastic wrapper like a crackerjack.

The more impersonal and immutable the room, the greater Haveabud's pleasure: the walls that could be wiped clean if you stumbled with your drink; the carpet that always absorbed quickly; the red light that blinked silently on the telephone like the beacon from a lighthouse.

Haveabud emerged from the bathroom in his undershorts, with the little towel balanced on his shoulder like an epaulet. Will was sitting on the shag carpeting, watching a car race, and Spencer was trying to master the one-armed push-up. When he got it down, Haveabud was going to cast him in one of his upcoming videos (a late-night treat for partygoers whom Haveabud chose to bring home) as a midget fingerpainter who had become the rage of the New York art scene.

"Are we going to have pizza tonight?" Spencer asked.

"I thought some Belon oysters with a white Chassagne-Montrachet," Haveabud said. "Perhaps followed by some carpaccio and a lingonberry soufflé for dessert."

"Pizza," Spencer said, not looking up.

"Sourdough bread with caviar-dill butter and yellow pepper gratinée," Haveabud said.

"We want real food," Spencer said.

"That's what my wife cooks me for dinner," Haveabud said. "Don't you feel sorry for me?"

"Yes," Spencer said.

"So: more pizza to cleanse the system. With nitrite-loaded crispy bacon, or pepperoni that may contain a small percentage of insect larvae and animal hair?"

Spencer stopped trying to do one-handed push-ups. "You're gross, Uncle Haverford," he said.

Will got up and walked next door to see if Mel was awake. He was not. He was snoring, though he must have awakened at some point, because now the air conditioner was on low. Will looked for another few seconds, then pulled the door closed. "He's still sleeping," Will told Haveabud glumly.

Haveabud's idea was that they take a swim in the pool. If Mel woke up and joined them, fine, and if he didn't, they would call the desk and see if there was a pizza place that delivered.

E L E V E N

Spencer wore red trunks with silver studs at the waist that made him look as if he were wearing a Western belt. He wore an ankle bracelet that some admirer had given his mother. Since an ankle bracelet was not her style, it would have been impossible to explain to her husband, so she had it fastened around her son's ankle, the way whores tattoo themselves in private places, or women carry lovers' pictures behind their children's pictures in their lockets. Spencer simply thought of life as a huge adventure in which he would be presented with unexpected gifts, sworn to secrecy about things that were for him, at best, enigmatic, and expected to intuit the moment's truth from his mother's expression. It was not a mode Spencer ever got clear on, so he developed the habit of suspending judgment and always found himself hoping that things would turn out for the best. Only an adult—in particular, his mother—could issue the final verdict, whispered the last thing at night, or delivered solemnly, with the implication that they were coconspirators and that outsiders must not be privy to their superior knowledge. What created anxiety in Spencer was not his mother, or the here and now, but an ultimate question, a question that no amount of research had turned up a clear answer to, but that was truly one of the essential mysteries of all time: What happened to the dinosaurs? Clearly superior, known to be of gigantic size and to have voracious appetites, high energy, and impressive abilities, the dinosaurs had just disappeared one day, as if they had always been the small-scale two-dimensional creatures of cartoons and coloring books who could be as easily dismissed as parakeets were when the cover was dropped over their cage. Was it possible that, as a protest against the current situation on earth, they had willed themselves gone? Could life have simply become, for the dinosaurs, an existential errand—time passed until the inevitable moment of extinction? Eat a few lizards, dive in a pool, snap up an insect. That might have been their version of eating a nightly pizza. There was a way in which Spencer knew that he and his family and friends were just passing time.

Spencer had nightmares—possible scenarios that explained the disappearance of the dinosaurs: a big-bang theory of doomsday in which clouds emitted choking blasts, and lizards, subjected to horribly contaminated food, in turn poisoned the Compsognathus, so they fell like rain, as helpless as puppets taken from the hand. Right now, this very minute, they should be devouring their prey. The planet, in spite of the media's constant update on its urgencies and its future, was at a standstill as far as Spencer was concerned—constantly vulnerable until the mysteries of the Mesozoic world were solved.

So they were headed south, to have a bit of fun along the

way and to deliver Will on a mission of importance—a visit to
his father and stepmother. They were as inconsequential as
dust. If the dinosaurs had been wiped out, suddenly and for
all time, what was so important about this mission? How
should they think of themselves as rational, energetic, even
superior creatures when the brightly lit buttons of the Coke
machine could be glowing a message that signified their im-
minent annihilation? How, in short, could anything be trusted
when something as calamitous as the mass extinction of dinosaurs had transpired, and when all that remained was conjec-
ture, idle speculation, TV cameramen filming scale models of
the earth before the great disappearance? What if they erected
a monument to extinct dinosaurs in Washington, D.C.? What
if the few token dinosaurs in the museums were taken outdoors, and others recreated full size? What if all those bones,
scales, and teeth were laid out in a line across the mall? *Then*
would people know what had vanished from the planet? Why
commemorate wars when no war could have been as deadly
and complete as whatever broke over the heads of the dinosaurs? What was *extinct* supposed to mean? That it was beyond people's dreams?

Will had worn his navy-blue boxer shorts into the pool.
Haveabud said no one would notice that he was not wearing
swim trunks, and Will was still at the age when he believed
whatever adults said about things like that.

Spencer, holding his breath, dove toward the bottom of the
pool, then rose to the surface to tread water. Haveabud started
to instruct Will in the dead man's float, demonstrating it himself with a buoyancy that made him appear more object than
human.

Will sat on the edge of the pool, dangling his feet in the
water. He was thinking of how exposed the pool seemed—a
flat expanse of water that except for minor disturbances of the
surface might have been a mirror reflecting the blue, blue sky.

Haveabud and Spencer were slick seals, and Will was waiting on the sidelines to applaud. That was the way it was when you performed publicly: You always owed the viewer an act that would please. It was why Will and Wag liked their tent's interior: because inside they could be themselves, on guard only against the possibility of some mother-anthropologist who would disturb the tomb. Being suspended in water and hiding in a tent were both a lot of fun, but the sheets enclosed you better than the water did.

Swishing his feet in the water, Will was biding his time as he waited for Mel to wake up. Mel and Haveabud were nothing alike: Haveabud talked a lot, and Mel was much quieter; Haveabud loved to buy souvenirs, which he thought should be put in a time capsule, but Mel only bought mints for everyone when they left a restaurant and postcards to send to Jody. Though Will did not know Haveabud's life story, he knew that Haveabud's mother made him nervous and he hated it when she visited him in New York. Haveabud said his mother lived in Siberia. Mel said Haveabud's mother lived in Cincinnati. The night before Will left on this trip, Jody talked to him about Haveabud. She told him that Haveabud liked to act wild, and that usually the easiest thing to do was to try to get into the spirit of things. It was obvious to Will that his mother made an effort to be nice to Haveabud. She was back in Mel's apartment, working on photographs that would be shown at Haveabud's gallery. Haveabud was like a wild boy in a sandbox, she had told him, but he had a way of tossing up things that were very important. Will had not understood that she was making an analogy; in the car, he had asked about Haveabud's sandbox and gotten a very strange look. Something about that puzzlement had let him know he should not ask more.

Will was thinking about his mother because Haveabud had been floating face-down and holding his breath for so long that his mother would have made him come up for air. As a younger child, when he first saw a metronome, he had cried with frustration. Now he was a child swinging his foot in the water as his older, more accomplished friend explored the depths and Haveabud tempted fate, and Mel sank deeper into his dreams.

Haveabud swam over to Spencer and lured him to his shoul-dertops. He moved around, in the area of the pool where his feet could still touch the bottom, bouncing Spencer on a bumpy ride. Water rose to Spencer's chin when Haveabud crouched. The water poured off him as Haveabud rose again. Will was offered the same ride, but he didn't want it. Finally, to prove to Haveabud that he was in the spirit of things, he went to the shallow end and floated on his back. That didn't last long because it was too bright to keep his eyes open, staring at the sky, and too strange a feeling to float with them closed. Wag had sent him a drawing of his neighbor's pool, which he could use any time he asked permission. His mother had told him that no matter who gave permission, he was not to use the pool unless an adult was present. He wondered who that adult would be. It would be a little strange to see Mrs. Vickers without his mother. He knew they missed each other but that his mother was less sad than she might have been because of the exciting things that were happening with her photographs and with Haveabud. Will looked at Haveabud and Spencer, giggling, just as Haveabud went all the way under, and Spencer swam free and kicked to stay afloat. Will thought it must be very sad to have your real father gone all the way to Europe. His mother had told him that Haveabud was so nice to Spencer because he was sorry Spencer's father had run away, and because Spencer's stepfather had no inter-est in him. Wayne was *his* real father, but Mel seemed more like his father. He wished that Mel could stay in Florida with him. He looked back at the motel, where two people were taking suitcases out of their trunk, arguing. Their words weren't audible, but it was obvious from the way they moved that they were angry. Will toe-hopped into deeper water and did the breaststroke, pulling himself up on the other side. He and Wag had taken swimming lessons together two summers before. He could hardly wait to be in the swimming pool with Wag.

Haveabud, out of the pool, rubbed the towel/epaulet over his chest and swiped the back of his swimming trunks. Dripping water, and gesturing for the two of them to follow, he pushed open the gate's creaking door and began walking barefoot toward the motel room.

"Bologna and apples!" Spencer hollered, running behind him.

"Liverwurst," Haveabud bellowed.

It was the daily debate about pizza toppings, starting from the most ridiculous and working toward something feasible.

Will called out that he wanted hamburger. He saw that something had bitten him in the crook of his arm: an itchy pink welt had risen. His mother would put medicine on a Q-tip and paint it over the bump. Mel would use his finger—if he had brought anything for insect bites. Will raised his arm and licked the bump. His skin tasted like chlorine.

"In here, in here," Haveabud called, motioning him into the room with a sweep of his arm. "In here, the person who wants hamburger on his pizza."

As Haveabud talked he entered the room and stepped out of his wet trunks. He was not tan, but his skin looked even paler when he took off his clothes. Haveabud turned around, scratching his pubic hair. He reached into his suitcase and took out a pair of black silk briefs and pulled them on as Spencer was closing the door. The pizzas he ordered by telephone were one medium with hamburger and extra cheese, and a large with shrimp and onion. Haveabud declined their

offer of a liter of RC cola for ninety-nine cents by saying that
he preferred to drink Jack Daniel's with his pizza. He gave the
name of the motel and his room number and asked that the
pizzas be billed to his credit card. He recited the number from
memory.

Spencer pushed the back of Haveabud's knees from behind
so his legs would buckle.

"They wanted me to commit suicide by drinking RC cola,"
Haveabud said, dipping a little as he hung up. "The stuff
tastes like rusted nails and cherry pits. You can get your bev-
erages from the machine outside, while I imbibe something
stronger."

Haveabud opened the canvas drawstring bag he had
brought into the room. Inside was the bottle of Jack Daniel's,
which he said was his only concession to currying favor in the
South.

"What's curried favor?" Spencer said.

"Please," Haveabud said, rolling his eyes. "It is all right for
you to be a child, but you have to also grant me my rights as
an adult. I cannot give a running narrative of the meaning of
all expressions. I keep telling you to remember that I like to
talk. It *seems* like I'm talking to you, but actually I am talking
to myself."

Haveabud switched on the TV. Gene Kelly was tapping
through puddles, singing his heart out. Haveabud changed
the channel: A camera zoomed in on otters sliding down a
waterfall. On the next channel, a blond woman in a dress that
made her look like a mermaid was playing with a telephone
cord, licking her lips as she pulled it this way and that, in-
clining her head, so that her flickering eyelashes recreated the
motions of the ascending and descending otters. She whispered a telephone number to call. "Let's party," the woman
said. This was followed by a commercial for Drano.

Spencer picked up Haveabud's bottle of Jack Daniel's and,

using it the way the woman had used the telephone, held the
neck to his ear and batted his eyes seductively, then held out
the bottle to Haveabud, who was coming out of the bathroom
holding a glass. Haveabud laughed. grabbing the bottle away
and pouring two inches of bourbon into the glass. Spencer
continued to mime the actions of the woman on TV, looking
at himself in the mirror. Haveabud reached into the clutter
that had materialized on top of the dresser and picked up
Spencer's Triceratops. He, too, pretended the plastic animal
was a telephone and shrugged his shoulder suggestively.
Then, from amid the clutter of keys and suntan lotion and
handkerchiefs, brochures of scenic attractions, a handful of
change, an aspirin bottle, and spare Missoni socks, Haveabud lifted a tube of lipstick in a silver case, removed the
cap, and stroked it on his parted lips. When he was done he
puckered his lips, and Spencer and Will both screamed with
laughter.

"Where did you get that?" Spencer said. "Where did it
come from?"

"It was in my overnight kit. I have no idea where it came
from. My wife must have dropped it in by mistake."

"Put it on my lips," Spencer said, jealous that Haveabud
had started toward Will. Will put his hands over his mouth in
protest, but actually Haveabud could see that he liked the
idea. It was Haveabud's notion that they could all be wearing
lipstick when they opened the door to take in the pizzas.

"Open your mouth like you're saying 'Oh,' " Haveabud
said. "I don't know how to put this stuff on other people very
well."

Will's smile disappeared when he opened his mouth wide.
Spencer sat on the bed and stared while Haveabud slowly
colored Will's lips. Will's eyes blinked every time Haveabud
moved the lipstick a fraction of an inch. When Haveabud had
finished, he got up and looked at his face in the mirror. Have-

abud had done a good job. His mouth was so bright that he couldn't focus on anything else—not even the other insect bite that had swollen on his forehead. He was afraid to talk for fear the lipstick would smear.

Spencer ran the Triceratops up Will's back and brought it to rest on top of one shoulder, its three horns pushing into Will's neck. Will swatted it away, examining his transformation. He had tried to walk in his mother's high heels, but he had never had on makeup before. It was going to shock Mel. Mel was going to laugh.

Haveabud was stretched out on the bed. With the remote control, he switched channels and stopped by popular demand when stampeding elephants raced across the screen, sending up clouds of dust.

"Elephants are no good," Spencer said to Will. "Why couldn't they have disappeared and all the Mesozoic creatures have lived?"

Spencer picked up the tube of lipstick and went toward Haveabud.

"Don't attack me with that," Haveabud said.

Spencer jumped on the bed and began to wrestle with Haveabud.

Haveabud got the lipstick away from him and held it tightly in the palm of his hand. Spencer sat on Haveabud's chest and pretended to be smothering him.

"Let up!" Haveabud said. "What do you want?"

"I want the lipstick," Spencer said.

"What are you going to do with it?"

"I'm going to put it on my lips," Spencer said.

Haveabud raised an eyebrow.

"I *am* going to put it on my lips," Spencer said.

Haveabud uncurled his fingers. Spencer pounced on the tube and held it aloft. Then his expression changed. "You put it on," he said.

"I'm resting," Haveabud said. "Go look in the mirror. You can put it on."

Spencer pouted. "Come on," he said.

Haveabud took the tube, and instead of putting it on Spencer's lips, began to dot it in concentric circles around Spencer's nipples. Spencer's eyes were wide. He started to pull away, then decided to sit still and see what he looked like with a painted chest. On TV, people in a Jeep were bumping through the forest, binoculars raised in the direction of stampeding elephants. Dirt got in one woman's eye, and she began to cry. "That's it! Your tears will wash it out, Stephani," her companion said. Dust billowed backwards so that by the time Will looked away there was nothing to see on the screen. Music played loudly and occasionally there were close-ups of the tires, bouncing through the rutted floor of the jungle. Will walked over to the bed to inspect Spencer's nipples. The lipstick looked much stranger there than on Will's mouth. Spencer asked Will if he wanted to have his chest painted too.

"Whatever you do, please sit somewhere other than my rib cage, crushing me to death," Haveabud said, pushing Spencer aside. Spencer braced himself and didn't move. He looked down at Haveabud and laughed. Haveabud sighed, turning his head, and stared at the television. For a few minutes they watched the dust storm clearing. Haveabud reached for the Kleenex on the night table, pulled one, and told Spencer to wipe off the lipstick.

"Suck it off," Spencer said, thrusting his chest closer to Haveabud. "Suck it off and your lips will be more lipsticked."

"You can put more on my lips if you want," Haveabud said. "Just don't sit on my chest while you're doing it."

"No. I want you to get it off," Spencer said, jutting his chest forward again.

Haveabud started to speak, then hesitated. Will looked at Spencer and Haveabud looked away. A commercial came on then: a woman rushing around trying to kill a cartoon ant with a broom. As Will looked back, Spencer bounced a little closer to Haveabud, and Haveabud began swabbing the lipstick off his nipples. At first Will thought he was just being careful, then realized he was rubbing it in instead of removing it, moving the Kleenex the way his mother lightly stroked the brush against her face when she was applying color to her cheeks. Haveabud continued doing this during the commercial, which ended when the woman put down her broom, got an aerosol can, and began spraying what was now a battalion of ants, who all died and were seen in close-up with big white x marks that looked like jacks over their eyes. When the show resumed, the woman who had gotten dust in her eye was sitting in a restaurant, raising a glass of champagne as the man, very dapper in a tuxedo, toasted her: "To you, my darling. And to your courage."

Spencer's fingertips were on Haveabud's nipples. He was not making the same motion Haveabud had made, but a light stroking motion, back and forth, the way the woman in the commercial had been sweeping before the cartoon ant jumped into her path. The pillow on Haveabud's lap was Spencer's seat cushion; Haveabud had drawn up his knees so that his thighs became a backrest. Spencer looked over his shoulder at Will, who was pretending to watch TV, and then went back to what he was doing. The air conditioner had been running for a long while, and the room was so cold that Will was getting goosebumps. He got up and put on Haveabud's shirt. Then, curious, he walked to the side of the bed where Haveabud lay with his eyes closed, Spencer's fingers lightly tickling his chest. Haveabud also had goosebumps. Spencer smiled at Will and said, "You do it."

Will sat on the side of the bed. He thought that Haveabud would open his eyes, but he didn't. The lipstick tube was on top of the bedspread, and as Haveabud breathed it rolled against his side.

"When is the pizza coming?" Will whispered, as if Haveabud were asleep.

Spencer shrugged, looking across the room to the door. Will followed his eyes. Nothing could be heard beyond the air conditioning. Will suddenly had a vivid image of the pool. Then an image of the room next door, where Mel was sleeping. Or maybe he was no longer asleep. Maybe any second he would knock, or if that did not happen, perhaps the person would arrive with the pizzas and soon they would be outside again, by the pool, with Cokes and pizza. Will's mouth felt dry. The bite on his forehead itched, but he remembered what his mother had said about scratching just making it itch more. He resisted scratching. He looked again at the door.

"I can show you how to do something," Spencer whispered.

Will stopped thinking about a knock at the door.

"He's asleep," Spencer said, tilting his head toward Haveabud.

Haveabud was very silent, but Will did not think he could be asleep.

Will sat on the bed and looked at Spencer. It was the same way he had sat dangling his feet in the water. The way he had been sitting in the backseat of the car. He thought it would be wonderful to be grown and to plant his feet on the ground instead of having them dangle. That was what was nice about the swimming pool: being able to swish his feet through the water.

"Lie down," Spencer whispered.

It was a queen-size bed. Will shifted and did what he was told, lying at the edge. Then he moved in a few inches so he wouldn't fall. He didn't know if he was supposed to imitate Haveabud, or what. Spencer climbed off Haveabud and slipped into the space between Haveabud and Will. "No," he said. "Don't open your eyes. Close them."

Will closed them and kept them closed, even when Spencer got up. For a few seconds Spencer was standing, but then he climbed back in the gully between them and put a pillow over the lower part of Will's body. Will shivered; the instant warmth made him realize how cold the rest of his body was. Spencer's fingers, as he began moving them on his chest, were warm, and when Will's nipples began to harden, they also felt warm. Soon the area between his nipples, which Spencer stroked, stayed warm when Spencer moved his fingertips from left to right and right to left.

"Put your hand on yourself, under the pillow," Spencer whispered. Will opened his eyes and frowned. In the second before he closed them again, Will saw that Haveabud's arm was under the pillow that lay over his own crotch. There was some slight movement even though the bed itself seemed still. Will put his hand on his penis. He waited for Spencer's next instruction, but there was only silence. Then Spencer shifted his weight on the bed and began rubbing Haveabud's chest. He chewed his lip as he did this. Will closed his eyes. After a minute or so Will felt Spencer's fingers on his own chest and, to his surprise, began to relax the minute Spencer's hand returned. Spencer stroked slowly with his palm, then gently rubbed Will's stiff nipples between his thumb and first finger. Will was falling asleep. It was what happened when his mother stroked his forehead, and because he felt hot and cold at the same time, he suddenly remembered being sick, his mother at his side, his mother sitting on his bed. He was conscious of the sound of the air conditioner. On the highway, a car slammed on its brakes and skidded—a sound loud enough to be heard in the room, but to Will it was like wind rustling in a tree, nothing to take notice of. Haveabud whispered to Spencer, and Spencer's hand abruptly stopped moving on Will's chest. Haveabud whispered to Spencer—and because Will's eyes were squeezed shut, his sense of hearing seemed more acute— that he should not stop, that he should do it even slower, much, much slower because . . . And then the bed jolted, and

Will opened his eyes. Spencer was on his knees, looking down at Haveabud, his cold heel touching Will's hipbone. Spencer stretched out beside Haveabud and curled on his side, but almost immediately Haveabud rolled out of bed and went toward the bathroom, inhaling deeply to get his breath.

In the bathroom, he mixed hot and cold water until it ran tepid, cupping his hands until they were partially filled with water. He smeared his damp palms over his penis and pubic hair before he cupped his hands and splashed water on his face. He reached for the towel and buried his face in it. Spencer got up and followed Haveabud to the doorway. When Spencer left without looking at him—when Will looked at the wide empty bed—Will had felt frightened for the first time. He got up and walked to the bathroom door. It was closed now, or pulled almost closed. There was a paper bathmat on the tile floor. Haveabud was on his knees, and this time he was licking Spencer's nipples. Will watched his mouth move lower, leaving a snail-trail of slime as it moved down Spencer's body.

TWELVE

Since quitting his previous job, Wayne had taken a job with a lawn-and-landscaping service. Also, on Friday and Saturday nights he delivered groceries to the big retirement complexes that had sprung up in the past few years: no big tips, but decent people who probably wouldn't put a bullet between his eyes the way loonies did when they got antsy in supermarkets. A month before, a kid bagging groceries had been threatened with a pistol, and another kid, loading groceries into a car curbside, had been robbed of what little money he had, and had gotten his wrist broken in the process. The first incident made the papers, but as far as he knew the second incident had merely gotten around by word of mouth, so Corky probably wouldn't hear about that. She already had objections to his working nights, and reports of violence would just fuel her anger, though she had quieted down since she had started to work two nights a week herself. If she had her way, he would quit smoking no matter how much weight he gained, never socialize with his friends, and sit around the house like Corinne's husband, who had been missing from the weekly softball game since his daughter's birth. The baby was suffering from jaundice. At first Eddie had recruited his friend Buzz to play catcher, but after three weeks he just resigned from the team. Corinne had pitched him a fastball with the unplanned baby (planned by Corinne, unplanned by Eddie, as Corky had told him, swearing him to secrecy), and now he was as in-tight with family life as a fastball hitting the pocket of a catcher's mitt.

He pulled into the hotel parking lot to take the short stroll across the sand to the Azure Skies, a thatch-roofed beach bar where every day there was happy hour from five to six: free Pepperidge Farm goldfish, free peanuts, and on Fridays a second drink provided gratis with the last one you ordered. A nice, simple, good-time sort of place that Corky, of course, wouldn't set foot in. The owner's twin brother ran the supermarket where Wayne had started moonlighting. It was from him that Wayne learned the supermarket needed delivery boys. It rubbed him wrong when Dalton said "boys," but he reminded himself that it was just an expression. Why get mad about that when things were so screwed-up in the world that now the person in charge of a meeting wasn't a chairman, but a *chairperson*. Hurricanes were now named for men. Next, people would be referring to sailboats as "he."

What sort of man would leave different women three times? Wayne was wondering to himself as he locked the door of the Toyota. He had taken off his socks and tennis shoes and left them in the car so he could feel the sand between his toes. A dip in the ocean would be even better, but if it came to a fast swim or a couple of drinks, his preference was the barstool. Just for the moment, he was entertaining the notion of breaking up with his wife. That would mean that he had left Carol Ann, and Jody, and then Corky. A man who needed to be independent would do that. A man who knew that he was better off on his own. A man tired of women's expectations.

For a few seconds the notion of being on his own made him feel powerful. Then he tried the flip side and decided that to walk three times meant that he had had unreasonable expectations of the women he had chosen. Probably some shrink could tell him the truth, but he had about as much intention of seeing a shrink as he did of swimming for the horizon. After a couple of Buds he'd feel either one way or the other: that he was entitled, or that he was a coward. If he decided he was a coward, he'd just have another beer before six o'clock; delivering groceries did not exactly require complete sobriety.

"My man," Dalt said, giving the high five. The fan above the cash register was blowing. Dalt was slightly cross-eyed. He was wearing one of his many baseball caps studded with fishing lures. Some of the caps had buttons with funny sayings on them, and one—a gift from his daughter, which the customers sensed wasn't to be laughed at—had a small heart-shaped frame above the brim that contained a picture of Dalt's fat-cheeked granddaughter, Melanie Rae. Customers found out the child's name even if they drank at the bar only one time. Large photos could be pointed out on the bulletin board above the cash register if he didn't have her silver-framed image riding high above his forehead.

Wayne gave the bar the once-over. Agnes was there, in a purple muumuu patterned with birds of paradise. She was barely tolerated at the bar, although she was a regular, and when she had one too many she was not tolerated at all; one of the people working the counter would load her across the highway, get the front-door key from under her doormat, and tell her to shower and stay home. One night after allowing herself to be taken home she had gone out and started thumbing. A week later—in an account she found more humorous than did anyone forced to listen to it—she found herself in Boston. That Agnes had hitched to Boston and back in one of the muumuus without encountering any harm was testament to the strange ways of the world.

"How's my brother treatin' you?" Dalt asked. Before he had his back operation, Dalt had played third base in the weekly game. Sometimes he still came to the field, bringing a lawn chair with him, impulsively hollering bets that he'd later make good on when the batter showed up at the bar. One such batter was there this evening, having a Stoli on the house to celebrate his home run. His nickname was Boat, and he installed tape decks. He knew everything that was new in the antitheft department. A few days before, the last time Wayne had been at the Azure, Boat had told him about the kid who got his wrist broken outside the supermarket. Boat's wife was taking a music-appreciation course at the community college, so he was free to drink as long as he wanted on Friday nights. He did what Wayne imagined was a very good imitation of the way his wife reclined in her chair, listening to classical music through earphones with a dreamy expression on her face. "Don't matter what kind of noise goes on, she don't react," Boat said. "Mower starts up, paperboy throws the newspaper against the door, nothing. Nothing but harps and oboes going into her head." It baffled Boat that his wife was taking a course in music appreciation. The only thing he obviously liked about his wife was that she had been part of a twenty-year union with him. Also in the bar this evening were two flaxen-haired girls flashing each other Farrah smiles and moving their eyes only between each other and their glasses of wine, a few tourists who had stumbled into the place, and Nick from the tackle shop.

"Your brother says things are really going to pick up when the store starts delivering pizza," Wayne said.

Dalt put a bottle of Bud on the bar in front of Wayne. He knew that Wayne didn't drink out of a glass. Then Dalt stretched and looked out to sea.

"How are you this evening?" Boat called down the bar. "Nice to see everybody in the world isn't swooning to Chopin." He pronounced the name as if it were two words. Agnes looked at Boat, and then at Wayne, as if she intended to join the exchange. When she caught Dalt's eye, she pointed to her empty glass instead.

"You gonna do all right with another one?" Dalt called to Agnes. "We don't want you setting off on safari or nothing."

"I'm doin' all right," Agnes said.

"What if you was to wake up at the top of Mount Everest?" Dalt said. He had not moved from where he stood after handing Wayne his beer.

"Bacardi and soda," Agnes called, as if Dalt didn't know what she had been drinking.

"Think she'd be a good pizza chef?" Dalt said. "Send her over to my brother, get her a job and make an honest woman out of her?"

"Your brother got a restaurant?" Agnes said.

"Now what are you doin' showin' interest in work?" Dalt said. "Didn't you move down to Florida to retire? Don't let me tempt you, Agnes. Ain't you worried I'll tempt you?"

"Not to work," Agnes said, her top lip curling in an approximation of a smile.

If you bantered long enough, Agnes always made some sexual innuendo. Sometimes Dalt played straight man just to please her. This was one of those times. He poured a Bacardi and soda and added it to her tab. Then he walked out from behind the bar and put it on her table.

"I told him he should open a separate pizza place, but he never listens to me," Dalt said, coming back to where Wayne sat and wiping the counter. "He's antsy. That's the trouble with him. He was born two minutes before me, and he's never let me forget it. But I tell him: I like the easy life. With him, it's hustle, hustle. I don't understand his life philosophy. I do a little fly fishing, he loves to go out deep-sea. He's got a different personality from me. If I had to deliver groceries for my brother, I'd sooner leave for Timbuktu." Dalt popped open two more beers and put them in front of Wayne, who had five minutes to drink them and drive to the shopping plaza before he'd be late. "Last call for happy hour!" Dalt said, then surveyed the suddenly eager faces. Dalt liked regular guys, and Wayne was a regular guy; he didn't come to the Azure looking for anybody's opinion, or to discuss anything in particular. Some of the customers were as predictable as the hand ticking around the clock: You knew just the direction they'd move in, and exactly the pace at which they'd proceed. You got to know the ones who had blowfish bladders, and the ones who started sliding around the barstool before the ice had even melted in their first drink. Wayne was a good-looking guy who never flirted with the women. He probably had an okay home life, even though—or hell, because—he didn't have any kids. He'd talk sports with you if that was what you wanted, and the week before he'd been a good enough citizen to jump-start another guy's car—a guy he'd just met ten minutes before.

It would have surprised Dalt to know that Wayne also had his doubts about Dalt's brother's character—so much so that he felt whatever he made off with was his due. He wouldn't touch money that wasn't his, but groceries were another matter. It was all very small-scale: He'd help Lee gather the groceries and throw a few items into a box that weren't on the phoned-in list, which he'd pocket before he delivered them. This meant that Wayne often ate smoked oysters for lunch, and exotic soups such as strawberry-melon. During the week, he fixed himself microwave chimichangas at the lawn-and-landscaping office and enjoyed bottles of pineapple-papaya juice.

As he hopped off the barstool, he and Dalt nodded. Wayne began to think up the excuse he would give to Dalt's brother, feeling that being late to work was also justified because his employer was a man whose own brother couldn't stand him. The car. He had never used that simple and expedient lie before. He would say that he'd stopped to change the tire.

In the car, he shook out half a stick of gum, unwrapped it, and began to chew, turning the radio dial to find a station that suited him.

Driving along, Wayne was rather pleased with himself for all the plans he had, all the decisions he had made at the Azure, and even for his good luck in living where palm trees always looked splendid in the light of a full moon. Briefly, he envied the person who cut in front of him on a Harley, but by the time he pulled into the shopping-center parking lot he was glad to be himself: a man who had just struggled to change a tire, and who had triumphed; a man lucky enough to have a wife who wanted more of his time; a man totally sober, so that every word he spoke was sure to be believed. A great Bob Marley song sped him on his way, socks shoved into his pocket, unlaced shoes on the floor behind his feet.

T H I R T E E N

A week before Will's arrival, Wayne paced through the house. It was Thursday night, one of the two times a week Corky worked late at Bathing Beauties, the new swimwear store that had opened last summer in Seabreeze Plaza. With her 20 percent employee's discount, Corky had already bought a lace poncho as a birthday present for her sister in Albuquerque; it hung from one of the bedposts. She had sewn a label with her sister's name embroidered in pink thread in the back of the neck. Some of Wayne's shirts had labels with his name sewn in, too, although Corky had stopped putting them in when she began laundering his shirts the second time the dry cleaner raised his prices in a little more than a month.

It had been a hot day, and after planting thirty rhododendrons with only one helper at the entrance to a new housing development, Wayne had quit early and come home to stretch

out and take Tylenol for his headache. When he was lying
down he was fine, but he felt antsy and kept getting up to walk
around the house. There was a lot of cleaning up to do before
Will came—clearing things out of Corky's sewing room so that
the sofabed could be opened, finding a place for the plants on
the glass window shelves so the curtains could be pulled,
putting things in boxes, and getting rid of the newspapers and
magazines. He didn't feel like working any more that day, and
he didn't like being told what to do and when to have his son
visit by his ex-wife. He was very glad Corky had gotten the
phone call instead of him.

He sat on the bed and opened the night-table drawer for a
pack of cigarettes. When Corky was around he smoked Van-
tage cigarettes. When she was gone he reached for the Camels,
which he kept hidden beneath the clutter. His one contribu-
tion to housekeeping was sorting, folding, and putting away
the wash. He had said when he married Corky that he would
do the wash, but it seemed that he never found time, or that
he washed the clothes wrong. By unspoken agreement the
plan got revised to Corky washing and Wayne folding. Putting away the clothes meant that he had a hiding place for his
Camels. As he closed the drawer, he saw the socks he would
be wearing next Christmas—the ones he wore every year,
imprinted with Santa in his sleigh, the nub of wool that was
Rudolph's nose glowing very red, in spite of many washings,
against the navy-blue wool. Because she had had the flu,
Corky's sister had spared them a Christmas visit last year, but
this year she would probably come, and her son, who had had
two operations on his crossed eyes, and her beagle, who would
wet the kitchen floor in his excitement any time anyone entered or left the house, and perhaps her estranged husband,
who had a way of showing up around holiday time, tempo-
rarily sober until the moment when the rum for the punch was
missing or he called from the police station after some skir-
mish in a bar. Wayne had once had to bail him out on Christ-

mas Eve. Everyone had piled into the car at the last minute, deciding to be forgiving, and Wayne had driven off into the night with a car full of unhappy people who had resolved to smile in spite of their sorrow. He had even played Christmas music on the car radio. As if that hadn't been bad enough, some other lunatic, in the throes of last-minute shopping, had run a stop sign and crimped his fender. Later, Wayne had said to Corky that they should have called the police and insisted that Jeremiah's eyes had not been crossed until the moment of impact. He often joked about the boy's affliction, which infuriated her. Then again, she was the one who had relatives who were like homing pigeons.

For no particular reason, he opened the bottom drawer. Corky kept her diaphragm in there, and the box of checks and deposit slips from their joint checking account. A sunset shone through from the background of the checks, fuzzily out of focus, the way Wayne's camera made everything hazy if he forgot to set the little button on the side for near, mid-distance, or far. There was also a ruffly pair of pink pants with a split crotch that she sometimes could be persuaded to put on when they made love. He had given her lace socks with red hearts sewn on the cuff and lace gloves made so her fingers would be exposed. She had worn those only a few times because she said that being naked and having her feet and hands wrapped in lace made her feel like a raccoon.

Wayne and Corky had been married for a year and a half, and she was beginning to put the pressure on about having children. She was years younger than he, so it was nonsense—and the doctor agreed that it was—to talk about the ticking of the biological clock at twenty-nine. On top of the night table was a brochure entitled "What Is Amniocentesis?" In matching brass frames someone had given them as a wedding present were pictures of her grandmother who lived in a nursing home in Wyoming, and Will, who had his hair slicked back. There was also a matchbook from the seafood restaurant

where he and Corky sometimes ate on Saturdays. This week
they'd have to skip it so they could take Will out a couple of
times during the visit.

The next-door neighbors were playing Patsy Cline at the
same time their TV was going. Through the slits in the venetian blinds he could see the bluish light flashing inside the
house. He knew Patsy Cline wasn't singing on TV because
the neighbors played that record night and day. Corky envied
Corinne (she was the Patsy Cline fan; her husband, Eddie,
liked what he called "living girl singers"). Corinne had a maid
who came once a week, and a two-month-old infant named
Debbi, who had been born with so much hair that a little bow
could be tied on top of her head. Ever since the child's birth,
by cesarean, Corky had taken them Sunday supper. The week
before, the four of them had eaten together, with the baby in
a plastic car seat on the center of the table and the Patsy Cline
record playing, as they watched the kitchen TV. The show
had been about treasure recovered from a sunken galleon.
There were diamonds amid the bubbles. Mossy urns with
snakes curled inside at the bottom of the sea. He knew that
afterwards Corky would say how much she wanted a baby.
He knew that Eddie regretted being a father. He felt sorry
for Eddie because he could still remember quite distinctly
the fatigue that came from living with a woman who was
always exhausted, which was a quite separate issue from
your own exhaustion. It was numbing, like trudging through
wet sand. It seemed that you had married a ghost, a wife
who would never again have color in her face, and whose
skin had strangely paled to match the baby's translucence.
Will had screamed for the first six months of his life: first
colic, then one allergic reaction after another when Jody had
to stop nursing because her nipples were so badly cracked.
Jody had made him get up half the time, in the middle of
the night, to soothe Will, and he had cooed and cajoled with

words that meant nothing to Will, rocked him, walked the floor. Other times he had stared in disbelief down his son's pink throat. He still dreamed about Will's gaping mouth, his wet, marble eyes, the pulse beating in his throat, his face turning purple. Many dawns Wayne had considered stuffing a diaper into his mouth, plugging the entrance to the cave of noise, or pinching him, holding him upside down, pushing a pillow into his face. He had never hurt him. Sometimes, except for holding him, he wouldn't try to console him, but he had never yanked a leg too high when changing a diaper or given him the vile formula without first testing a drop on the inside of his wrist. The most horrible thing about a baby was that it robbed you of dignity. They were just like the Army officers who urged you to succeed by berating you so much that you would either triumph or be totally beaten down. In all those late-night moments with Will, he had felt the opposite of what he had been led to believe a dutiful father would feel. He had felt humiliated, weak, a coward, and, finally, expendable—the person who was only a stand-in for the child's mother. When Wayne walked the floor with Will, it was the pacing of the prisoner in the courtyard; when he bounced Will on his knee, he was an idiot dandling a doll.

As Wayne smoked the last of his cigarettes another thought came into his mind. It was to get up and close the blinds and masturbate—not come, just get excited, then make himself wait until Corky came home. As he stubbed out the cigarette, though, an image of Will came clearly to mind: Will wailing as he lightly rubbed his gums where his teeth were beginning to come in. Remembering touching the little lumps in Will's mouth made the life go out of his cock. Then he had an image of Corky turning away from him, which is what she most often did when Will visited because she was afraid they might be overheard.

Patsy Cline was singing "Sweet Dreams," Wayne's favorite, the one he never minded hearing. The baby was crying with all the lusty misery Patsy Cline tried to choke down as she sang the song. He looked at his watch and saw that it was quarter to nine. It would still be at least forty-five minutes until Corky got home. There was still time to do what he had put off doing all day: open the manila envelope from Jody, one of the mystery envelopes she sent every so often that contained souvenirs of her life. He went to the hall table, where Corky always put his mail without comment, got the envelope, walked into the living room, and sat on the floor and opened it. The envelope contained everything from flyers from the health food store detailing the advantages of various kinds of juicers to postcards she had received from friends on vacation. Between the lines, or because he began to recognize handwriting, or because some items were constant, he would eventually begin to piece things together: who was important, what was happening, even what Jody might be thinking. It was a form of flirtation, surely, but also an annoying and childish thing to do, like dropping something from a high window onto someone's head and then ducking out of sight. He found a thank-you note from Jody's father (he and her father had never gotten along); a 3-D postcard, mailed to her in New York City care of her lover, Mel Anthis, of King Kong with a screaming blonde in his big arms, and the message "You are safe with me," signed simply J.D.O.; a letter from a fruit shipper saying that she had forgotten to enclose a check with her order for tangerines; notice of a bounced check from Midas Muffler; and one of Will's drawings (which must have been done awhile ago, because Will's recent drawings were much more realistic): two crayoned lines intersecting in the center of the piece of paper with four ovals on one side and on the other a Christmas tree that looked as though it had been made with a shaky cookie cutter. Above that was lettered

FOOTBALL, and then, in an adult's hand, FIELD. He had not known that Will was interested in football. It would be something to talk to him about—it was always awkward for a while, until he found out what Will's interests were. In the bottom of the envelope, like the penny in the toe of a Christmas stocking, was a little slip of paper—a fortune-cookie fortune that said, "For the new year, you will have to wait until good luck." He kept the drawing separate and stuffed the other things back in the envelope, which he threw away in the kitchen. Jody had been with Mel Anthis for years now. He wondered if she saw him exclusively and, if so, whether they would marry. It had been because of her that the pregnancy didn't end up an abortion; it was her fault that a distraction, and a big responsibility, came into his life just when he might have been able to decide which direction his life should take, instead of which direction it must take. There was nothing to do but walk away from people like that. She was probably still a person whom so many people thought different things about because she was such a chameleon. That was why her mother kept her distance, and why so many people poured their hearts out, trying to get her attention. She would send him personal letters that she had not cared to open! A series of letters that added up to the realization that someone was flirting with Jody, although she would not even respond to the increasingly distraught messages. (Did she think it was funny that the vice principal of Will's school sent her so many notes asking her to account for his absences, and eventually asking her if she realized the problems she was causing by not responding?) Jody was a person who would enclose a sales slip for a two-hundred-dollar pair of shoes and a notice of a bounced check in the same envelope. He had liked her nerve, at first—the way she felt that she didn't have to explain anything to anyone, or that she would do it in her own time. It made sense that she started a business, because she could only work for herself and not for anyone else who would expect things of her and tell her what to do. She was always good at improvising, and at flattering people, so that they'd gladly lend a hand. What he had understood, though, years before, about her being mischievous had by now established itself as mean-ness—assuming that was what she intended by sending the envelopes. There was no way to be in collusion with a prank-ster. All that remained of being tied to Jody was Will. Instead of rolling out the red carpet, he would be carrying stacks of old newspapers to the edge of the driveway for the next day's trash collection, cleaning the room Will would stay in, giving the illusion that there was space and time enough for Will to make an impression.

F O U R T E E N

Corky filled the sink and took a whore's bath, squeezing the washcloth and rinsing it after cleaning her armpits and crotch. She let the water out of the basin and soaked the washcloth a final time under a stream of water from the faucet before wringing it out and hanging it on the towel rack. The sink emptied quietly. Something was wrong with the pipes leading to the bathtub; if you showered for more than a minute, it began to sound like someone was playing the bagpipes.

She opened the door, pausing to see whether the creaking hinges had awakened Wayne. The bedroom was quiet. She reached behind her and turned off the lights, then went on tiptoe down the hall. In the bathroom, she had not been tempted to look in the mirror. She knew that after a long day at the store her hair needed to be washed and her makeup would be smeared. The little bump she had first sensed when she was driving home had by now risen under her bottom lip until it came to a head, hard and tingling.

Some days it seemed to Corky that she and Wayne had been married for years, and other days it seemed that she was living with a stranger whose moods she couldn't predict and whose emotions were never revealed by his actions—only by what he said. She thought he would be angry about her signing on to work Thursdays and Fridays, but when she came home he had embraced her—almost run to put his arms around her. He had pulled down the bedspread like a triumphant magician, eyes aglow, to reveal the secret of mismatched striped sheets, on which he would have her stretch out. Because he was so clearly delighted to see her and to have sex, she now thought that his silence over the last few days might have been because he was worrying over Will's arrival. If he suffered because he did not see his son more often, she wasn't aware of it, yet she didn't think this indicated anything negative about her future with Wayne. She thought that if she and Wayne had a child of their own, Wayne would love the child and probably relax and be quite demonstrative. He and Will were always a little on guard and awkward when they were together, but she supposed that that was quite normal, given how infrequently they saw each other.

Corky caught herself doing what her mother had so often objected to: making everything all right in her mind. All through her adolescence there had been a running argument—no, only her mother's harangues; it was never an argument—in which her mother urged Corky to expand her horizons (her mother's term), to look around her at the damage being done to the environment, the inhumanity of man to man, the awful politics of the AMA, the streets filled with people in need, ignored by a society that did not provide enough affordable medical care, a society that created gas-guzzling cars that fell apart, and that provided its citizens with no reasonable can-

didates in presidential elections. Corky's mother would have
been pleased to have Jane Fonda as her daughter. Adele Da-
vis's books were her mother's bible. Sometimes while she
waited for dinner to cook, her mother would step into the
pantry to toss a few darts at the Richard Nixon dartboard, a
disc so pocked that Nixon was almost unrecognizable.

Corky's father left when she was ten, after overturning every piece of furniture in the ground-floor apartment and drag-
ging the mattress off the bed and throwing it over the porch
rail. Corky and her mother were locked in the bathroom, and
at the time her mother was shouting insults at her father, she
had her hands over Corky's ears. To this day, Corky could not
wear a hat that was pulled over her ears or sleep on her side
with an ear against the pillow. She slept on her back, like a
corpse in the morgue, Wayne said. She could still remember
her feeling of helplessness as her mother, who had a way of
fixating on one thing, insisted, after her husband fled, that she
and Corky get the mattress back into the apartment. Her
mother became as insane as her father had been during his
tirade, yelling at Corky even though Corky was a frail child
who couldn't lift her end of the mattress from the ground.
None of the neighbors came out to help, but someone called
the police. Her mother then fixated on her hatred of the police, insisting that there had been no shouting, and that she
was simply airing the mattress. Into this scene walked Corky's
sister, Vera, eight years old, who had been at a Brownies
meeting, sewing a crayon pouch. Vera had a way of being
absent from the beginning of things and showing up at the
very end. As an older girl, she would show up at the movies
when the last show was ending. When Vera was sixteen she
ran off with a construction worker named Ricky Lattanzi, and
nine months later added twin boys to the family he had already provided her with (two girls, from his first marriage).
By the time her mother found her sister, she was, as her

mother said, "in deep," so she never enacted the threats she had made in Vera's absence: to commit her; to send her to a convent; at the very least to have the marriage annulled. During her mother's long illness, years later, it was one of Ricky Lattanzi's daughters who nursed her. That was also the only time she ever let Ricky Lattanzi into her apartment. On her deathbed she still maintained that Ricky was too old a man to be a suitable match for her daughter.

Corky and Vera had become closer in recent years because Vera had learned how to type. Every couple of weeks a typed letter from her sister, with a little drawing one of the twins had done, would arrive in the mail. It was the only personal mail Corky ever got, unlike Wayne, whose Army buddies, and even his ex-wife, often sent things to him. Lately, her sister had begun to hint that she would help out with the airline ticket if Corky came to visit. Since she had married Wayne, she had never gone anywhere without him. Wayne didn't like her working two nights a week, so what would he think about her taking a trip to see her sister?

In the side room, Corky considered all the clutter that remained, even after Wayne had thrown out the newspapers and she had put away her sewing things so Will could color on the table. A year ago, on a rainy day, she and Will had played a game that had amused both of them. Corky would hide things, and Will had to guess where they were, either going on intuition or guessing because she gave him a hint. Will didn't act like a sissy, but she wondered if he might be a mama's boy because on the last visit he had wanted her to teach him how to embroider. He and Wayne were both loners: Wayne would stand on the pier with his hands plunged in his pockets, watching the fishermen by the hour; Will would sit on a bench and swing his feet, looking at the pelicans. You never knew what silent men were thinking. Corky expected the worst from silence. The man Corky had dated before she met Wayne had suffered from migraines and always wanted as much quiet as possible. All the time she knew him, the man insisted that people leave their shoes in the hallway when they entered his house, and he bought Squeak-Ease to squirt between the wood strips of the parquet floors. Sometimes when he was suffering from migraines a friend of his who lived next door and taught Buddhism at the local college would come and sit with him. That man had recently opened a small store that sold crystals in the shopping center where Corky worked. Inside was a poster of a smiling blond woman with her hands extended and various crystals placed on each palm. Asterisks floated above her hands like gnats at a backyard barbecue. The various crystals and their powers were identified at the bottom of the poster. Corky had bought a crystal keychain for Vera. The man told her that someone had once come in with a leather steering-wheel cover for her sports car and asked him to stud it with crystals so she could move her hands over them as she drove. The man called this "human folly." He also studded the wheel cover for her. The crystal shop might be an interesting place to take Will. She wasn't sure how long Will would be staying, and she was the sort of person—she admitted it; Wayne didn't have to tease her into confessing—who liked to have plans and alternatives. She thought that this tendency, which Wayne made fun of, would actually be beneficial to good mothering. What was wrong with knowing what you were having for dinner the next night, or what you would do with a child if it rained? The last time Will visited, Wayne had picked up a few things at the last minute, and what an odd assortment of things they had been: a water pistol, a calendar of women in swimsuits, a chocolate bar as thick as a brick, and a hammer—an adult's hammer, which Corky first saw when Will grasped it in both hands and banged it on the table. It left an indentation and made the biggest part of the chocolate bar fly off to the side, landing in her sewing basket. Later, she was tortured when Will went around the house running the hammer over everything as if it were a feather duster. Wayne had not let her confiscate the hammer because he had given it to Will. Until it was proven that he did damage with it, Wayne thought, it was perfectly fine for him to have the hammer, so Corky just held her breath as he ran it along the Formica counter in the kitchen. It wasn't that he was destructive—it was just that a hammer was a strange and potentially dangerous thing to give a young child.

With a sense of pride, Corky imagined herself to be the most responsible adult Will encountered. She had never met Jody, but from the way Wayne presented her, she was one of those attractive, insulated women who waited until life came knocking on their door, and who had a sorceress's power to see that it would. Apparently, she had had no interest in Wayne's carpentry and thought that a college education was the only respectable way to go. Wayne said it was Jody's fault that he lacked self-confidence; he had wasted precious years in exile because she wanted to live in the country, and commuting into the city became more of a hassle than it was worth. She already had a degree; *he* was supposed to work all day in solitude and then drive for miles to night classes in Washington and come home and do all the work in his spare time, which was never spare time because he was always on call as a handyman. Then she got pregnant—on purpose, he suspected—and insisted on having the baby, although the timing was bad and their relationship was already shaky. Corky could understand Jody's position, though—others could do what they wanted, but Corky personally felt that abortion was a sin—yet she did not argue with Wayne. Instead, she tried to persuade him that the time was perfect for them to have a baby, that he shouldn't generalize from one bad experience. Yesterday morning she had put a booklet about amniocentesis on the bedside table, and earlier in the week she had asked

Corinne not to tell Wayne that Eddie had fainted moments before they performed a cesarean; she was pretty sure Eddie wouldn't tell an embarrassing story about himself. Why tell someone like Wayne every plan, express every misgiving?

It did seem clear to Corky that if she hadn't married Wayne, she would have left Florida by now. She missed the seasons in the North. She didn't like tourists. She felt—though this was impossible to articulate, even in letters to her sister—that living in a place where the sunsets were so intense, she didn't have a future. That the sun had a future, but she didn't, and that hers was a life of little consequence. The sunsets were like the last lines of novels that let you know a sequel was planned, and that made her all the more uncertain—in spite of her hopes for a long, happy marriage to Wayne and her desire to have a child—about what would really happen to her. Sometimes, on the weekend, she would go to the pier with Wayne, and while he studied the sinking sun she would be thinking not that what she saw was romantic, but that the colors—the ever-deepening silver streaks and shades of pink and lavender—were exhausting in some way.

She always said yes reflexively when Wayne said the sunset was beautiful. There was no reason for him to know that she was avoiding looking at it, or that evening, so exhilarating for most people, made her sad because the enormousness of the sky made it clear that she was only a speck, a mortal speck, and that everything might end before she had what she wanted.

That day, feeling worn out, Corky had gone to her boss's doctor for a shot of vitamin B_{12}. The doctor asked no questions and the nurse asked her for fifteen dollars in cash as she was leaving. As far as Corky could tell, the shot really had been a pick-me-up. Why else would she be up when Wayne was asleep, turning over so many things in her mind? Photos of three grinning towheads had been framed above the doctor's desk. Like archangels, they had hovered above his head as he wrote a prescription for Ativan, in case Corky had trouble sleeping. Except for taking medicine for menstrual cramps, Corky never took pills. Corky went into the kitchen, took the bottle out of her purse, and placed one of the tiny white pills on her tongue, establishing a bond with her employer, who took the pills throughout the day, not just to help her sleep. Marian said that Corky was her best employee, and that soon she wanted to start training her as a buyer. Of course, it was understood that if Corky got pregnant, taking care of herself would take precedence over anything Marian might have in mind.

Corky picked up a few more things, looked in the cupboard to make sure the sheets for the fold-out bed hadn't started to smell musty since they were last in use. Wayne would never think to check something like that, but it was important because children hated funny smells, and Will would have enough problems adjusting, coming from the cold winter weather into the humidity and sun. But of course, she thought, as she opened the closet door, that would be a nice thing for a child, coming from gray days into a sunny world; it was like being born. Why couldn't she be Will's mother? Why was Jody blessed with motherhood, with Wayne's child, when her home and Wayne's was childless? Why *did* she try to convince herself that everything was for the best?

Tears welled up in her eyes. The sheets smelled of mildew. The mattress she and her mother had tried to move years ago smelled the same way. Corky could remember feeling infinitesimal next to the mattress, and smaller still as one of the cops hoisted it and helped her mother carry it back into the house, saying, "Lady, I'm just real glad it's not a body."

She knew very little about Wayne's childhood, and he knew very little about hers. She liked it that Wayne didn't want to pry into her past—an unusual attitude for a man, in her experience. What men always wanted to do was banish the other people—cap the lid on their existence, like placing one checker on top of another. Men wanted to make other men—of course men didn't care about your childhood friends, only about other men—into understandable clichés and then dismiss them, pick them up and take them off the board. You could help them by mentioning only the nasty one-liners, remembering only rainy days, producing a picture of the person in which the former beloved foolishly held up a fish not big enough to brag about, or one in which he was flanked by his friends, who had previously been described as villains. Wayne had surprised her, though, by not being curious. It made her wonder what he might have done that he didn't want her to inquire about. How bad had things been, that he would rather not mention those people, or those years? Sometimes she felt that he was too handsome to be interested in her, that she had gotten lucky too fast. They had met at a garage sale when he stopped to look at hubcaps and she was flipping through a twenty-five-cent *National Geographic*. Instead of buying the magazine, she bought a book of Sherlock Holmes stories—she still had the book and hadn't read it, but meant to one day— and he bought a hubcap and a frying pan. She figured that he was a single man because of that purchase: No married man picks up a frying pan at a garage sale. They had glanced at each other as they paid for their purchases. Walking toward their cars, she had sneaked another look, and later he confessed that he had walked slower than usual so that he could more or less keep pace with her. His car was parked in front of hers. As she was opening her car door, he had hollered something that she didn't quite understand. She looked at him quizzically and heard him the second time: He had *National Geographic*s in the trunk of the car, and they were hers, if she wanted them. She walked toward him, feeling the hot-faced shyness she had experienced as a little girl. He smiled and opened his trunk. There were six *National Geographic*s he said had been in the trunk when he bought the car. There had also been newspapers tied with string, he told her, and a couple of cinder blocks—none of which were there when she looked in—and he smiled when he told her it was only some time after buying the car that he had figured out the previous owner must have put them there to stop the car from fishtailing. Then suddenly he was telling her how much faster the car guzzled gas if a bag of sand was in the trunk, and she was complaining about the battery she had bought that went dead one month after the warranty expired. While other people had a book of matches or a drink stirrer or some other little souvenir of the night they met, Corky had a pile of *National Geographic*s. She would have to put them in the closet so Will didn't think they were something he could play with. As silly as it might be, she did feel a great sentimental attachment to them. When she looked at them that first time, flipping through nervously as she and Wayne had coffee, she had felt elated, as if the African tribesmen and egrets on the wing foretold their exciting future together. If Will's round-tipped scissors had begun to cut anything out of the magazines, it would have been like cutting out her heart.

Children meant no disrespect; they just thought that whatever they discovered, they could have. Girls usually grew out of that notion, but boys did not. Boys continued to think that the world was accessible, whether they went after what they wanted with scissors or with guns. Corky hoped that if she had a child, it would be a girl.

‌‌‌‌
It is a mistake to leave a child alone in the dark, under the weight of the blanket and the heavier weight of your reassurances, when the child knows perfectly well that the monster is still in the room. As long as the shutters stay open—and they must, so the moonlight can stream in—the tree branch will be endlessly transformed into the shadow of a bat, whose wings will stir in the breeze the moment the door is pulled shut. The robe draped over the chair, straightened so that the hood no longer casts the shape of a huge arrowhead on the wall, will become a mummy intent on sucking the child's breath away if the child should be foolish enough to close his eyes.

Telling the child that you will see him in the morning, and smiling down at him, is as unconvincing, and as little to the point, as standing on the deck of a sinking ship and applauding as the lifeboats are lowered. As if the sea didn't churn. As if something benign presided over our destinies. As if words could palliate so real a darkness as *night. The feathers shift inside the pillow and sink. The leaves of the plant curl until morning light. Sleep is like life in the city: Everyone is in danger who moves while others are still. How can we continue to tell the child, or any other skeptic, that night settles like lush, soft velvet, when it's as insidious as the swirl of the bullfighter's cape? The cape swishes and the bull escapes for a while, but soon enough the dagger plunges in and there is blood on the velvet, blood on the sand.*

At night, the furry fox cub in the storybook sprouts fangs and gnaws the wire coiled in the boxspring. The jack-in-the-box, having popped up, continues to grow, towering until it touches the ceiling, and then ducks its head, the eyes two globes dangling from the lighting fixture, the mouth smiling or smirking, obliterated by darkness.

Things are hungry at night. This is when animals stalk their prey. When fish sleep with open eyes. When fevers rise. When a sheer drop may be just ahead, and there is black ice on the highway.

For children, the metaphor exists, not the simile, and at night they see what we see, without dreaming. How interesting to always see potential: the thing transformed, before it is even understood.

At night, the child and the adult try to puzzle out the same thing: In order to comply, does one also need to smile? If someone is gone, are you the same person? Will people still call? Wasn't there an understanding that you belonged to each other? In the future, just once, could you have a guarantee? What will there be to say if the person returns sadder, or perhaps seeming younger or older, surprised by something, changed? What if, when you next see your lover, he has a scar on his cheek, or she has cut her beautiful curls?

He opens his eyes wide when fairy tales unfold and when myths are made to seem real, but the child's surprise is no less intense than ours. Why did Orion die, and what was it like for Diana to be tricked? Was Diana's brother sorry that he told her Orion's head, above the waves, was a ball floating? Or was he happy his prank turned out just as he wanted? What a perfect myth for the late twentieth century—the story of a man who dupes a woman, and a woman with the power to turn her mistake to splendor, while poor Orion, become a swashbuckler of the sky, finds that death means only that by the simple process of transformation he has lost his life and become, instead, a work of art. An unhappy bedtime story, though one likely to be remembered by the storyteller staring out the window, observing the stars' configuration in the sky.

Nighttime. How pleasant to think of the child, at least for a while, questioning nothing and dreaming the unimaginable. He is snug in his bed, still as a mummy. The monsters are at bay; the bull does not snort; his beloved and tattered blue blanket is clutched in his fist. The blanket is as necessary to sleep as the puffed parachute to the skydiver's safe fall.

The way we think of the child at night—our image of him as calm and sweetly sleeping—is a necessary delusion. It's romantic and also a little sad, like a love letter carried by hand, or being in love with a person who lives in another city. We are all vulnerable to darkness and to silence. Yet something has to be imagined. Something has to be said. In the dark room, every night, our last whispered words are always—and only—"Good night."

FIFTEEN

Wayne and Kate tumbled on the beach. Not sex, tumbling. Wayne on his knees, holding her thighs so she couldn't get away as Kate tried to jerk sideways, out of his grip, the sea breeze blowing her hair forward and obscuring her view every time she looked down.

In spite of the laughter and the insincere curses, it wasn't really a game. Wayne felt that he was holding on for dear life, like a drowning person who doesn't know his own exhaustion until he grabs hold of the rope. This wasn't water, but sand. He wasn't sinking, but buoyant. This wasn't his wife, it was a thirty-two-year-old divorcée from New Jersey offering him a tumble he was eager to take. He had met her earlier that evening, when he was delivering groceries. They had flirted then, and after work he had returned for her. Now he held on to her legs because he wanted to show her how strong he was.

He held on because that allowed him more time to fantasize, and what he imagined was getting more interesting by the minute.

She lay on her stomach in the sand, head resting on her arm, and he was on top of her, his penis erect in his pants. He knew instantly this was the person he had wanted all his life to meet. She was the person fate had sent: a cocky woman with every assurance of how attractive she was, giggling mischievously at what she had caused to happen so quickly.

Instead of going to the Azure, where they would be seen, he took her into the Hyatt, where a mirrored ball that rotated on the ceiling sent flashes of light around the room and four musicians played songs from the sixties. He moved his chair in close to the table and put his hand between her legs, under her skirt. Her skin was still sandy, even after they had brushed each other off back on the beach. Wide-eyed, she ordered a gin and tonic, staying as still as possible so that the waitress wouldn't notice Wayne's probing fingers. A bowl of peanuts was lowered to the table. She took his free hand in hers without objecting to the location of his other hand. He was *exactly*—except for the scar above his eyebrow and the long, straight nose—*exactly* like the car mechanic she had flirted with all year back in New Jersey, who never did call, except to say that her car was ready to be picked up. Now a man who could be the mechanic's twin was going to save her from a depressing, claustrophobic week with her mother, whose diabetes was under control, after all, and whose opinions could seem all the more ironic as they came up against Kate's mental images of this night. She could think of them playing in the sand while her mother talked about savings bonds. She could remember the bits of revolving light mottling his face as her mother talked about Oliver North's bravery. When her mother urged her to eat cereal in the morning, she could—hopefully—think of Wayne coming in-

side her. She bumped an inch closer on the blue vinyl ban-
quette. He took his hand out of the bowl of peanuts and
held out his fingers so she could lick off the salt. Before he
went back to the apartment complex to leave his car and go
off on what she called "an adventure" in hers, Wayne had
found a cash machine back at the shopping center and had
withdrawn one hundred dollars, which was burning a hole
in his pocket. In fact, he felt sweaty, his fingertips tingling,
his lips dry, his forehead so moist he suspected he might
actually have a fever.

"Don't tell me your last name," she said, kissing his thumb.

"Don't tell me yours," he said.

The waitress put a gin and tonic in front of Kate and a
Molson and a beer glass in front of Wayne. She picked up the
half-empty bowl of peanuts and lowered another one to the
tabletop. She had on a pink skirt and a paler pink blouse with
black polka dots and a lace collar. She was long-legged and
wore black fishnet stockings. Quite different from the service
Wayne got at the Azure.

"Are you married?" she said.

He hadn't been expecting that question. He missed a beat,
then shrugged, able neither to lie nor to tell the truth. He
poured the beer, letting a big head rise. He looked up and saw
that she understood he was married.

"You weren't wanting to get married to me, were you?" he
said.

A couple passing their table looked down at them as he spoke.
The woman looked over her shoulder after she passed by.

She took a sip of her drink, then put the glass back on the
table and fished out the little piece of lime. Instead of squeezing, she licked it, then turned it cut side down, rubbed it
around the rim, and dropped it back into the glass. She took
another sip, looking at him as she drank.

"So what's your story?" he said.

"Were we telling stories?" she said.

"What are we doing?"

"What do *you* think we're doing?"

"Having a drink," he said. He was trying not to let on that she was unnerving him. What sort of game was she playing? There was an edge of mockery in her voice. He asked, "What do you think we're doing?"

"We're flirting," she said.

He cocked his head to look at her sideways.

She had lovely eyes, with eyebrows lightly penciled into dark arcs. Her lipstick had disappeared. Her lips were pale. He leaned forward, and she also leaned forward and surprised him by kissing him lightly on the lips.

"How come we're flirting?" he said.

"Truth? We're flirting because we happened to meet and we were attracted to each other, but I'm also flirting because you remind me of someone."

He hadn't expected that, either. He waited to hear more.

"Except that I don't know him," she said. "You remind me of somebody I don't really know."

"I'm a stand-in?" he said.

"The way I'm a stand-in for your wife," she said.

Touché. He smiled, giving her that one.

She leaned back. "I like the music," she said. She took off her shoes and put one bare foot on top of his shoe, then moved it up the side of his ankle.

"Why don't you get us a room?" she said. "Unless you have to get home to your wife."

"Oh, I don't know," he said. "You seem to like sitting here, chatting about my wife. Are you sure you want me to get a room?"

He was on automatic pilot. He had probably realized when she was driving him around in her car that they would have to go somewhere, but until she mentioned checking in to the hotel, he hadn't really thought it through. What would it cost? And was there any possibility that they'd go to the room and she wouldn't let him touch her? Was it possible that this was some strange game she played, and that she was just a cock tease?

"You're frowning," she said. "Do you and your wife have children?"

He shook his head no. He thought about the amniocentesis booklet. About Will—but she didn't ask if he had ever had children.

"You have children yourself?"

"I can't, if that's what you're worried about," she said. "I've got scarred fallopian tubes."

It was more than he needed to know. Women had so many problems. He hoped she wouldn't elaborate.

"You're not interested in whether I'm married?" she said, running her toes up the back of his calf.

"No," he said. "Who do I remind you of?"

"A car mechanic in New Jersey," she said.

The flatness with which she answered took him aback. Not a movie star. A car mechanic?

"So," she sighed.

"So what?"

"So I guess it's my turn to ask a question."

"Go ahead," he said. He would have liked to toss down a big swallow of beer, but he had already drained the glass. The waitress stopped at their table and asked if they'd like another.

"No thanks," he said. "Just the bill."

As the waitress started to walk away, Kate said, "I might have one more while he's gone."

The waitress scribbled something, nodded, and walked toward the bar, swinging her hips. The "So" was obviously decisive: He was to get a room. The change from the hundred dollars was all he had—the MasterCard was at home in a drawer, where Corky insisted it be kept so they wouldn't buy anything impulsively. He couldn't charge the room anyway, because Corky would find out. How much did three drinks cost? Was the change going to be enough? In any case, he would have to wait for the waitress to come back, pay the bill, and go with cash in hand to the front desk.

Kate had on bright pink nail polish. He let his eyes drop to her chest. Nice breasts. The waitress had seen where he'd been looking. She put another drink in front of Kate and handed him the bill. He took out his billfold and paid her. She fished in her money belt for the change and put it on the table. He picked up a five, folded it, and handed it to her. The waitress had on shiny orange lipstick that clashed with her blouse. Nail polish, too, although her nails were bitten to the quick. She looked like a lot of women in this part of Florida: women who had wide hips even if they had slender bodies. He had tipped her five dollars, which was almost 50 percent. At the Azure he left a dollar, whether he had one beer or five. He pocketed the money and walked away, out of the bar and into the overlit lobby. A child was getting off the elevator as he passed by. The child held a pink inflatable palm tree and ran ahead of his mother and father.

"Andrew Bornstein, you come back here," the child's father called, stressing all syllables of the name.

At the desk, the clerk was reading a newspaper. He put it down and looked up pleasantly as Wayne approached. Wayne considered asking directions to the seafood restaurant he sometimes ate at with Corky—asking directions, thanking Mr. Clean-Cut Smiles, then walking out the door and going home and telling Corky that he had been having a beer with a friend. He looked at his watch. Whatever he told her, she would be furious. As long as she was going to be furious anyway, why not sleep with Kate?

The room was affordable. There would even be money left

over. He got the key and turned and looked at the elevators, where Mr. Clean-Cut Smiles pointed. The doors were opening again, and a group of laughing men were coming out. They turned left and went into the bar. When the clerk had asked for a credit card, Wayne said that he would like to pay the bill in advance. Even this was done smilingly. Would he also smile when Wayne and Kate checked out, an hour later?

Reentering the bar, he was happy that Kate did not know his last name. He put the key on the table, and she picked it up and smiled. Her drink was empty. They walked together out of the bar, away from the already drunk laughing men, who had settled at a table in the corner. The waitress's eyes met Wayne's, and he realized that she knew perfectly well what she was caught between: a group of wild men who were going to act crazy and probably stiff her, and a man and a woman who had decided to go fuck. He knew that she knew he and Kate weren't married.

But that was the way of the world. That was the way of the world. And Wayne suddenly felt quite . . . cosmopolitan. He touched 3 and the button lit up, and the two of them rose, side by side, to the floor where they would turn, stop in front of a door, put the key in, and then what? Images he had had at the desk tumbled like a jigsaw puzzle falling off a table, leaving big gaps everywhere: Kate's soapy breasts, an image on the TV rolling and rolling, horizontal lines on the TV, the plaid bedspread, Kate jumping away, the mouse leading the cat on a deliberate chase.

She started the game—the flirtation—as he reached out to insert the key in the lock. She put her hand over his and stopped him from turning the key, puckering her lips so he would have to stop to kiss her. He could have turned the key anyway, but he let her have the kiss. Her lips were soft—he was feeling skin, not oily lipstick—and he was also feeling her nice breasts, or one of them anyway, pushing against his chest.

He started to get hard. She put her hand on his hip, and curled her fingers into his pocket. He tried to kiss her again, but she wouldn't let him. She wouldn't move and she giggled and wouldn't let him. Then she wanted him to look into her eyes, and he did, and it seemed he was seeing through to something. A couple came out of their room, closed the door, and passed by, pretending not to notice them. The man had on a shirt patterned with starfish. The woman wore a halter dress. Her bare back made Wayne raise his hand to Kate's back. His hand felt heavy. He moved his fingers to the side of her breast and pushed gently. She moved closer, and he turned, taking his hand off the key, and stood facing her, knowing she felt his erection. She reached back and turned the key.

Inside, he pinned her hands to her sides. He gave her one very long kiss, after which she reached behind her to close the door and they settled themselves on the floor. Their bodies locked together, fast, and, as he pulled down her panties and pushed inside her, surprised and panting, feeling as if he were sixteen again, he suddenly wanted to know whether she was going to be in Florida for a day or a week, what her last name was, where in New Jersey she lived. Her dress was raised over her hips, her panties tangled around one ankle, and he was still fully dressed, his snap unfastened, the fly of his jeans unzipped.

"Come on," she said, wriggling out from under. "We'll tell them the room is too close to the Coke machine, that we didn't like it."

"What?" he said. "What are you talking about?"

"We'll get a refund," she said. "We'll get a refund and to-morrow night we'll do the same thing, somewhere else."

"What do you mean?" he said, wiping the sweat from his face. "They're not going to—"

"I'll take care of it," she said. "You go sit in the car." She smiled. He saw that his zipper had left a red welt on her thigh. "I hate hotels," she said. "I know my way around desk clerks. Particularly wimpy kids like that."

Wayne's knees felt weak. She closed the door behind them, and they walked to the elevator. The elevator door opened. There were several people inside, so they did not talk again until the elevator descended to the lobby.

"Hyatt can afford to give us a quickie," she said. "We didn't even use the john."

A couple was registering at the desk, and the clerk didn't look up when Wayne passed through the lobby. It had all happened so fast that he thought he could still be where he had been just a moment ago, debating between returning to the bar or going home. She was going to get the money back! He was giddy, thinking about it. And the next night . . . What next night? Corky was already going to kill him. He decided that he didn't care. He'd lie to her, and if she didn't like it, tough. The next night. Somewhere else.

She came out as he was still getting his breath, smirking and holding out the wad of money. "It's minus a ten-dollar tip," she said. "He very nicely ripped up the record of renting the room." Her smile faded. "Listen, I've got to go home," she said. "I told my mother I was taking a walk. I've got to get back."

"What about tomorrow?" he said, as they walked across the parking lot.

"You must know the hotels better than I do," she said.

As he opened the car door, she smoothed her skirt under-neath her. Smoothed it as if she were a modest lady, not someone who had just hiked it up to her waist to fuck on the floor. Her hand slightly brushing the bottom of her skirt made his cock tingle and start to go hard again. It was really like being sixteen. He could hardly wait for the next night: an-other hotel, another closed door. The next night they could skip the drinks. Let her tip *twenty* dollars—who cared? The money would last for nights.

As he started the ignition, Florida began to look different. Like a botanist to whom a field is not just a haze of green but a very particular, complex world, Wayne saw the hotels and motels lining the highway as loaded with hope and possibility: stage sets for fantasies he and Kate could repeatedly create.

When he got home that night the situation was better than he could have imagined. Corky had gone to Corinne's house because the electricity had gone out. A miracle! No electricity! The note taped to the front door told him he should come get her.

He went in, flicked the light switch up and down—no electricity! *No electricity!* He washed his face and then went next door and knocked, telling Corky that he had been so worried until he had found her note, which had fallen down at the side of the steps. With his arm around her shoulder, he led her back to the house, and they found their way upstairs in the dark.

Everything he and Corky said was all talk about another world. Wayne was sixteen, and his life with Corky didn't really exist, let alone his first marriage, and his marriage to Jody. There was no Will. The next night he and Kate would be in another hotel, behind a quickly closed door. He heard the door closing. Slamming, in fact, though the sound was inside his head: a pounding headache that had come from exhaustion, drinking, guilt, and from holding his breath so long, earlier that night, while his body exploded.

The door closed over and over, creaking.

"Do you think you could find your way into the bathroom to get me a couple of aspirin?" Wayne whispered from beneath the noise of the crashing door.

Corky slipped out of bed and slowly began to grope her way down the hallway in the dark.

SIXTEEN

The day of Will's arrival Wayne was shoveling mulch around bushes planted on an incline—some rich person's last-minute thought about landscaping the hillside on the north side of the pool. The lady of the house liked Wayne. If it weren't for Kate, he might even have been interested. He was amused—giddy, almost—that after years of putting out signals and hardly getting a head to turn, he now had a lover who was almost a nymphomaniac.

Zeke, who worked with Wayne, was slender and pockmarked. This was his first job since getting out of the Army. As he was marching one day, his arches just collapsed, leaving him with flapjack feet and a set of discharge papers. His family wouldn't take him back; for two nights, when he was between places to live, he had camped on Corky and Wayne's sofabed. But recently Zeke was much happier: sharing a place with another guy at Breezy Palms trailer park just off the highway, dating a waitress named Susan who was almost ten years older and had dyed black curls and an appetite for sex that drove Zeke mad. He had her picture—a photo-booth square, laminated— along with a small silver cross and a miniature rabbit's foot, hung on a chain that was tucked under his shirt, the way he used to wear his dog tags. Wayne was amused that Zeke thought of him as a family man (even if Corky was his family), a stay-at-home who must envy Zeke his wild adventures.

Wayne made it a point never to drink on the job. Zeke took Wayne's lead, always, so the two of them were drinking lemonade out of paper cups. The pitcher was on a metal table under a striped umbrella. The good life, minus the person who made the money to buy the good life—the big-bucks businessman husband who commuted to New York. This weekend his wife would join him up North, and she had offered Wayne the use of the pool. He thought that he would take her up on it. It would give him something to do with Will, though he wished that instead of being with Will he could be swimming with the beautiful nymph Kate.

"How many women have you been in love with?" Zeke asked Wayne.

"Seven," Wayne said. He always answered automatically, though he rarely ever spoke seriously to Zeke. Zeke thought that Wayne was approachable and forthright.

"Seven," Zeke said, thinking it over.

"Why did you ask?" Wayne said.

"You're five up on me," Zeke said. "I wanted to see what the older generation had on me."

Wayne looked at Zeke. "Put your hat on," he said. "They have to cut any more skin cancers, your nose is gonna look like a potato with all the eyes cut out."

"Sun block," Zeke said, tapping his nose. "Susan bought it for me."

"Probably hoping for an exchange—a diamond ring," Wayne said.

"Shit," Zeke said, shaking his head. "You won't even give her credit for giving me a good present."

"I give her credit for knowing *you're* a good present," Wayne said. "I don't care what you do as long as you don't get hooked up with her." Wayne wiped his forehead. "Why don't you get the truck and back it up?" he said. "Put some of those wood chips around these bushes."

Zeke did whatever Wayne told him to do. He left the shovel sticking in the ground and started toward the driveway.

How many times have I been in love? Wayne wondered. He had loved his first wife. Only after this many years could he admit, grudgingly, that he had also loved Jody before they were married and for about a year afterwards. Corky was like a salve. She was what most people would think of as ordinary, although her kindness was exceptional: an empathy that could etch circles below her eyes in your presence, a dogged kindness that made him feel protected. Rather than being in love with Kate, he was addicted to her; he had felt that way about women many times, and he had always fallen hard, then struggled to break the addiction, though each time he succeeded, the success assured that he would fall harder for the next woman. He had thought that marriage to Corky might break the pattern. Before he met Corky he had lived briefly with a woman who pitied herself so much he would sink in her sadness as if it were quicksand. When he was completely submerged some odd moment always transpired between them, as if they were two fish all alone at the bottom of the sea deciding to give each other a look. They would make love and, panting, dash for the surface. It turned out that she had been two-timing him with a scuba diver. When he met Corky—the day he pulled off the road to go to a garage sale to see if they had hubcaps he could use—he had felt something like a shock

of recognition: Here was a woman with a liveliness in her eyes
that he had forgotten. To exorcise his self-pitying former
lover, he had slept with someone who was physically similar,
but who was not her. He had decided, by the time he met
Corky, that this time around he would put no premium on
talk. No asking about her past, her regrets, or even how she
felt right that minute. He would take it easy and see if she
would respond in kind. He would take what he wanted in
calm moments, instead of moments fraught with emotion, and
see if she found that allowable. He would ask no questions and
hope that she wouldn't speak of problems she expected him to
solve. Corky did not see herself as particularly put-upon. She
could adapt to things—thank God for that, because she would
certainly know better what to do with Will than he would.
She was going to make cupcakes for his arrival and planned to
take him to Bathing Beauties to let him play in the store, and
at lunchtime she would take him to the rock store—rocks, or
something like that—and introduce him to the owner and buy
him some things. Wayne knew that Corky wanted to show
him what a good mother she would be, and how manageable
a child could be. The truth was, having a child made it harder
to leave. He would have left Jody sooner for being such a
ball-buster, telling him what to do with his life and disdaining
him if he didn't do it, if it hadn't been for Will. Now it was
difficult to remember what his scenario for staying might have
been: him suffering her silent criticism, and Will shooting up,
like fast-growing bamboo, until he was a stake that stabbed his
father's heart? If Jody thought the way he did things was so
unimpressive, see if she didn't give him credit for being able to
inflict a little shock when she woke up and he was gone, no
explanation, no "I'm sorry" that implied *she* should be sorry—
just gone, and the next thing she got would be a telephone
call, when he was good and ready to get in touch. In leaving
he had scored his point. Though he had to concede that in

coping—not even calling the police to report him missing—
she had proved hers.

But beyond all this, there was Will. Will, who, when
Wayne saw him, always seemed to be surrounded by Jody's
aura. Men cheating on their wives are advised to be careful
that they do not carry home the smell of hairspray or perfume
to betray them. What about the telltale signs of a mother on a
child—those smells trailing memories of the mother's scent,
the child's clothes selected in *her* favorite colors, the Mercu-
rochrome on the scratch painted by her professional hand?
Something was coming clear to Wayne: that the child was just
a springboard for the mother, a launch pad from which her
presence could shoot up to hover hugely over the scene. As
long as Will existed, Jody would be larger than life. She had
seeped under Will's skin as surely as a ghost passing into the
walls of a house. If she could not remain in Wayne's heart
herself, she would send an envoy to penetrate his world.

As if he could read Wayne's mind, Zeke reappeared with a
question about Will. "Your kid," Zeke said. "What's the deal
about the pool? I'll bring an inner tube, and what else do you
want us to bring? I forget."

Wayne rolled his eyes. "Us" meant he was going to have to
endure a day of swimming with Susan.

"I just thought that if you had a tube, the kid might like to
float around. I don't think he swims."

"Maybe we ought to get him some of those arm-float things
you strap on," Zeke said. "Maybe that would be better."

"He's not a doll we're dressing up," Wayne said. "Bring the
tube. If the kid's not interested, we can use it."

"You know, in Texas Susan used to go down some river in
a tube. One of those places you enter one place and end up
another, and they shuttle you back to where you started. She
says she really misses Texas, but, you know, her grandmother
she was living with had to go into a rest home, God rest her

soul, and she figured makin' the move to live near her sister
was the best thing to do, since she wouldn't be livin' with
family no more."

"Her grandmother died?" Wayne said. Every girl Zeke
dated had a history as long as *War and Peace*. How he ever
managed to get any action except talk was a mystery to
Wayne.

"No, she didn't die," Zeke said. "I told you: She went to a
rest home."

"Didn't you just say, 'God rest her soul'?" Wayne asked.

"Hey, it's just an expression."

"It's not just an expression. It's what you say when somebody's dead. Like 'Happy Birthday' isn't an expression. It's
what you say on somebody's birthday."

"God better look out for those folks in the rest homes,"
Zeke said, hating to be corrected.

Wayne sighed. A bee buzzed his hat. The job was almost
done. Soon he could have a final shot of lemonade, and then
he would head home to wait for Will's arrival. Corky would be
there, frosting cupcakes. He should think about what his first
line would be when the doorbell rang. How he should act.
Every time he saw Will it was awkward. He always hugged
when Will wanted to shake hands, or bumped his forehead,
leaning down for a kiss. The holier-than-thou bodyguard
would be with Will, too: Mel, with a proprietary hand on
Will's shoulder.

"You remember the stuff I told you about Susan's parents,
right? About how they had this foster kid that they used like
a servant, and somebody got wind of it and before you knew
it, zip, that kid was out of there, and Susan went to her
grandmother, and if the father hadn't drowned, he might be in
the slammer today, because—"

"You told me," Wayne said.

"Which really makes it mysterious, since now we know he's

no great lover of kids, and Susan's mom's so sloshed you don't know on any given day whether she's gonna make it out of bed, whether that brother of Susan's really died in his crib, or—"

"This is like a fucking soap opera," Wayne said.

"It's her life, Wayne. She showed real get-up-and-go to relocate herself to Florida. Susan's a devoted family person. When things took a turn for the worse with her grandmother, naturally she got in touch with her sister, and—"

"God rest Susan's soul," Wayne said.

Zeke looked at him, puzzled.

"It's just an expression. God rest her soul *if* she dies," Wayne said.

"I don't think that's funny," Zeke said. "Saying something like that, you might bring bad luck to Susan."

"What's the grandmother's story?" Wayne said, knowing that he could derail Zeke.

"Her father was an immigrant from Italy," Zeke said. "They had five children, and two that died at birth, and the mother . . ."

Zeke was off and running. Wayne adjusted his hat and smiled to himself. If only dealing with Will could be as easy as dealing with Zeke. Zeke was just like a baby: When you dangled something in front of him, the hysteria would end; fascination would make his eyes widen and bring a big smile to his face. Just dangle the possibility of another story waiting to be told, and Zeke would reach up and touch it—it was all so real to him, it was as though he could touch it—and then, for as long as you could stand to be involved, there would be peace and tranquillity. A reward and a respite.

"The way you feel about Susan," Wayne said, shaking his head as if a great revelation had dawned on him. "The way you feel, you can probably envision spending the rest of your life with her. Am I right?"

Zeke narrowed his eyes. He cleared his throat. He looked at the bushes they had planted as if Susan might be hiding behind one.

"Well, I don't know about marriage," Zeke said. "You know yourself, Wayne, that marriage ain't so easy."

"What makes you say that?" Wayne said.

Zeke's eyes narrowed again, this time to slits. How long had Wayne been putting him on?

S E V E N T E E N

hough Corky knew the story all too well, Corinne was telling her, again, about Eddie's deception: On the day Corinne went to the hairdresser a friend recommended, that same friend lured Eddie to her apartment and jumped into bed with him. Hearing about the situation made Corky uncomfortable enough, but Corinne's bleak view of women had really begun to depress her. Corinne had almost every woman they knew categorized as a vile, untrustworthy witch. Corinne did not say "bitch" because she had made it a household rule, once the baby was born, that there would be no more swearing. "Witch" seemed an appropriate-enough term, however, because Corinne suspected even the nicest women of manipulating others by putting spells on them. She did not think they literally did this, but she did believe they had terrible powers.

Corinne had just finished discussing her new hairdresser.

She grudgingly admitted the woman was a good hair-cutter, but being there earlier in the day had reminded her of women she called bogus big sisters, who would fawn over you by twirling one of your curls into a perfect ringlet when they actually hated your good looks and wished you'd disappear. Women who slipped out of their own high-heeled shoes and begged to slide their foot into your flats weren't compliment-ing you on your good taste but expressing symbolically their wish to crush you as they crushed the backs of your shoes. Women were treacherous. They would think nothing of doing anything they pleased behind your back with whatever man you were with.

Corky assumed she was exempt from Corinne's scenario but wasn't sure how she had been spared. Perhaps it was because her horror had been so genuine when Corinne first confided in her about Eddie's dalliance. She had also been horrified that Corinne would use her anger as an excuse to throw out her birth-control pills, though she knew better than to criticize Corinne—especially when she was upset.

Right now Eddie was in Pittsburgh, where he had flown the night before, to act as a pallbearer at his father's funeral. It pleased Corinne that the Sunday before his father's sudden death the minister had preached about how transgression could lead to a series of terrible things. She hoped that some-how Eddie connected his father's death with his afternoon at the witch's apartment. The minister had been trying to subtly assure the parish that he was a finer person than Jimmy Swag-gart, but Corinne hoped Eddie registered the minister's point about sin and understood that it was his fault their child had been born with jaundice. What did Eddie think, now that the dog had been hit by a car? What about his father's unexpected death? And was it clear to him why she was no longer inter-ested in sex?

Corinne fanned out a match and dropped it on her saucer.

She took a puff of her cigarette and exhaled high above the baby's head. The baby was in a plastic car seat that was usually in the back of Corinne's car, but Eddie had taken the car to the airport, and she was always afraid that anything left in a car for any amount of time might be stolen. Ganglia of straps and buckles trailed on the Formica table.

"I want to raise her to trust other women, but the thing is, I don't trust other women myself," Corinne said.

"I think it's harder to raise a girl than a boy," Corky said. "Harder, but for me it would be much more fun."

"Well, the thing is, you've got to figure out what to tell them and what not to tell them about other women," Corinne said.

"Just like what husbands have to figure out: what to tell us, and what not to tell us," Corky said. She instantly regretted joining in with Corinne's cynicism; she got up and opened a cabinet door. "There's a real good drink I can make that's like a sombrero, only with club soda added," she said.

"Mmm," Corinne said. "I might as well, because I'll be up by my lonesome all night anyway, doing the night shift."

"Have you heard from Eddie?" Corky asked. She was pouring batter into rainbow-striped paper cups. She had bought another muffin tin so she could bake the whole recipe for cupcakes at once. An extra muffin tin could always be useful. For your jewelry, for one thing.

"He told me his mother was all upset because she found his dad's Christmas stocking, which had been missing for years, in a drawer of his tool chest, stuffed with girlie magazines. She hunted high and low for the stocking, and he always said she had thrown it out by mistake with the Christmas wrapping."

Corky giggled. She shook her head.

"So I don't know," Corinne said. "Things are better between us now that that witch is out of the picture, but I hate to not trust somebody. I talked to the minister and what he says is to trust him: no reason *why* I should trust him, just that it would be a nice thing to do."

Corky filled the rest of the paper cups with batter. A few drops landed on the center of the muffin tin; she wiped them off, then ate them. Corinne opened the oven door, and Corky placed the muffin tin beside the other one.

"Christian charity, right?" Corky said.

"Probably. The truth is, I don't half listen to what he says anymore. I think he doesn't half listen to what's said to him, either; he just starts kicking his legs and waving his arms like one of those wooden pull-toys. He's a very physically active man for a minister. I find it a little distracting. When Eddie and I had our appointment with him, we went downstairs and he was there pushing his fingertips into the wall—some kind of exercise, he said. Not that there's anything wrong with exercising," Corinne said. "But it's a little strange that he's always out of breath from riding his bike to the church on Sundays, and you always see him jogging around town with his face as bright as the sun, or collapsed on some bench. I saw him purple in the face, panting on a park bench. I really did." Corinne stubbed out her cigarette. "That's a funny way to find your minister is all I'm saying."

"Well, I guess so many of them are alcoholics, we should be glad he's not one of those," Corky said. She stopped, hearing her own words: making everything all right in her mind again.

"Speaking of alcoholics, how about one of those drinks?" Corinne said.

"Oh, sure," Corky said. "Should I put on some music, or would that disturb the baby?"

"This baby won't be disturbed until it's time to go to sleep." Corinne put her hand over the baby's cotton bootie. Small meteors streaked across the baby's instep in an arched trajectory toward the side stitching. The booties were a present from Marian, who had sold her a maternity bathing suit. Corky turned on the radio. She always kept it tuned to an easy-listening station. For a few seconds, she mistook "Yesterday" for "Raindrops Keep Falling on My Head." She looked at the kitchen clock—the grinning black-faced cat with a swishing tail that had been a present from her sister—and saw that Wayne should be getting back from work any minute. Then Will would arrive. She felt bad about not being able to ask Mel if he wanted to stay the night, but Wayne had said that he drew the line at entertaining his ex-wife's live-in lover. There were times when Wayne was judgmental in ways that surprised Corky. She wondered what he thought of Eddie and Corinne's marital problems—whether Eddie had even told Wayne. She didn't want to say anything herself because she feared Wayne might think that women used babies as retribution, or as a way of shaming men into staying. She had probably already hinted at too much to Wayne by saying that Corinne tricked Eddie. She only wanted to point out her own maturity, but it might have backfired.

There was a nice aroma in the kitchen as they had their drinks. Corky hoped it would linger, and that Will would come into the house knowing there was something good for him to eat—something special. She thought about getting out the icing tube but decided that frosting the cupcakes with a spatula would be good enough.

"And do you know what Eddie thinks?" Corinne said. "He thinks I'm sweet on the minister. He honestly seems to think that."

"Well, at least he agreed to quit the softball team," Corky said.

"That's true," Corinne said, taking a sip of her drink. "Umm," she said. "An adult milkshake."

One song fed into another. The song now was "Cherish."

"Have you had any luck talking Wayne into a baby?" Corinne said.

"I think that he really wants one. He's just scared," Corky said. "But if he and Will can start to have a better relationship, maybe that'll pave the way for another baby."

"Will's not a bad boy, is he?" Corinne said.

"He's always been a nice child. I know that as boys get older they get more troublesome, but I think a lot of it has to do with how you treat them. I have to say that his mother seems to have done a good job."

"It's none of my business, but why did they get divorced?"

"He says they just married too young. And that she was always intent on having a career. You know, he was married to another woman before her, and she died in a car accident. When something like that happens it can make you very afraid of the future."

"A car accident?" Corinne said. She put her hand on the baby's bootie.

"She and Wayne were having a trial separation. She was in the car alone, somewhere in the South, where her parents lived, and they think she missed a turn—ended up at the bottom of a ravine. I think it was raining."

Telling the story, Corky realized she did not know the details at all. If it hadn't been raining, why would such an accident have happened?

"And then he married—what is her name?" Corinne said.

"Jody. He was still grieving when he met Jody, and they were too young to be married, because apparently she was very independent, and she didn't understand how important carpentry was to him. She just wanted him to be an intellectual."

Her own voice stunned her. She was making up stories. And it was easy to do! No malice was intended. She just filled in the blanks with whatever seemed appropriate. Her heart went out to him: His heart had been broken when his first wife plunged into the ravine. In trying to disentangle himself from his sad fate, he had acted too quickly, married impulsively, let himself be drawn into a relationship in which a

woman expected too many concessions, too soon. That he had
emerged as little scathed as he had was testament to his solid-
ity. His fine values.

Corky had finished her drink. The timer went off, and she
inserted a toothpick into the cupcakes, careful not to burn her
hand on the top of the oven. The toothpick came out clean.
The cupcakes were baked. As Corinne moved her chair aside
to escape the oven's pulsing heat, the doorbell rang. Corky
stopped, oven mitt suspended in midair.

"That can't be Will," Corky said.

The doorbell rang again.

"Where's Wayne?" she whispered.

She went toward the door. Simply rushed forward, as if she
needed fresh air. She thought again of the day she stood with
her mother in the side yard, and of her mother's words: "I'm
just airing the mattress. Is it a crime to air the mattress?"

Mel stood in front of Corky, taller than she remembered,
pale and obviously tired. Standing beside him was Will, the
small boy who would determine her future. Corky bent forward and kissed Will on the cheek. "We're so happy you're
here," she said, realizing as she spoke that there was no *we*.
She folded her arms around him. What would she say when
she let go?

The awkward handshake with Mel. They never knew
whether to embrace or to shake hands.

Beyond Corky, Will saw the baby on the table. He wondered if he had a brother or a sister. He wished that Wag
could be his brother. As they came up the front walk, Mel had
made him promise that he would not ask about visiting Wag
until the next morning.

E I G H T E E N

should of brought my camera," Susan said. "I put it out and everything, and then I just forgot it." It was the end of the day and everyone was in good spirits. To Wayne's amazement, Corky actually seemed to enjoy talking to Susan. If he had overheard correctly, Corky was going to see if Marian was hiring anyone else for part-time work at Bathing Beauties. He felt a twinge of gratitude toward Corky, not because he cared anything about Susan, but simply because Corky really did have a good heart. She cared what happened to people who were down on their luck. Wayne knew that, in a way, both he and Will were down on their luck. He was grateful for her affection toward them. It seemed that she and Will had really warmed up to each other after their day of exploration in the gem store. Will wore a small bluish crystal around his neck. The crystal was crisscrossed with thin leather cords and dan-

gled like a miniature papoose. He gave Corky credit for knowing what Will would like. He would never have thought of
cupcakes and crystals.And the boy could swim! He was really
pleased when he saw that—as pleased as a parent learning that
his child had tried out for, and made, the Olympic team.
Maybe one day Will would: Will, butterfly-stroking on TV,
with a muscular body the girls would all adore, a body that
would make the men take it easy on the buttered popcorn.
Right now Will was a little skinny.

Wayne wished this could be his life. That being at a pool
with people he liked, on a sunny day when no one had to
work and everyone was in good spirits, could be the norm
instead of the exception. Of course, it was also very pleasant
to know that Kate was pining away for him, waiting for the
moment when he could sneak away. And it was because
the lady of the house was sweet on him that they were all at
the pool. Zeke had let that be known, in a none-too-subtle
way. Who could figure it: Instead of being jealous, Corky
had actually been proud to find that Wayne's attributes had
been noticed.

Susan had brought a cooler filled with cans of Hawaiian
Punch. There was also a pint of rum, which was added to the
adults' drinks in big splashes that made the bottle dwindle to
almost nothing after the first round. There were chicken salad
sandwiches. Corky had even been smart enough to put in two
slices of white bread, in case Will objected to the pita pockets,
which he had. She really understood small children. Wayne
had thrown in two tins of stolen anchovies and a tube of
tomato paste—a wonderful combination, spread on Saltines—
to get into the spirit of the picnic. Zeke had brought home-
made pickles, which had been delivered to the doorstep of his
trailer by his mother. Every week she dropped off food and a
written progress report on her lobbying efforts to get his father to forgive him for having been thrown out of the Army.

In her notes she always referred to his father as "Ret. Col. Pyke."

"You know what heaven would be?" Zeke said, looking over at Wayne from the diving board, where he was sitting. "Surf 'n' Turf," he said. "Heavy on the butter with the Turf, too. And a side of steamers with broth to dunk 'em in to clean out the sand."

"I think heaven for you would be the certainty of your convictions," Wayne said. "Not having to check with anyone to see whether they'd bear you out. Not caring if other people felt the way you did. Not caring jack shit, unless you felt like considering their opinion."

It was more of a response than Zeke expected. It was also a bit puzzling, as many of Wayne's replies were. It was Wayne's tone, more than the words: that cold way Wayne pronounced on things, though you could tell by his expression that he didn't care passionately, at all, about what he was saying. It was almost pugnacious, as though the other person had asked a question looking for a fight.

"Because I think eatin' what you want is a big part of the pleasure of life," Zeke said. When he did not know what to make of Wayne's replies, he usually just ignored them, or reasserted his opinion.

"Stayed in the Army, you'd be eating cow-flop hamburgers and seaweed spaghetti," Wayne said. "Lift those paddles up. Those things you call feet. Let's see your marks of disgrace that got you out of the mess hall and into this great society where you can wolf down a steak and chew one of those rubbery lobsters all at the same meal, every time you can pay for it." Wayne crossed his eyes. His arms were extended and his hands rather convincingly bent to look like lobster claws. He pursed his lips. He could see through his squint that Will was looking at him from the shallow end of the pool, smiling. He turned the lobster claws toward Will. Will did the same imitation of a lobster. A lobster with a little-boy belly that stuck out above his bathing trunks.

Wayne stretched out on the chaise longue—the only one at the pool—groping for the bottle of rum to tilt another splash into what remained of his Hawaiian Punch. That done, he recapped the bottle and sloshed the can a few times before taking a drink. Zeke looked at him, biting the inside of his cheek. Wayne was going to be the tannest person at day's end. He was the one who never got stung by a bee and was rarely bitten by mosquitoes. His back was muscular and smooth— no pimples, no big smear of a birthmark, just a long, glowing expanse of skin. Even when he was lying on his stomach, you could tell that Wayne was handsome. Still, Zeke thought, not every woman would be attracted to such a strange man. A lot of women liked younger, quieter men, such as himself. Susan, for instance. And he didn't have Wayne's track record, either: two divorces, living with more women than you could count, a period in his life when the IRS had put a lien on his bank account, two rounds of clap. Hell, he might even know more about Wayne than Corky did. Working side by side with him for so long, he'd heard a lot of things. Maybe they should know that in the CIA: A person made to plant rhododendron bushes day after day will tell you anything.

Zeke held his breath and slipped off the edge of the diving board into the water. It was chilly and had an oily feel. Where the shadow fell across the pool the surface was inky blue. Zeke smoothed his hand over the top of his head. It was like putting ice on fire. He ducked under the water, came up, and smoothed the hair out of his face. No one had paid any attention to his entrance into the pool except Will, who was butting the inner tube with his belly in the shallow end, talking to himself as he sent it scurrying along. Zeke began to swim toward Will, clowning as he stroked, eyes bulging and jaw dropped. Will stopped playing with the inner tube and looked at Wayne, a hesitant smile on his face. Zeke must be nearer his age than his father's. Zeke's teeth sparkled like the big white teeth the Tooth Lady brought into Will's classroom twice a year so that she could show everyone how to brush their teeth with a whisk-broom toothbrush. Then she poked between the teeth with a piece of rope, making the same sawing motion adults made rubbing their backs as they dried off. As Zeke came near him Will smiled, partly at his approach, and partly because of the memory. The Tooth Lady's teeth were big enough to be the entranceway to a medium-sized dog's doghouse. The Tooth Lady herself had small white teeth, and enormous breasts that made the boys laugh. The Tooth Lady, Nancy Spears, was nicknamed Bicycle Pump because of the sixth-graders' assertion that she pumped up her tits with a bicycle pump. All through her presentation, the boys would push their hands down to the floor and raise them and push them down again, giggling, and the girls would hang their heads in shame. Will did not know, as Zeke neared him, that Zeke's shiny white teeth were false. Gum disease had necessitated the pulling of all but two top teeth and the molars, though when he was in the Army Zeke had chosen to say that a jealous husband had knocked out his teeth.

"Hop on," Zeke said, backing up to Will. "King Kong will take you for a swim."

Will could not imagine Zeke as King Kong. He was too thin and too white. Also, King Kong didn't hang out in swimming pools.

"You're not King Kong," Will said. He came nearer, though. Zeke looked over his shoulder and saw Will take a few steps forward.

"Well, I don't know the names of any monsters of the deep," Zeke said. "Just pretend I'm one of those. Oh—wait—I know: I'm the monster from the black lagoon. Black lagoon or blue lagoon. Something like that." He gestured toward his back.

There was a birthmark on Zeke's back, shaped like a crescent moon. Haveabud had moles on his back. Will remembered Haveabud rolling out of bed, and the sprinkling of moles across his back—so many that Will had squinted, the way he squinted to see the pattern stars made in the night sky. Haveabud's moles, though, were more like measles than constellations. Will had only one mole, at the side of his knee. His mother had had the doctor look at it. He wondered what a doctor would think of Haveabud's back. Though the water was not cold, Will shivered.

"You afraid of monsters?" Zeke said, smiling over his shoulder. You had to coax kids a little, Zeke knew. Kids and women. He had to take Susan to dinner six times before she would even let him feel her up, but the next time he really scored: right from first base home. Now, any time he wanted it. He looked at Susan, stretched out on the towel. From this perspective, her thighs looked like mountains. Will thought that maybe Haveabud's moles had flown onto Zeke's back like iron filings attracted by a magnet. Maybe hidden current moved through Zeke's body, like electricity. It might not be safe to climb on his back. It would be just like Haveabud to find a way to get rid of something he didn't want. Whenever he dropped anything out the car window, Haveabud always said, "It's organic." Kleenex were organic. The crossword puzzle, torn from the magazine in the motel room, was wadded up and thrown out the window once it was finished because the crossword puzzle was organic. Also the tabs Haveabud pulled off cans of Schweppes ginger ale. When they had driven far enough south so that the windows could be opened because it was suddenly so warm, Haveabud had let his socks flap out the window: little lavender-and-green argyle flags, snapping in the wind. Then he had just released them, not looking back to see where they went. "Ya-hoo!" Zeke screamed, as Will mounted his back. Zeke's cry sounded like Haveabud's shout when he released the socks. He remembered the look on Mel's face as he sat in the driver's seat, turning to look at Haveabud as the socks went snapping out the window. It was the same look his mother got when she found him stamping in two inches of water in the bathtub. Or the look she gave him when he said a bad word. Spencer had paid no attention. He was used to Haveabud's enthusiastic shouts. He heard them when Haveabud concluded a successful business call. When they watched the Mets play. When Haveabud knocked down all the sand monkeys sitting on a shelf at the carnival and won the stuffed-snake prize—a superlong bright green snake that Haveabud later wound around the coatstand in his office, after moving the philodendrons from the reception area and putting them around the stand, so that the snake appeared to be coiling out of a forest.

"An Anatosaurus," Will said suddenly, remembering the name of a monster of the deep.

"What?" Zeke said.

"They're dinosaurs with big bony heads. Anatosaurus means 'duck lizard.' They swam in the water and had big bills, like a duck. Dinosaurs hung out in the water. People just think of them running all over the land but actually the water was full of them, too. The Anatosaurus had a head shaped like a wheelbarrow. Great big wheelbarrow heads on enormous bodies in the water."

"Holy shit," Zeke said. "Don't tell me that stuff. I'll have nightmares."

"They're gone," Will said. "The dinosaurs are all dead, even though people say they've seen them. Those pictures they take are faked. They're fog looking funny when it rises from a lake. There aren't any dinosaurs, and nobody knows the mystery of where they went." He was saying just what Spencer had taught him. Spencer wanted to be proven wrong, though—you could tell that. He had books and articles about dinosaur sightings, and even though he said he didn't believe what the people saw, he still kept a list of sightings and possible explanations, using the person's own words in one column, and commenting himself in the far column.

"There's no Loch Ness monster, either," Will said, bobbing through the water on Zeke's back. "And did you know that one time an albino was photographed with a fish-eye lens in a thunderstorm, but the magazine that bought the pictures found out and never printed them?"

"Stop talkin' about this stuff," Zeke said. "I've got enough monsters in my nightmares."

"Dinosaurs aren't monsters," Will said.

"Yeah? What are they? Harmless, like cheerleaders?"

"They're *gone*," Will said. "You'll never see one in your entire life because they aren't on the planet anymore."

Spencer had been very emphatic about this: The dinosaurs were gone, every one, in spite of their size. They were gone, and nobody could have any sense of them except people who went to museums and saw their skeletons. Will kicked his heels lightly against Zeke's sides. The dinosaurs were gone, but it was still possible to go giddyup on a horse. Zeke was a horse in the water. That was what you might see now, instead of dinosaurs. His mother had talked about the wild ponies at Assateague, saying that one day she would take him there.

"What are you two doing?" Wayne said, rubbing his eyes.

"We're ghosts from the prehistoric world here to haunt you," Zeke said, bobbing and weaving as though a basketball were in play. He approached an invisible hoop, retreated, feinted, submerged himself in the water. Will was starting to enjoy himself. What if Zeke really was a monster—a too-tall, lanky monster who was a *real* monster in spite of putting on a charade, a person whose spine had magnetic powers? Zeke went down, Will shot up; Zeke submerged himself entirely,

Will rose up as though leading his team to victory, waving his arms.

"Be careful with him," Corky hollered from the sidelines.

"He can swim," Zeke said and, giddy, Will shouted that he could. Zeke was bobbing and weaving, the imaginary ball suspended for longer than would have been possible, the crowd growing restless. Will's knees became Zeke's earmuffs. His hands on top of his head became his helmet. Will's shrieking became the roar of the crowd. Will was riding on Zeke's slender shoulders and Zeke was a man with a purpose, a man in motion, a person about to reach the goal—which was the far side of the pool, the side near Wayne, in deep water.

Suddenly a car pulled into the driveway at high speed, the radio blaring. A sandy-haired man got out of the driver's side, leaving his companion in her seat. She turned the music down. The man peered over the roof of the car for a few seconds, then started toward them. As he walked, the woman inside the car threw open her door. She extended one tanned leg. She had low, pointed-toe white boots, Wayne saw, as she swung her other leg out of the car. The car was a Mazda RX-7—the car Wayne thought was the sharpest thing next to a Jaguar. The man walked toward them hesitantly, pushing his sunglasses to the top of his head and squinting.

"Hi. What's going on?" the man said.

"It's a swimming party, is what," Zeke said. Zeke didn't like the way the man was walking toward them. If the man took them for rich folks, he might think it was a fine time to rob them and take off fast. There was something hostile about the way the man moved.

"What can we do for you?" Wayne said, standing. He, too, wondered what the man was doing there. The music coming from the man's car was "We Are the World." Cyndi Lauper's voice cut through the air.

"Just wondering what was going on," the man said. "I was

going to take a dip, and I wasn't expecting to find anybody."
He hesitated, looking at the women. At Zeke, who had turned
his back on him and was bobbing, with Will, toward the other
end of the pool. The man looked at Wayne and frowned. "Are
you friends?" he said.

"Are we friends, or are we friend*ly*, do you mean?" Wayne
said.

"I mean: Who are you?" the man said. "This is my mother's
house." Only when he spoke the last words did his voice take
on an edge. But Wayne was relieved to know why the man
had stopped. He hated it when he was stopped by a cop and
had to watch the cop approach the car.

Wayne extended his hand. "I'm Wayne," he said. "Your
mother was kind enough to offer us the use of her pool for the
day."

The man shook his hand tentatively, still frowning.

"She's in New York," Wayne added. That was the thing to
do: tell her son that she was in New York. So why was he still
puzzled?

"Please. Go right ahead," the man said. "If you'll excuse
me, I'll just go in the house and call New York."

Zeke stopped playing with Will.

"Sure," Wayne said, sitting down. He was thinking that the
pool was his for the day. She had said that it was theirs for the
day. *It was theirs by right.* He watched the man walk toward
the house. Tight-ass, he thought. Why make a federal case out
of everything? He looked like his mother, but on him the high
forehead only seemed conspicuous. His mother had a pretty
widow's peak, and nicely arched eyebrows. Her face looked
very clear. Her son was a tight-ass who was balding.

Corky came over to Wayne. "Nothing to worry about,"
Wayne said. "Why's he making a big deal? If he wants to call
Mama, let him call Mama."

Theirs by right.

He watched the man open the back door. He would be going to the phone in the Florida room, filled with white wicker and hanging plants with little red flowers that looked like open mouths with forked tongues spitting. The nursery Wayne worked for did not have those plants. He had looked for them, out of curiosity, to see what their name was. Who did her son think they were? Criminals?

Mine by right, Wayne thought. Maybe she hadn't known that Will would be at the pool, and Susan, but could she really care that there were five people instead of three? He had been up-front. He had let her know earlier that he was married. She wouldn't have thought that he was going to have a swim without his wife, would she? And most couples had children, didn't they? *Mine by right*, he thought again, but this time he was fueling himself in case there was any problem. He understood that it wasn't exactly his by right. Corky sat on the towel next to Susan again, but their conversation was strained. They would not have a good time until the man came out of the house and gave them his blessing. What does he think—he's the fucking pope, because the old lady's got some bucks? Wayne thought.

In a few minutes, the man came out of the house. Now he was trying to appear casual. Wayne looked at the man walking toward him, his hands in his pockets. What kind of man was he that he'd leave his girlfriend in the car in the heat? His high forehead gleamed in the sunlight.

"Well," the man said, shaking his head as if he had very much amused himself with his folly. "That'll teach me not to reconfirm my plans with my mother, I guess."

"Hey, stay and have a swim," Wayne said. "Water's great."

"Honey!" the woman in the car called.

"No. Sorry to interrupt you. I guess we'll be pushing on."

I could have fucked your mother if I'd wanted to, Wayne thought. You unhappy to see me and my friends in the pool? What if I had fucked her?

The man bent to shake Wayne's hand. Wayne was damned if he'd rise a second time. The man had wanted to know what he was doing there? He'd told him. He wanted to check? He checked. Furthermore, even if the pool wasn't his by right, at least he was swimming there because the lady of the house was smitten with him. He could make the beast with two backs with the lady of the house as soon as she got home. Maybe on the floor of the Florida room, on the cold tile, with that ceiling fan going around and around. The room he had stood in as she wrote a check, asking: "Do you get tired of flowers? When you see so many, do you—does a person—get tired of flowers?"

The next time he saw her he would take her up on her offer of something "more substantial" when he finished work. Send Zeke back in the truck. Have his own car, then fuck her, fuck her for her pretty eyes and her high forehead and because she wanted him to, and now because she had a son who wouldn't like that.

Corky and Susan were talking louder. The man was almost back in his car. See? Wayne thought. You get those big-buck guys, they leave you sitting in the sun like you were a piece of tumbleweed on the desert. You think rich people have good family lives? Her husband's always in New York, and she wants to fuck the guy who's planting bushes on the hillside, and her own son didn't know she was in another city when he stopped by. You think that was his wife in the car? A wife with white boots who calls him honey?

Will wanted to know who the man in the flashy car was.

"Nobody important," Wayne said, and tried to mean it.

"He should of stayed and gone swimming. We're not lepers or anything," Susan said, combing her black hair.

Wayne jumped into the pool and kicked water high in the air, wetting Corky and Susan at the side of the pool, making Susan yelp and Corky run for cover. He meant to bring back the spirit of fun. The man and his girlfriend had driven away. Let them have their sports car and let him have his keys to Mama's house. *Mine by right*, Wayne had started to think again.

Will was giggling, sitting on top of Zeke's shoulders. Watching them through the geyser of water he kicked up, Wayne was happy that Will was having a good time. In his heart, he always trusted that he could amuse him. If his friend was the temporary stand-in, so be it. Wayne stopped kicking and swam to where his feet could touch bottom. Then he peed, luxuriating in the scalding rush of urine around his legs, staring at the fixed point of Zeke standing in shallow water with Will balanced atop his shoulders. If it were his house and he had the keys, he could have gone inside to pee. As it was, the only thing to do was jump in the pool and do it in the water. A little urine wouldn't hurt anyone, diluted by all the chlorine. And—like everyone who pees in a pool—he was convinced that he wasn't the only one. Like everyone else, for the umpteenth time in his life, Wayne was just going with the flow.

N I N E T E E N

It did happen on the floor of the Florida room, after Wayne had two shots of Chivas on the rocks, drunk out of crystal glasses that acted as prisms as the day drew toward evening, throwing marbly bits of light on the wide white columns separating the sliding glass doors. A quilt had been pulled from the sofa. She was more drunk than he and informed him the quilt was versatile. That her husband liked things that were versatile. Her son, she said, was simply wrong about the date.

Elliott had had surgery. There was a scar low on her belly, on the right side. As she lay back, her earrings clattered on the tile floor: long silver-and-agate earrings. She told him what agate was. He was licking the stones, and she said, "Does the agate feel cold on your tongue?"

He didn't ask where she got a name like Elliott. People who had money often named baby girls for their uncles, deceased.

Or they gave babies an important surname they didn't want lost when a woman took her husband's name—they put it first, like a person with a sweet tooth who eats the dessert before the meal. As a baby, did they call her Ellie?

Jody was going to name the first, he was going to name the second, but there was no second.

Elliott said: "My husband likes me to wear freshwater pearls. Pearls are different colors, you know—not just white. They can be silver-gray. Many different colors. But the way a pearl feels—it isn't hard, like a diamond. Some irritation causes pearls to form. Something deep inside that couldn't be gotten rid of. He thinks of that, I know, when he tells me to wear pearls."

"What does your husband do?" Wayne said, kneeling between her legs.

"Arbitrage," she said. "He wears socks that come up to his knees. He sleeps in them, the way Mormons sleep in their undergarments."

The ceiling fan.

"He pushes them down around his ankles when he's in bed, but he keeps them on. He gets up at six o'clock. He has his back worked on by an acupuncturist. Little porcupine quills. He relaxes with a Magic Slate: making squiggles on a Magic Slate, then pulling up the top sheet, sloooowly, like someone removing a bandage with a lot of adhesive. Sometimes he gets up at five-thirty in the morning. All his socks are black."

Wayne was not used to making love to women who talked. Her legs were the smoothest he had ever felt. There was not even hair on her thighs. He rubbed his hands down her legs, feeling the muscles under her slick, soft skin. She lived in Florida, but she was not tan. He leaned toward one nipple, licking around the areola, his eyes closed. A few tiny hairs surprised him, like seaweed when you were swimming. Her legs were hugging him tightly. He was not yet inside her, but his penis was hard, horizontal over her belly as he kissed between her breasts. Little kisses. Baby-step kisses. One two three. It took five little kisses to get from the left breast to the right. Her fingers gently touched the head of his penis.

"Amber takes a high polish," she said. "It's vegetable resin."

"You're teaching me things?" he said, inserting the tip of his penis. Pearls would be shot inside her. He pushed another inch deeper. She was smiling pleasantly, as if she had run into someone on the street whom she knew. When she came, she winced and looked unhappy, as if the person on the street had quite unexpectedly stepped on her foot.

He had his shirt on. As she rolled away, she tugged the material. His pants and his undershorts were on the wicker chair. He opened his mouth to breathe. She went into the bathroom and came back wearing a pale blue robe. The sash dangled down the front. A stain had seeped through, high up, over her thigh.

"Who's your wife?" she said, as if no time had intervened between his asking about her husband and her reply.

"My third wife," he said. Let her think him a three-time loser. Women liked wild cards.

"Oh?" she said, raising her eyebrows.

He walked over to her. She was standing behind a large teakwood bar with a blue glass top. She picked up a camera and pointed it at him. "Oh no you don't," he said, taking it out of her hand. "No souvenirs." He put it back on top of the bar.

"A chaser of champagne, or beer?" she said.

Beer.

She took a beer out of the refrigerator under the bar. A small bottle of champagne, which she handed him. He undid the wire and took it off. It would make a good muzzle for a box turtle. He dropped it on the bar and turned the little bottle until the cork popped. The glass she held out was shaped like a tulip, and he poured slowly, stopping an inch from the top.

Their last anniversary, he and Corky had had champagne.
She clinked her glass to his bottle. Both swallowed. A warm
rush went through his body and settled in his penis. He was
standing behind a bar without any pants on, drinking with a
woman whose husband slept in his socks. He took a long, cold
drink of beer. It had a metallic taste—the taste that had lin-
gered on his tongue after licking her earrings. She pushed her
hair behind her ears, which made her look younger. She was
probably fifty. The fan was turning.

She was running her hand through her hair. Pretty, the
color she had painted her nails. As though you could dip your
hands in fruit and keep the color. She had finished the champagne. He reached for the bottle and poured the rest into her
glass. "Take one sip," she said. The transparent tulip moved
toward his lips. He took a sip. The beer had numbed his
tongue; he could only taste fizz. The bubbles danced in his
body for a while before sinking to prickle inside his penis.

As she sipped, she unfastened the robe with one hand. She
had on a low-cut black lace brassiere with a tiny red flower
over the front clasp. She finished the champagne. He was
getting hard. The fan was turning. What had happened to
account for his sudden luck with women? It was as though
angels had plotted to please him. The little red flower made
him think of impatiens. Hoeing the ground. Digging with the
trowel. Setting in little impatiens plants. White, salmon, and
red. Last week's work. His hands were on her hips.

"I do have a bed," she said.

The bedside clock was ticking. Will had had a toy—a piece
of laminated cardboard shaped like an alarm clock with bells
on the top. He would spin the hands, making them go round
and round. Babies always parted their lips when they played.
Wayne had shown Will how to click his tongue. It had taken
a long time to teach him. He was glad that he didn't have to

be the one to teach Will to whistle. He could not remember if he had taught Will to click his tongue over the Giddyup Pony book, or to make the sound of the ticking clock. He would be going home to Will and Corky.

Elliott stretched out across the width of the bed, and again he kneeled and looked down at her. For fifty, she was in very good shape. She would have to be fifty, give or take a few years, because of the age of her son. "Did he have that girl with him?" she had asked. He had not even reached them in New York; he had left a message on their machine. Susan had asked why they didn't join them for a swim. "We're not lepers," she had said. Elliott's son fucked a girl who wore white cowboy boots. In Wayne's imagination, they had taken on sterling silver tips, cleats, and silver spurs. She kept them on when they fucked. She lay naked on top of a lasso, a *Penthouse* beauty photographed through a haze filter. Then she sat in a sports car, a Mazda RX-7, in a driveway in Florida. She had called "Honey" with as much of an edge as she would let creep into her voice, considering that she wanted to please the man so he would marry her. She had certainly not been his wife sitting there, in that car, in those boots.

Wayne took Elliott's smooth feet—even those were smooth!—and brought them to his chest. He ran his hands down the sides of her thighs. He was smiling at her, and she was smiling at him. The bushes were planted on her hillside. There would be pool parties, which he would not be a part of, when she and her guests would drink champagne and notice— vaguely notice—that things were in flower. The day at the pool would probably stay in Will's mind longer than in the minds of any of the people Elliott entertained. Will would tell Jody. She would ask what he did, and he would tell her that they went swimming at a big pool, and what could she think but that Wayne had friends who had a swimming pool. He looked down. A little wisp of hair blew over Elliott's forehead, sent aloft by the turning fan. She was rubbing his pubic hair, her thumbs moving up and down the sides of his crotch, her fingertips rising high to stroke the part of his body where the hair ended and his own smoothness began. Impossible to imagine Will in such a position. Will kneeling in front of a woman. Though he would, of course. By that time, would magazines offer the same orchestrated fantasies seen through smoky lenses? Victorian ladies in their bustiers. Cowgirls naked except for white boots, pouting with bee-stung lips, hair spread out on the pillow? Maybe by then space helmets would be erotic, and the hourglass figure, which had been replaced by the anorexic figure, would be something else entirely. Nipples might not be points of fascination, but the clavicle. By the time Will was grown, Jane Fonda might be leading the archangels in aerobics, or using all her muscle strength to leap through the fires of Hell, if she hadn't been forgiven for what she did in Hanoi.

He had powdered Jody's buttocks with a big powder puff and then pulled her ass into his stomach and gone inside her, the powder leaving two small moons on his body.

Hanoi. So long ago, it might have been the Civil War.

On the rug, playing with baby Will. Not sure-footed at all. Those hard baby shoes, laced up, that they put them in. Like they'd plunged your tiny feet in rigid ski boots and you were trying to run. No flexibility. No way to run fast enough to win, even though Daddy could only move so fast on his hands and knees. The palms could take it, but not the knees. Trousers helped. Baby knees, going up and down like a carousel horse. Up-down, up-down. Trying to run, but how, with feet in ski boots? Knowing you're going to be caught. Just knowing it. Squeal and run, work your knees, but you're as stationary as an animal on a carousel. Big bear will get you, smiling in the disguise of Daddy. Run in circles. You'll be caught.

He cupped his hands over Elliott's hipbones and pulled her ass against him, entering her.

What had Jody thought, when she realized that he wasn't coming back?

Would he be coming back here? To Elliott's?

He was prepared for Kate to leave. From the first, he knew that she would leave and go back to New Jersey. That allowed him time to prepare. The good thing about fucking other women was that when you left them, or they left you, whatever you had done could be recreated with your next partner, and she would be grateful. Interested. He had powdered Corky's bottom, improvising a little, years later, by spanking her first. And she had liked it.

What is amniocentesis? flashed into his mind.

Corky was letting him know that she was having a good time with Will. He could see his son growing close to her. She had bought him a little tube that would break the world into bits when you looked through it.

Tick tock.

He fucked Elliott harder this time, three or four hard strokes, slowly withdrawing until only the tip of his penis was inside, moving his fingertips to her nipples, gradually accelerating his thrusts as his grip on her breasts tightened. Tick tock. In out. It seemed silly, child's play, if you thought about it. Two adults in odd positions. No wonder children were frightened when they looked into a room and saw what they shouldn't see. Sometimes the people *were* hurting each other. And if they weren't then, they might be somewhere down the line. Hurt if the other person refused to do it every day. Or if the person left. Or if you left, and tried to forget the person. Your body would remember.

He could not remember the names of all the women he had fucked. For a while he could. Now he couldn't. And if things kept going the way they were, there was sure to be more amnesia. Though he hadn't even wanted to fuck the girl in the Mazda—the girl who said "Honey" with an edge in her voice—it would be an interesting idea to have Corky keep her shoes on, her high heels, which she could wear as she crouched over him.

He had planted rhododendron bushes on Elliott's hillside. Maybe she would look at them and think of him, and of the turning fan, the phone that rang and was answered on the second ring by the answering machine, the ice cubes clattering into the bin.

He could hear them clattering again, as he came. So much fucking always gave him a headache, so that what he heard was partly the imagined avalanche, and partly the sound he made, a groan uttered as much from pounding pain as pleasure.

This was what he was doing as Corky took care of Will. Exhaling. Kneeling on a bed with a woman below him who turned over, her arm bent, thrown across her eyes. He kissed her elbow. He kissed her only there, then stood and waited to see if she would look at him. When she did not, he turned and started toward the other room to gather his clothes. When he got there, he went behind the bar and helped himself to another beer, tossing the cap on top of the bar. While the refrigerator door was still open, he took one of the little bottles of champagne and put it in his jacket pocket. He felt sure that she would not hug him goodbye. That even if he decided to go into the bedroom to bend over and kiss her, she would not feel the bottle.

He was right. He went back to the doorway. The fan was turning. She had rolled onto her stomach. He went to the bed and kissed the top of her head, tousled her hair. He also kissed her spine, at the small of her back. Then he went away, having had a premonition from the first that this was the way he would depart.

He left the front door open. When she saw the open door, she would have to think of him.

The bottle was a little ice pack. He could remember Jody telling him, when Will was an infant, that if you stand in cool water, it cools your whole body. That in the winter, if you cover your head, you will be warmer, because so much heat is lost through the head. She kept the blue stocking cap pulled down low, to Will's eyebrows. Around every body there were invisible currents of air—hot air or cold air—spreading out, dissipating.

He stopped for a minute and looked at the pool. He went closer and saw that a bee was floating, struggling for its life. The water was quite still. If the bee made it to a long green leaf a foot in front of it, it might have a chance. He thought about pushing the leaf farther away, but didn't. He looked back at the open door and wondered what insects would enter the house.

A man who had picked the wrong woman three times was the only kind of man who would leave three women.

He looked at the leaf. A maple leaf, very still in the water.

He went to his car and got in, taking the cool bottle of champagne from his jacket pocket, dropping it on the passenger's seat.

There were moments in life—rare moments, but they happened in every life—when you knew clearly what you did and did not want, and why. You could know the minute you took off in a car that you would not have to test-drive anything else, that this was the one for you. Apparently, all women could tell in a split second if a dress was right or wrong for them. You could know that because the butter on the popcorn you got in the movies was rancid, you would never be able to stand the taste of popcorn again. Wayne could remember the moment, as a small boy, when he had put his washcloth on top of the soap dish, thinking: This is ridiculous. I can wash my body with my hands. I will never again use a washrag.

Today was another one of those moments. Alone in the car, he knew that whatever Corky wanted, and no matter what price he had to pay for refusing her, he did not ever again want to look into a rearview mirror to check the expression on his child's face as he drove along. A child who would die if he rolled up the windows and left the car in the noonday sun. A child who would be limp when he was lifted out. Whose little mouth he would suck up into his own, breathing. Breathing.

Such things happened. They didn't make the papers, but they happened time and again. Children dead in their cribs. Suffocated in cars. Born to nuns and thrown in the garbage. Snatched into the tiger's cage at the zoo, or pulled underwater by an alligator, which was eventually hunted down and split open, the dead child inside.

All of those things would be horrible, but worst of all would be transporting a sleeping child, slumped in its seat, buckled in as if things were so safely arranged that if the car became a rocket and shot into orbit, the child would not even suffer whiplash. You could pull over and check a million times, if you let yourself. The motion of the car would put the child to sleep. The child, asleep, might be dead. He would never again sing or talk in the car—talk to himself like a madman—to try to keep a child awake. He would never again break into a sweat as he pulled off the highway to check for that tiny expulsion of breath from the child's nostrils as its head lolled to the side. He would never again fumble with straps, thinking he had only seconds, only to have the child open his eyes, quizzically, wondering why Daddy was frantic. Was Daddy suddenly digging like an animal getting ready for winter, in mid-July? Was Daddy playing a game? Was the baby's navel, which Daddy's fingers seemed to be tickling, the nut, and was Daddy a silly squirrel?

You were always seen as being out of control with children. At the shoreline, not realizing that your voice would carry so well, you would shout too loudly. Heads turned. On the roller coaster you acted insane, clutching the child with both hands, so you felt unsafe yourself as the speeding car swooped down. You squeezed the child too hard, hurting him.

Never. Not ever again. Better that the needle go into your own heart and pierce it than prick the womb in which a fetus lay curled.

The note Corky had left on the kitchen table said that they had gone to watch a movie on Corinne and Eddie's VCR. It gave him time to sit in the kitchen chair quietly. To concentrate on breathing evenly.

He had left her stretched across the bed, the fan turning, the door open.

He pushed the bottle of champagne on top of the clutter on the second shelf of the refrigerator. He could lie so spontaneously about where it came from that he didn't even need to bother thinking about that.

Part of the exhaustion he felt must have been because of the fucking, and drinking, and fucking again.

He had planted rhododendrons on her hillside.

He closed his eyes and imagined a bee buzzing in Elliott's bedroom. A bee, above her naked body, carried like a leaf, airborne, blown by the currents of the ceiling fan.

Maybe she would smile when she saw the open door. She liked it that he was cocky. That he had stood there, in the Florida room, letting her know with his eyes that he realized she wanted something more than to give him a check to take back to the landscaping service.

Deciding to take his time about getting Corky, he took a quick shower, then dried off, went back into the room and pulled a beer out of the refrigerator and threw the twist-off cap in the trash. Cardboard was in there. Corky had bought Will a set of jacks and a ball.

When he went next door and shouted hello as he opened the screen door, Corky's voice and Eddie's hollered back.

They were watching *Dirty Dancing*.

Corky gave him a bright, false hello.

Will was sitting on the floor, turning the little ball he had gotten earlier over and over in his hand like a worry bead. That afternoon he had gotten a call from Jody. Jody wanted him to do her a favor. She wanted him to return to New York early—before he saw Wag, because if he returned when she needed him to return there wouldn't be time to see Wag—so he could be photographed with her for the July issue of *Vogue*. She was going to be one of five women photographed with her child—a full-page picture. And her show opened in July. He would be doing her a great favor. She would return the favor by promising to have Wag for the summer—the whole summer—if Will would leave Florida early, so that they could be photographed together for *Vogue*.

Everyone was pretending there was no foregone conclusion.

Will rolled the little red ball back and forth across the floor as though he were rolling dough. The whole reason he had come to Florida was to see Wag. Why didn't she know that?

He didn't know his father.

Corky tried too hard to please.

He would tell his mother—and only his mother—about Spencer and Haveabud in the motel room.

Although he would not tell his mother unless she asked. Sitting at the side of his bed, when he returned, she might ask.

Will looked past his father, out the window. The darkness was a huge mole on a giant's back. The giant had backed up against the window. Inside was what was happening in houses, and outside sat the giant. What the giant looked at, Will couldn't be sure. It was possible that the giant could see all of history. That he sat just the way Will sat in a school chair, studying all of history, which moved in front of him like an endless movie. Maybe all the world was a movie, and the giant was looking at dinosaurs snapping up lizards, wading into ponds, pulling up bushes to eat.

T W E N T Y

Into Will's suitcase went the ball and jacks, which Corky had put in a Baggie and tied with a yellow twist tie. Also the T-shirt whose front depicted a sandy beach with people stretched out on striped towels, water lapping the shore, seagulls swooping. On the back of the shirt were three more seagulls, but this time, instead of rising up against a blue sky, they hovered on white cotton. Corky had let Will pick out any shirt he wanted, and he had picked the shirt with the seagulls.

Corky bought Will flip-flops to wear to the beach. His mother had not even packed beach shoes. Corky thought she might ask Will whether he would like to keep the flip-flops in the hall closet, along with hers and Wayne's, but then she thought no: What was his was his. If he wanted to feel that there were things left behind in the house that were his, he would have said so.

Corky put Coets on either side of the pyrite and agate she had bought Will at the gem shop: little white cotton pads, like sandwich bread, to protect the slices and discs.

She was sorry for him. She would have driven him to see Wag—gone back and forth in one day—except that both the other salesgirls were out sick, and she was the only one who could help Marian. She was glad she had not raised the possibility of the trip with Will, because he would have been further disappointed.

Corky and Wayne and Will had watched the fishermen, and seen the sunset, and eaten fried shrimp at the seafood restaurant. Will's dinner, ordered from the children's menu, had been called The Captain Nemo. He had been allowed to go to the treasure chest and select a toy. He brought back a plastic camera. Looking into it and pushing the button, you saw first a starfish, then a whale, then a school of silvery fish.

"How do shrimp see?" Will asked.

"They have heads. When they clean them, they take off the heads," Wayne said.

"When they clean lobsters they don't take off the heads," Will said.

"They don't clean lobsters," Wayne said.

Now Corky looked at Will, who was sitting on the bed, watching her put things in his suitcase. New York had pigeons and Florida had seagulls and pelicans. Nobody had dinosaurs. What Haveabud and Spencer had been doing might have had something to do with dinosaurs. There were no more dinosaurs, but maybe Haveabud and Spencer were involved in a ritual to bring them back. That was why the ritual had to be private. Secrets had to be whispered. It went without saying that he should have sealed lips. But if his mother asked. Was Haveabud's ritual similar to what went on between his mother and Mel? Some night ceremony, to bring back the dinosaurs? If he could see what they did. If his mother asked. On television, Perry Mason asked people questions in court. When Perry Mason heard an answer he didn't like, he looked to the side, with his bird-bright eye. Another, more difficult question followed.

"I'm putting in your flip-flops," Corky said, a slight question in her voice. Will knocked his toes together in his stocking feet. He was not supposed to wear shoes when his legs were stretched out on the bed. It was really not a bed but a sofa that turned into a bed. At first, he had been afraid of the dressmaker's dummy in the corner because it looked like a warrior, waiting for the signal to do battle.

G.I. Joe was back in the zippered bag he had been in when he arrived. Like a body bag, Corky thought. She asked Will if she should leave the bag out, so that he could have it on the plane. He nodded that she should. Wayne was trying to help Eddie start his lawnmower.

Lobsters probably got to keep their heads because they were bigger. Lobsters would fight, because they were big, but shrimp wouldn't fight, because they were small. In a fight between a lobster and a shrimp, the lobster would win. Beady black eyes would win. Haveabud and Spencer had dark eyes. Brown eyes with black pupils. Haveabud was a lobster and Spencer was a shrimp. Spencer would be afraid to fight with Haveabud.

Why couldn't his mother give the magazine one of the pictures she already had of him?

Corky put Will's shorts and underwear in the suitcase. She had laundered them. His mother had folded his socks. Corky put them together in a different way, pulling the cuff of one over the ball made by the two rolled socks. That was the way his socks would go home, to show Jody that this was her way.

His mother had packed a white shirt and a bow tie. Corky thought Will would look like a midget businessman if he wore those things. The only pants Jody packed were jeans.

Seersucker pajamas. Little boys would still allow you to put pajamas on them. When they got older, they would sleep in their underwear. When they left their parents' house, they would sleep naked.

Will watched Corky fold the seersucker pajamas. Running your hand over seersucker was like moving your hands up and down your body when you had insect bites.

Into the suitcase went the plastic camera from the seafood restaurant, which was now stuck on the picture of the whale, and the book about gems that Corky had bought him. A place mat imprinted with a map of the area. A penny that had been pressed into an oval souvenir of Florida. Maybe Mel could think of a way to attach the flattened copper penny to a chain so his mother could wear it as a necklace. Before they left New York, Mel had shown him an ad in a magazine for diamond rings and asked him to guess which one his mother would like best. Mel pointed to the small type at the bottom of the page: All the rings were enlarged to show detail. Mel could buy his mother a diamond ring, and he could give her a bright, thin penny on a chain.

Purple was amethyst. Green was jade. Though pink also could be jade. The man in the crystal store had given him a piece of smooth pink stone. While Corky worked, Will walked through the mall to the crystal store and crayoned a picture for the man on a legal pad. In exchange, the man gave him the smooth stone, which he proudly gave to Corky. In the crystal store, you could buy chains with little discs on top and tubes of glue so that you could make anything they sold into a keyring. Will suggested to Corky that she do that, and she had said that it was an excellent idea.

The dressmaker's dummy was more like a skeleton than a warrior, as she had shown him, turning the light on and turning the headless body. What harm could it do without a head?

Dinosaurs in the museums were skeletons.

The dummy had no head, like a shrimp whose head had been removed.

It was harmless: a shape, a shadow. Nothing at all.

In the tent in Virginia, he and Wag had made Martian dolls: Kleenex boxes standing upright, with upside-down saucers on the end to look like heads, and strings from an old mop held on to the saucers with masking tape. The boxes did a dance, illuminated by flashlights placed behind them that pointed up, backlighting the forms, which danced on a field of white Kleenex. The flashlights were the sun rising, while the box-Martians had a secret ceremony.

If all the dinosaurs had gone into caves. If they came out again someday, the way bats flew at dusk.

His mother had told him that the man who would be king of England did not come right out and ask the woman he wanted to marry to marry him. The king said "If I asked . . ." so he could find out in advance what she would say.

If his mother asked.

Corky reached under his pillow and took out the Bugs Bunny with a flexible orange body. Bugs held an orange carrot with a spray of green plastic at the top. His big front teeth were white. Bugs probably cleaned according to the advice of the Tooth Lady, flossing every night.

Corky asked if she could pack Bugs. If she left Bugs under the pillow, she would forget to pack him, she was sure. He nodded yes. But no: He did not want Bugs dropped in the zippered case with G.I. Joe. G.I. Joe would be insulted, the way any soldier would be insulted if asked to share quarters with a rabbit. If the rabbit was a pet, that was one thing—but Bugs was the same size as G.I. Joe, only skinnier. He would have to go in the suitcase. Tucked in the pocket of the white shirt he had worn on this trip was fine.

Corky held the bow tie over her top lip, and Will laughed. A lawnmower started outside. That meant that his father and

Eddie had triumphed. The people next door always played the same record. If he played a record more than once, his mother objected. When you grew up, you could play any record you wanted, any time you wanted. The lawnmower drowned it out, though. Grass had to be cut. This was a fact. A Virginia and a Florida fact. In New York, there was just the snapping sound of the hedge clippers, when the sister of the man who lived downstairs came to cut branches. You also heard firecrackers and gunshots in New York. In the video arcade, at the mall where Corky worked, he had heard New York sounds. He had led her inside to investigate. Sounds of exploding asteroids and speeding cars that collided. Helicopters that failed to clear the tops of buildings and exploded. Bells and sirens. A spray of dots fired into descending targets that fell in no predictable pattern.

Wayne sat on Corinne and Eddie's front step, sipping a Schlitz. He raised the can as if toasting Eddie, who shook his head from side to side, pushing the mower. If Wayne hadn't been able to get the mower going, Eddie's ass would have been in the doghouse; Corinne had begged him to charge a new mower. She had just *known* that when people were invited over the mower would quit on them again, and the shop wouldn't get to it for a week.

Corinne was in a good mood now, standing in the doorway, looking at Eddie as admiringly as if he were driving the Indianapolis 500, the baby resting against her chest. Wayne turned and said something to her, and she smiled. Wayne was probably *not* giving her the word that Eddie was going back on the softball team.

That was how they all were: Eddie, confident that the mower would keep going just by the sound of it, began to mow the grass in earnest; Corinne stood outside the screen door; Patsy Cline sang; Wayne tilted the can of Schlitz higher, hurrying to finish, because he never found it easy to make conversation with Corinne.

Corinne was the first to notice the police car. The car was moving slowly, with the windows down, and you could hear the two-way radio: fuzzy words and crackling. It passed by and stopped at the curb in front of Wayne's house. She patted the baby's back, as if to soothe it, and watched as both cops got out of the car. One carried something thin and rectangular. Both looked at her, standing in the doorway. Their faces were expressionless. She did not think that they were collecting for the Fireman's Ball. But *of course* policemen would not be collecting for the Fireman's Ball. Firemen did that. Police collected for . . .

Fear gathered in the back of Wayne's throat. It was there like food that had gone down the wrong way.

Eddie looked at Wayne, and at the policemen walking up Wayne's walkway. He had helped Wayne put the flagstone down the summer before. Wayne had wanted to leave too much room between stones. Weeds would have grown. Eddie was glad that he had taken his advice about placing them closer together. He stopped mowing the lawn.

Corky opened the door. Wayne could have headed them off, but it was all so sudden. And you couldn't head off cops. The closest thing Wayne knew to that was a guy he used to work with, years ago, who kept a Masonic ring in his glove compartment and fished it out whenever a cop stopped him for a traffic violation.

Corky pushed the door open and turned and looked at Wayne, sitting on the step, holding a Schlitz. It was the last drink he would have before his life changed. She was looking at him across the distance between houses and he looked back as if she were a lighthouse and he were a boat, receding. She suddenly seemed that tall, as he looked up at her. There were fewer and fewer lighthouses. Things were done electronically.

He had thought about getting a boat. Just a small boat, to keep at the dock. Even a rowboat would have been fine. Tie it with a chain. Down at the dock, where the fishermen fished.

He nodded that he was Wayne, when the cop asked.

The other cop looked like somebody who'd steal your girlfriend. Handsome, and with no compunctions. It was hard to imagine which role he'd have if the two of them played Good Cop/Bad Cop, because if he played the Good Cop, men would still resent him because of his good looks and his fuck-you expression; if he played the Bad Cop, he'd be poorly suited to the role. Bad people didn't look like that. They didn't look like they should be in the movies. If this was a movie, suspense would be mounting. Everyone would have his fingers in the popcorn bag. Wayne put down the can of beer.

There was a photograph. A small photograph on a clipboard, of Kate.

He nodded when asked if he knew her. He was holding the clipboard like somebody giving a speech, looking down to refresh his memory. Now Corky was standing in front of him. What would this speech be about? There was not one thing on the clipboard but a picture of Kate, smiling.

The other cop took a pill bottle from his pocket. Wayne frowned. He was standing now. When he stood, both cops stepped back. Eddie had come up alongside one of the cops. The lawnmower was in the middle of the yard. The grass behind it was mowed, and the grass in front of it was tall. This was a bad situation. What was the cop showing him?

A pill bottle, with Corky's name on it. He didn't know she'd been sick. It was her name, and her address—were they here to ask her about that? Not with a picture of Kate, they weren't. Kate's smile seemed utterly inappropriate.

The handsome cop asked Corky if Kate's picture was familiar.

She looked at Wayne. The woman was Wayne's lover. He

had picked a woman who looked nothing like her. She shook her head no.

Wayne asked if there was some problem about the pill bottle.

Where it was found, they said. In a rented car. It had rolled under the seat. There was also quite a bit of cocaine in the car. Did he know anything about that cocaine?

Cocaine?

Cocaine. He did know the woman in the picture?

Kate.

The cop with the clipboard nodded. The other cop could have been posing for photographs: square-shouldered, noble chin. Tall and trim in his uniform.

Corinne was praying that Eddie was not involved in this. She always knew Wayne was trouble. A sulky person. One of those men who're buddy-buddy with the other guys and look at a guy's wife like they're peering into a bread basket: one more piece of bread, cut on the angle. No surprises. Wayne was trouble. Standing there listening was like watching an accident: It wasn't a nice thing to do. But it was impossible to move on. Wayne and Corky's future was transpiring in front of Corinne's eyes.

Eddie didn't know what to do. Earlier, he and Wayne had talked about his rejoining the softball team. Was that going to be in question now?

Patsy Cline was singing "You Belong to Me."

Everyone looked at Corky. It occurred to Police Officer Pasani, as his partner read Wayne his rights, that it was a shame they had her Ativan pills, because she might be needing them. In the movies, the woman in the picture would be hiding in Corky and Wayne's attic, even as they spoke. Pasani looked at the house. No attic—maybe a crawl space. Only in the movies would a woman who looked like Kate be in the attic.

"You going to trust what some motel clerk said, or should we take the missus in, too?" Pasani asked his partner.

Suddenly, Wayne lunged. Wayne lunged, and Pasani just stepped aside. It could have been a cartoon, the way Wayne rushed forward into thin air. From the first, Pasani had thought it would be a good idea to cuff him. This, now, was their chance. The handcuffs really did make a sound. Clink: just the way they sounded in the movies.

Will was in the bathtub, having a bath with Bugs, whom he had removed from his shirt pocket, and several thimbles from Corky's thimble collection. Letting him have the thimbles to play with had been something of a problem. She didn't really believe that he would make the mistake of swallowing one, yet he seemed too young to be given thimbles and too old to be told to be careful with them. He was pouring thimblefuls of water out of the thimbles. Putting Bugs across his knees and pouring tiny amounts of water on his teeth and on his carrot.

Mel had given him a radio that could be played in the bathroom without any danger. He had brought it with him to Florida. It sat on top of the closed toilet seat. A film director was being interviewed. Yes, the director said, such things had happened to him; he had tried to repress them, but eventually he knew that he had to make a film. Yes, it was upsetting, but also in some ways wonderful.

Will had gotten good at hitting the target: Bugs's teeth. However high he raised his hand, his aim was usually still good. It was just that a thimble held only a very small amount of water, so the scooping up would have to start all over again. The bubbles were disappearing. He took the bottle and squeezed more bubble goop into the water, kicking with his feet to make suds.

Outside, as Wayne spat on the ground, Pasani looked over his shoulder and asked Corky if their cat was missing. His partner was steering Wayne toward the car.

"We don't have a cat," she said.

So the cat that had been found dead in the car was not theirs. It was just a hunch. You went on hunches when you found a rental car in the parking lot of a shopping mall and inside the trunk were boxes—ordinary cardboard boxes—filled with cocaine. A shopper who knew the cat was in distress called the police. Ironic: all those people sticking Garfield to their car windows with suction cups, and in this case someone had left a real cat that had died because of the car's internal temperature. Who had that much cocaine and simply walked away from it, in a parking lot, with a cat locked in the car? The woman who left the car in the parking lot had not boarded any planes in the last twenty-four hours under her own name, but of course there were many ways to leave Florida besides flying, even if she was holding a ticket. Her mother said that she was holding a ticket. She showed them the calendar, with her daughter's time of departure noted in pen, not in pencil: It was something her daughter had been sure about.

The old lady crying at the police station had been a pathetic sight. She had become hysterical at the thought of arranging for the cat's cremation. A cat, as she said, that she had never met.

Corky's bottle of pills had fallen out of Wayne's jacket. She often wore his blue nylon jacket, now that oversized jackets were in fashion. She had thought she lost them somewhere in the house. She didn't really know for sure that they were missing, since she hadn't been taking them. She frowned, as if the pills had brought on this disaster.

Going away in handcuffs was a disaster. Eddie had a sudden unexpected vision of Wayne choking up on the bat to bunt. Two hands sliding forward. The ball dropping dead. It would bring in the guy from third, put Wayne out at first.

Pasani and his girlfriend had gone dancing at the same Hyatt where the desk clerk remembered Wayne and Kate. If it had been the movies, they might even have crossed paths one night in the bar, Pasani taking Jeanelle for a swing around the dance floor, wearing the Italian shoes with the thin soles she had given him for his birthday. Gigolo shoes he called them, but he secretly thought they were stylish. He would like to wear such shoes every day. He liked to dance with Jeanelle and to watch her sipping a pink drink: a strawberry daiquiri. Her lipstick on the rim was only a shade darker than the mixture inside. They might have been there the night Wayne and Kate were having a night on the town.

As Wayne walked toward the car, he thought of the door at Elliott's house: the open door. He wondered if he would be behind bars. Whether they would believe he knew nothing. All his life, he had found that if people assumed you were guilty of one thing, it naturally followed that you were guilty of another.

Dialogue from the director's movie was being spoken by actors, on the radio. The interviewer approved of their words. He was amazed, he said, at how well the director had captured these people. People that—if he was correct—the director had not seen since childhood. Ah, but that was a time when everything was so intense, said the director. And when the movie was being filmed—what had it been like to return to that country? It was my country and is still my country, the director said. Though people do not necessarily realize this, it is still true: You carry your country with you. Your country is stamped on you, like a birthmark; or inside your body, like a rib. A heart.

Though only the interviewer saw the gesture, the director was tapping his chest with his fingertips. It was sincere—an honest gesture, however clichéd—and it made the interviewer like him. He decided not to throw him a curve by reading him part of a bad review. To keep on with something positive. He decided to ask for a physical description of the country. The director began by speaking of the mountains.

Will looked at his hands. The skin was wrinkled on his fingertips, and his cuticles were very white, as were the moons that rose just a bit above the cuticles. His hands felt funny when they touched each other. He rubbed his fingers up and down his legs. He had been in the tub a long time. Corky was true to her word: He was big enough to bathe himself, and she wouldn't bother him.

Out of respect to Bugs, he had wrapped him around the waterspout when he began to play with his hands, instead of letting him sink in the tub. Was there any contortionist in the world who could twist around in a complete circle, the way Bugs was twisted on the waterspout? If so, Will might see him at the circus one day.

Ah, but the blight that hit the chestnut trees, the director said. His sentence faded out. Then he wondered aloud if he was being too nostalgic: if he was talking about life as though spring were the only season, and everything of importance always happened underneath the chestnut trees.

The interviewer, who was fascinated, said nothing.

But then again, the director said, it would have been ludicrous to paint other trees to look like chestnut trees, or to have imitation chestnut trees brought in as props.

The director concluded by saying that of course that had not happened, and except for him, probably no one noticed the absence of the chestnut trees. "We are not Hollywood," the director said. But even that he said lightly. He did not mean to indict Hollywood. He was just saying something that was to him quite apparent.

Will stood up carefully. He could almost hear his mother's voice, telling him to rise carefully from the bathwater. He could almost see Mel's expression as he extended a hand to steady him as he rose. He was happy that Corky had not worried aloud about his getting into or out of the bath.

When he was standing he turned the dial and got music. It

was classical music that sounded like what his mother played in the darkroom when she was developing photographs.

He pulled the stopper but did not unwind Bugs. He meant to, but once he stepped onto the bathrug—a rug in the shape of a strawberry that fit without an inch to spare in the little space between the tub and the wall—he looked out the window, and what he saw got his complete attention. He saw Corky's back, and the neighbor's backs, and his father's back, as he bent to get into the backseat of a police car. For half a second, he wondered if his father was looking for something, but then realized that he could not be looking for anything with his hands in handcuffs, because what would he do if he found the thing? The police had come for him, which was what they did when a person was a criminal.

The car pulled away. It pulled away and disappeared, without the light's turning and without any noise except the sound of the motor. If his father was in the police car, something must be very wrong. When he thought of the worst thing he could imagine, it was that his mother was dead.

Then the thought came to him that it might have something to do with Haveabud. Why had Haveabud refused to come to the house, saying that he and Spencer would go to a comic-book store? Was that an alibi? Was there some reason why only Mel had accompanied him to his father's house?

His father was in the police car.

His father could not be in a police car. How could his father be gone, when he had come to visit him?

The police would bring him right back.

They wouldn't; Will had seen enough television to know that his father would not come back.

Corky and Corinne were crying. Holding each other and crying. The only man on the lawn now was Eddie, standing there, looking down the empty street.

No, his mother couldn't be dead. The police would not

have come to his father's house and taken him away like that if she were dead.

He waited at the window to see if he might be wrong, and the car might come back.

Black dots representing strawberry seeds were spaced evenly across the rug. Will lifted his foot and looked at the seeds that had been beneath his foot. Then, keeping the towel over his shoulders like a shawl, he sat on the closed lid of the toilet seat, to think.

He held the radio on his lap, turning the dial from station to station. He missed the classical music and tried to find it again, but he couldn't. He moved his thumb slowly, and one time he thought he had found it, then realized he hadn't. The tempo had shifted to allegro, but he didn't know that and kept trying to find the same music. He had been in the darkroom with his mother enough times to remember that classical music changed, just when you liked something, it changed, but he was distracted and he didn't remember.

The music sounded wrong.

Something was wrong if Corky and Corinne were crying.

Through the window, he had seen what was wrong.

If someone did not come into the house soon, he would have to go outside and ask what had happened, because he was still worried that his mother might be dead.

For the moment, he sat with the towel around him, in silence, having given up on finding the song. He remembered, very distinctly, the way his father had looked at the man who showed up at the swimming pool the other day. Did that have something to do with this?

He bit his cuticle. He got up and unwound Bugs. Bugs waited with him.

Let's say that the child knocks the radio off the shelf, where it has been sitting above the worktable in your garage. That you were prepared for the child to hurt himself because he is somewhat clumsy, never alert enough to danger, always intent upon what he wants to do, no matter what may be in the way—a radio cord, or whatever— so that when there is a mighty crash and the room goes silent, you look up expecting that the chainsaw you do not own has cut through the child, or the lawnmower has started up again and run him over. No, you see: It is only that he has attempted to walk through the space where the radio cord is stretched to go into the wall outlet. He reaches down and puts the plug into the socket again, and as he does that, you look at his quick concentration and know that you have lost him for all time. His hair has begun to change from gold to dark brown, his hands have real dexterity and are no longer the bobbing-octopus fingers of a baby. Suddenly he is neither angel nor devil, but a person doing a quite ordinary thing, and hoping his mistake will not be unduly remarked upon. What have you been doing all these years, anyway, in shaking your head sadly from side to side every time he forgets to screw the lid back on the jar, in admonishing him to get on tiptoe to put his cereal bowl in the kitchen sink and run water in it? You have devoted great amounts of time to worrying, to talking when you would have been happier to remain silent, to instructing someone who was bound to learn things whether you informed him of them or not.

Not wanting to betray your impatience, you have nevertheless been trying to speed him along.

Wanting to stand his ground, he has lagged behind.

Trying to be kind, you have told him jokes simpler than those that amuse you.

Understanding that compulsive talking is your nervous tic, he has patiently allowed you to rattle on.

You have explained to him that some words that can be said in front of you cannot be said in front of his mother.

He has understood that secrets bond men together.

You have done everything possible to give him the impression that although men and women may be different, women are every bit as intelligent and capable as men.

He has told you he knows fifteen words for women's breasts.

You have told him, in terms he can understand, about sex.

Sex becomes a great mystery.

When questioned about fine points, you have not backed down.

He has spared you information about playing doctor with the boy next door.

You finally realize that the day has come when you can let go of his hand as you are crossing the street.

In his peripheral vision, he sees the red sports car he wants one day to own.

Being ever so subtle, you drop into conversation the name of your alma mater.

He tells you to stop pressuring him about where he will go to college.

One morning the child sees you smelling a rose and looks at you questioningly. You feel like a doddering old man, straightening up from smelling the flower.

He has more information about cars than you have.

You read Car and Driver *at the barbershop, instead of* Time.

He wears a larger size shoe than you.

You can't believe it.

He sings snatches of a song you've never heard before.

You find yourself humming a song you used to sing when you rocked him to sleep, and you look at him nervously, thinking he may think you sentimental.

He tells you that you can relax: There is nothing he wants to know about sex that he doesn't know.

You tell the barber not to take so much off—that you are letting the sides grow.

He gets a cough he cannot seem to shake, and you fear that it is pneumonia.

Your wife tells you that it is an ordinary cough.

You insist that he visit the doctor.

He looks at you the same way he did the day he saw you smelling the rose. It is just a cough, he says. Nothing to worry about.

You think, in the night, that you hear him coughing. You go down the corridor, to his bedroom, but all is silent. You must have been dreaming. Only when he is grown do you acknowledge your terror about ordinary childhood maladies: measles, mumps, sore throats, infected cuts, and bulging bruises. It would have been the greatest tragedy if anything terrible had happened just as he was starting to come home with jokes that made you laugh, the quite-inventive whispered profanities he'd learned from the older boys, if he disappeared so his eye would no longer suddenly meet yours when his mother got upset.

Imagine this: You love someone whose birth had nothing to do with you, whose features are too striking to resemble your own (although something in your bearing may account for people's observation that the child looks just like you), whose presence is potentially threatening because of its power to leach away all of his mother's emotional energy. You love someone whose mother has admitted, on occasion, to wishing him away so that the complexities of her life would become simple matters. She pursued fame, and left it to you to pursue baby-sitters. And the closer you and the child became, the more she withdrew, as if that was what she had wanted all along: a clear road, space, time, the people around her happily involved. You would expect a little jealousy. More guilt. But that isn't the way it was.

Your worst fear about the child is that he will never let you in.

He sits on your shoulders and puts his hands on top of your head to steady himself when you start running. Feeling his cupped hands, you think to teach him the word "yarmulke."

You think that his mother will not marry you.

You get married.

You become melancholy, sure that you will die before the child is grown.

You live.

You fear that the world will treat the child unfairly.

The child, rarely intimidated, proceeds on his way quite well.

Struck by lightning, then. Something cruel and sudden.

Lightning does not strike.

He wanted more G.I. Joes; you lobbied for another child. His chances of getting a toy were always higher than your chances of talking her into having another baby.

He wanted to daydream; you thought about changing careers midstream. He daydreamed whenever he felt like it, but you stayed in the same profession after all.

He trusted you; you worried that although he was right in his judgment of you, he was generally too accepting of people and things.

He wanted a dog; you wanted a dog. She said she wanted to be free to travel, and that she did not want to feel guilty all the time she was gone about some sad-eyed dog hanging its tail between its legs in a kennel.

He would make up stories about people at her openings; you would repeat all but the most scandalous gossip to him. She looked across the room and smiled at the two of you, and you thought your heart would break.

In short, you lived, with this child, the most ordinary life, suspecting in the back of your mind that virtue might be rewarded, giving thanks that you had found each other in this world, trying to avoid sentiment, dutifully planning for his future. And if, miraculously, he did not end up hating you, perhaps you could one day ask him what he thought about his life. Not fishing for compliments. Just finding out what were high points for him that might have gone unnoticed by you. Or things you were curious to know: How many times did you hear your mother and me making love? Did you envision it, when you heard the bedsprings creaking? Did you want us to get it over with faster? Did it make us seem more childish? Vulnerable? Remote? Might it as well have been a sneeze? Were there times when you coughed or got up and went to the bathroom on purpose to make us whisper and wait? Do you have any memory of when you were still quite small and came to listen at our door at night? You stepped out of your bedroom slippers, so in the morning we found them there, in front of our door, like shoes left in the corridor of an expensive hotel. Do you remember how you managed to find poison ivy in New York City? Do you think that Haveabud and your mother had a sexual relationship? Do you think I ever stepped out on her? Did you ever fear that we would divorce, like everybody else's parents? Did you think that one or both of us might die? Who would you rather had died? Did you know that I defended your decision to say your prayers silently at night, and that I honestly didn't think that you meant to stop saying them? How many arguments did your mother win, and how many did I win? Was my favorite color obvious, or did I tell you at one time what it was? How interesting that you learned all my sizes, as if memorizing necessary mathematical formulas, but you might not know my favorite color. In time, you certainly disliked Haveabud much more than I did. What about that scare when your mother went in for the biopsy? Did you think of her as disfigured? Did you know the worst that could happen? Was it helpful or harmful to be told your I.Q.? Did you sense, in your mother, a bit of misogyny, and in me a bit of homophobia? Am I making up questions to provoke you? Did I do that raising you? Did I condescend? Did I convince you of things, even when you argued? How often does chance intervene, and how often is "chance" a term used loosely about an incident that is self-generated? Did you think that your mother had a rather bleak view of life, considering her photographs? Was it wrong of her to discuss her family in print? Did she tell the truth about us? Did she know the truth? Do we know the truth about each other today? Does it seem calculating, her getting a puppy at this point in time? I suspect she will spoil it when she's around. That in getting it, she's also thrown me a bone.

I came into your room one night and found that your mother, seated at the foot of the bed, was reading you Blake's sunflower poem. A poem that I could only think would be obscure to a small child. Perhaps you liked the rhyme. Her presence. You seemed not to criticize what she read, but you complained if I varied my intonation from one night to the next.

We would not have had Christmas trees, except at my insistence. She would have let you grow up without Christmas trees. She knew that was terrible, and always gave in. Hanging the decorations, she acted as if it were the most pleasant thing possible. Then, the next year, she would not want a tree.

My guess about Haveabud is that he would do anything that was expected of him by an important person, but if that thing went unstated, he often overreacted.

It was more difficult than I thought to live with an artist. Is that the primary reason why things have sometimes been difficult?

She loved my ears. She would bite the earlobes lightly, and nuzzle the ear with her nose, as if she meant to enter my body there.

I hated buzzing insects. She hated anything that crawled.

Enough of the past tense.

Today, the sun is shining with a brightness that would seem to obliterate the words written here. I like overcast days, when you don't have to squint. Days of pale clouds.

There would not have been this house without your mother. Or any you, of course, without your mother. So that when she travels, it seems strange: Things seem to have been abandoned, to exist without context. I realize that when you agree to something, it becomes your world. I may be disingenuous in saying that she determined so much. What I am really saying is that she put a border around my life, as if we lived within a photograph.

Think of the things she has photographed that I have never seen. Sequential shots, like the blinking of an eye. Think of how many times I have looked at her face as she blinks, and how many times those eyes have closed and opened to my presence in her world.

There were years in which I could have devoted myself to writing if I had wanted to. It is commonly known that everyone looks back and regrets not following through on more things that mattered to them.

What will you think of these ruminations, which started out with such surety about the wonders of childhood, filled with Ben Franklin-esque advice to the wary? I look back and see that what I recorded as sound advice was often only a prediction. Probably I had in mind passing on something eloquent, pretending to myself that it would be useful, but secretly hoping you would be surprised by my sensitivity. Maybe I have ruined my chances merely by writing that sentence. Maybe written words could never guide you and this information about childhood could not mean any more to you than your mother's photograph—of which you are so fond—of your shoes kicked off in a field where champagne glasses sparkle like huge diamonds and the rain has misted the grass and deteriorated the paper napkins as fast as acid.

Her feeling has been that people do things, then abandon the worlds they have created. She is interested in what remains, after the fact. No doubt she also feels abandoned. All artists are involved in personal quests, regardless of how well they seem to be investigating larger matters. Also—no different from cowboys or saints—they will be drawn to what reinforces them. I have recently read, and smiled over,

*this passage from Valéry: "It seems to me that the soul, when alone
with itself and speaking to itself, uses only a small number of words,
none of them extraordinary. This is how one recognizes that there is
a soul at that moment, if at the same time one experiences the sensation
that everything else—everything that would require a larger
vocabulary—is mere possibility."*

*We all like simple rhymes, spontaneous smiles. We are all so much
alike, which is rarely remarked upon by artists.*

*I see now that what started as a private record took a trajectory of
its own. I might have let it fly away, of course; or perhaps because it
was dear to my heart I held it close. The trouble might simply have
been that I was wary of creating something. A child—I would have
created a child; the physical creation of something didn't scare me—but
words . . . perhaps I was reluctant to let language transport me.*

*It seems to me that the problem with diaries, and the reason that
most of them are so boring, is that every day we vacillate between
examining our hangnails and speculating on cosmic order. Should we
simply record any thoughts we want, and judge them along the lines
of Valéry?*

*Questions and question marks. This is being written at night, the
light and the muttered expletives of the day having faded into darkness
and silence. The dog curled nearby. Leaves brushing the window. An
archetypal scene of the room in which the writer writes.*

*As always, the writer is secretly waiting for something else. To-
morrow night, your car in the driveway. You will close the door and
walk toward a house that was once called "the retreat," when we still
lived in the city, but that now, when we are older, is the only home
we own.*

*Though I have decided to give you a key and to tempt you to read
my words, finally, I think that the flashlight I bring into the driveway will be your primary help, in terms of illumination.*

*Enough. There have already been enough conclusions. You have
always been so smart about implied questions, ever since you first
looked up at me and seemed, in that first glance, to take in everything*

I wanted. Then you became the questioner, not me. When I came into your mother's life, I recall distinctly, you didn't make a scene. You stayed calm, as any intelligent adult would in the face of an intruder. Maybe you thought I'd sneak off under cover of darkness, taking only the jewels—or the cameras, in this case. Maybe because you knew only what happened day to day and didn't have a clear idea of what your life would be, you considered me not so much an intruder but a phenomenon, like a flash shower or a sudden gift of new Keds.

If your wide-eyed wonder was resentment, I never knew it. You came to love me—that much is clear. Though I have done other things through the years, I still think of myself as the person who knelt so many times to tie your shoelaces. Who needed to see them double-knotted, and to know that you were safe, again, from tripping. I could have identified your feet—and still could, I see them so clearly— in a lineup of a hundred children.

Off we marched—maybe even hand in hand—to whatever was ahead of us, which I sometimes had no more idea of than you. But you thought I did. You may also have thought that it came naturally to me to bite my tongue when I felt like cursing, or that it was easy to stop when the caution light flashed yellow, instead of gunning the car.

Do you see all this as altruistic? Of course it wasn't that, however much I might like to imply, now, that it was. I didn't see you as a hurdle: You were the simple stepping-stone to her heart. Then, to my surprise, I started to love you.

I remember taking you out in a brook to fish, and finding that the rocks were slippery, and that the water moved faster than it seemed to from the shore. I went back and got our shoes, yours and mine—I had to take care of you, after all—and endured your protests that only sissies wore shoes out on the rocks. Later, I got in trouble with your mother for getting your new shoes soaking wet.

Who was the real child? Who was naïve? Let the current rush around us, I thought, heady, as I often was, with my certainty that we'd stand firm. That we'd make it. Always. Every time we tempted fate.

PART III

CHILD

TWENTY-ONE

It sits on the piano in the living room—the *Vogue* photograph taken twenty years before. When the picture was shot, Will was urged to look not at the camera but at the photographer's raised hand, fingers wiggling like tiny fish splashing in the air. It is a photograph in which he looks somber and his mother beautiful. Her eyes could have bored through the lens. As he nestles in her arms, naked from the waist up, Will's skin looks like porcelain. Turned only an inch farther to the left, Jody's lips could have grazed his fashionably long hair. Previously, the picture sat on Jody and Mel's night table, but in recent years it has moved first to the Biedermeier chest, then to the piano. Except for the times Will visits Connecticut, he forgets the photograph, but once he enters the house he finds that he gravitates toward it. It is a conventional portrait, in its way— the people are attractive, the photograph well lit, but still: not as evocative as the photographer had hoped.

He is so in love with his wife. Through the living-room window he can see Amanda, standing on the lawn talking to Mel, swaying slightly to keep their baby relaxed as he slumbers in her arms. But actually, it must be out of habit that she cups her hand behind his head and shifts gently from foot to foot; the baby has been sleeping deeply almost from the moment they left New York. The motion of the car puts the baby to sleep.

Today is his mother's birthday, and he and Amanda and their son are putting in a command performance. On his birthday, Will usually receives only a card. Amanda's birthday often goes unacknowledged. Jody has been consistent through the years: Her time and energy are still reserved for her career. She is more expansive with the hangers-on than she is with Will, Amanda, or Mel. The house is often filled with adoring acolytes or journalists who stay an extra hour or an extra day, during which time everything goes off the record and they hear Jody's version of how she became so successful. For years, to all but family, she has been known simply as Jo.

Revisionism set in long ago. As she tells it, although Haveabud conceived of himself as divinely inspired and always pirouetting on the cutting edge, he was really a rather fatuous neurotic whom she successfully manipulated, knowing better than he what the marketplace wanted.

Haveabud. It is amazing to Will that even at Columbia University, where Will is an art historian, Haveabud's name sometimes comes up, or appears as a footnote in some book or article about contemporary American art. He is in Paris now, reunited with some former painters he once represented whom he turned into performance artists. Apparently, he became something of an overnight sensation abroad. Several years ago, Amanda found a photograph in a magazine of Haveabud, at a fund-raiser in a private home on Avenue Foch. Like all people the media elevate to stardom, Haveabud learned how to smile.

Will still exchanges Christmas cards with Corky, who is a nurse's aide in Coral Gables.

Wayne has not been heard from since at least fifteen years ago, when he sent Will a postcard from Mexico City.

Wagoner died at sixteen, drowned with another boy when their boat capsized.

Though Will and Amanda were almost two hours late, Jody was not prepared for their arrival. Her distaste for schedules and for doing the expected has become even greater with the passage of time. Looking around the living room, Will reflects that there is not even a particular chair that might be said to be her favorite. Mel has had to fight to keep his old blue chair, though she still threatens to give it away. She alternates between teasing Mel and being so conciliatory that Will can only think her attitude is condescending. ("Darling," she said to Mel the last time Will and Amanda visited, when he told Amanda, in great detail, about his desperate courtship of Jody, "it's perfectly all right to be conventional. You know I've always found it charming.")

There is a puppy. After so many years of protesting, Jody is now so fond of the puppy that she takes it into the bathroom with her when she bathes. She is upstairs now, calling downstairs that she will be down momentarily. He can hear water draining from the bathtub. The puppy whining to be let out.

Will goes into the kitchen to get something cold to drink. Mel's medicine is kept in the refrigerator. He looks away and takes a glass from the shelf. It is a wine goblet, but what does it matter? He shakes the orange juice and pours half a glass. Closing the refrigerator door, he thinks: Florida Sweet. That was the brand Corky bought. Florida Sweet orange juice. He had been so helpless. Helpless in the motel room with Haveabud and Spencer. Helpless when the police led his father away—the beginning of the end of Wayne's marriage to Corky.

Jody was absent too many times and wanted to hear too few

things. If not for Mel, he might have been sent to Florida more
often. Years later he found out that when Mel got the call to
come get him, Mel was furious, because he had wanted all
along to stay in Florida in a motel and wait while Will had his
visit. If only that could have happened. If only Mel could have
been there in fifteen minutes, instead of the next morning.
Corky had clutched him and cried—the two of them alone, in
that sad house.

On the other hand, Mel was hardly a hero. He should have
made Jody face up to the fact that she was his mother. Or was
it to Mel's advantage that she let him take over? Was that part
of the bargain—Mel's caring for Jody's child as a condition of
marriage?

Years ago Will had started to tell Jody about Haveabud, and
she had shushed him. Nothing negative could be said about
her manic mentor.

He had been so close to Mel. Why hadn't he told Mel?
Perhaps he had tried, and he had blocked out Mel's response.
Or perhaps—this was the way he remembered it—Mel had
been so shaky when he arrived back in Florida that Will realized he should not bring up anything that might cause further trouble.

The dog comes bounding down the stairs, tail swishing,
sniffing its way to Will, in the kitchen.

This is what will happen now: Jody will descend the stairs,
and soon there will be exclamations about the baby's beauty
and compliments on the dog's amusing energy. Mel will open
a bottle of champagne, and the birthday cake on the kitchen
counter will have its three candles lit (one for the last year, one
for the next, and one to grow on), and then Jody will make a
wish and blow them out.

The rest of the day, though, will not be so predictable. As
they take an evening walk, Mel is going to give Will a key, and
tell him that there are papers he wants him to know about, in

the event anything happens to him. Nervously, Will will put the key in his pants pocket and try to change the subject. "They're only things I've written—not official documents," Mel will say.

Things he's written?

Later that night, he will know what those things are. Having opened the locked metal box in the carriage house where he and Amanda always sleep, he will sit on the floor and untie the string around a heavy cardboard envelope. He will flip through a few pages, then read only the first paragraph before sitting in a chair to read more. He will read:

Of course you do not want the child to be a ventriloquist's dummy, but if there could be a bit more sitting on the knee, a little less of the back of the head and more of the profile as you spoke, that might be all the better. The child that reminds you of your own mortality needs so much tending to—so many wisps of hair brushed off the forehead, so many dollar bills handed out, so many anklet cuffs turned down, so much humming to accompany the soprano-sung solo—that it is almost impossible to decide whether to be as quick-talking as an escaped convict, or as patient as a penitent.

For hours, Will will not put it down. He always knew the care Mel took raising him, but now he will also sense a sort of narcissism difficult to separate, at times, from true involvement: an almost militant desire that things go well, or at least have a rationale, after the fact.

All those years Jody was photographing, Mel was writing.

But what does Mel want? To explain that everything was more difficult than it seemed? To impress with his sensitivity? To have his writing published? Because Jody's notoriety would certainly mean that such a manuscript would be of great interest.

No. Mel never misled him. If Mel wanted the manuscript

published, he would either have said so or have done it himself.

The next day, should he say that he read Mel's writing? Should he awaken Amanda? Or crawl into bed and nestle against her? Or just sit there with his eyes closed, listening to the breeze blowing through the trees?

With his eyes closed, he remembers a moment earlier in the evening—sees it as if he could at once be part of the scene and also absent himself from it to take a photograph. He smiles at this strange desire. Is the desire to photograph genetically encoded—or at least entirely predictable when parents have young children? Will has his imaginary photograph but knows that others would see him differently.

They would see a young man standing on a wide green lawn. His eyes are quite brilliant when he first looks up. Only when he fixes a more even gaze on you do they gradually become less intense: what most people call kind eyes.

Mel has given the baby a bright red ball. The child holds it, unsure. He looks at his father.

Across the distance, Will smiles and speaks. He nods, holding out his hand.

The child's knees bend as he does a skittish little dance. Then, holding his arms stiffly, fists behind his hips, he jumps high and lands slightly crouched, looking something the way penguins did before they became extinct.

"Throw the ball," Will says, smiling in an attempt to persuade the child. "Come on. You have to let go of it sometime. Come on, baby, throw me the ball."

ABOUT THE AUTHOR

ANN BEATTIE lives in Charlottesville, Virginia, with her husband, the painter Lincoln Perry.